# INVENTIONS *of the* HEART

## Books by Mary Connealy

### From Bethany House Publishers

The Kincaid Brides

*Out of Control*

*In Too Deep*

*Over the Edge*

Trouble in Texas

*Swept Away*

*Fired Up*

*Stuck Together*

Wild at Heart

*Tried and True*

*Now and Forever*

*Fire and Ice*

The Cimarron Legacy

*No Way Up*

*Long Time Gone*

*Too Far Down*

High Sierra Sweethearts

*The Accidental Guardian*

*The Reluctant Warrior*

*The Unexpected Champion*

Brides of Hope Mountain

*Aiming for Love*

*Woman of Sunlight*

*Her Secret Song*

Brothers in Arms

*Braced for Love*

*A Man with a Past*

*Love on the Range*

The Lumber Baron's Daughters

*The Element of Love*

*Inventions of the Heart*

*The Boden Birthright:*
A Cimarron Legacy *Novella*
*(All for Love Collection)*

*Meeting Her Match:*
A Match Made in Texas
*Novella*

*Runaway Bride:*
*A* Kincaid Brides *and*
Trouble in Texas *Novella*
*(*With This Ring? *Collection)*

*The Tangled Ties That Bind:*
*A* Kincaid Brides *Novella*
*(*Hearts Entwined *Collection)*

THE LUMBER BARON'S DAUGHTERS :: TWO

# INVENTIONS *of the* HEART

MARY CONNEALY

a division of Baker Publishing Group
Minneapolis, Minnesota

Published by Bethany House Publishers
11400 Hampshire Avenue South
Minneapolis, Minnesota 55438
www.bethanyhouse.com

Bethany House Publishers is a division of
Baker Publishing Group, Grand Rapids, Michigan

Printed in the United States of America



Library of Congress Cataloging-in-Publication Data
Names: Connealy, Mary, author.
Title: Inventions of the heart / Mary Connealy.
Description: Minneapolis, Minnesota : Bethany House Publishers, [2022] |
Series: The lumber baron's daughters ; 2
Identifiers: LCCN 2021053579 | ISBN 9780764239595 (paperback) | ISBN
9780764240164 (casebound) | ISBN 9781493437337 (ebook)
Subjects: LCGFT: Novels.
Classification: LCC PS3603.O544 I58 2022 | DDC 813/.6—dc23/eng/20211105
LC record available at https://lccn.loc.gov/2021053579

Scripture quotations are from the King James Version of the Bible.

This is a work of historical reconstruction; the appearances of certain historical figures are therefore inevitable. All other characters, however, are products of the author's imagination, and any resemblance to actual persons, living or dead, is coincidental.

Cover design by LOOK Design Studio
Cover photography by Aimee Christenson

Author is represented by the Natasha Kern Literary Agency.

Baker Publishing Group publications use paper produced from sustainable forestry practices and post-consumer waste whenever possible.

22 23 24 25 26 27 28 7 6 5 4 3 2 1

To my grandchildren:
Elle, Isaac, Luke, Katherine, Lauren, and Adrian.
The absolute lights of my life.
It's almost the weirdest kind of pure luck that the
six smartest, sweetest, most beautiful children in the
world ended up all being my grandchildren.
What are the odds?

CHAPTER

# ONE

**JULY 1872**
**TWO HARTS RANCH**
**DORADA RIO, CALIFORNIA**

"AT LEAST YOU KNOW YOU CAN TRUST ME." Michelle Stiles slashed a hand about an inch from Zane Hart's face.

They sat in his kitchen. His roof over her head. His food in her stomach. And safety thanks to him. Still, the man was so stubborn. She wanted to help, and besides, she was bored, and she knew she could do this job better than anyone else.

Zane slammed both fists down on the table, and his dark blue eyes flashed like summer lightning. "This subject is closed. Don't you have a husband to find?"

Michelle never should've told him about the terms of Papa's will. He'd been goading her about it ever since. And anyway, he shouldn't be able to torment her so smugly about her finding a husband after he'd kissed her.

She shoved her dark curls out of her eyes and tried to

overpower him with the force of her will. "I don't need to find a husband right away. Things are better now."

Zane glared at her, looking remarkably un-overpowered.

She thought of what a terrible job her stepfather, Edgar Beaumont, was doing running Stiles Lumber, the vast company her father had founded and raised her and her sisters to take over.

When Mama married Edgar, their lives had turned ugly. They discovered Edgar's plot to marry his stepdaughters off to loathsome friends of his and had no choice but to run.

And because he had them virtually held prisoner in the mansion her parents had built on top of a remote mountain, the fastest way to escape had been to ride down a flume in half barrels. They'd survived the reckless escape and found a place to hide on the edge of Zane's ranch.

And Zane was right about marriage. Each sister inherited her one-third of the company when she turned twenty-five or when she married. Now with Laura married, all Michelle needed to do was round up a husband, and she and Laura could combine their shares of the company and take controlling interest in Stiles Lumber. Jilly could be next to get married, of course, but she seemed overly resistant to the idea, and Michelle couldn't guess why.

Their company was still in danger from Edgar. But Zane didn't need to keep bringing it up. The fact that he was right only made it more irritating.

"At least Mama isn't in danger anymore. And Laura is all safely married and back there with Caleb and Nick to protect her and Mama." Michelle trembled to think of Edgar's violent anger toward Mama when he'd found the girls gone.

They'd tried to bring Mama along, but she'd fallen and

sprained her ankle, and they had no choice but to abandon her.

Michelle had hated it.

But then they met Zane and his cowhand Nick Ryder, who knew of the Stiles Lumber dynasty and had worked for them last summer.

When Nick heard Mama was in danger, he jumped on his horse and rode off to the rescue.

After that, they found gold near Purgatory, a rough settlement on Zane's property.

"Let me run the mining operation." There was no mining operation yet, because when Laura had found the gold and told Zane, all of them had known gold caused trouble.

No one had figured out what to do about a gold strike, so it remained a secret. Michelle wasn't just offering to run his mining company. She was offering to create the company, work the mine, and count, ship, and sell the gold. She'd figure out security and how to protect the gold. She had no doubt in her mind she could manage it.

She wanted to do it all.

"You're leaving," Zane said. "I need someone permanent."

"Let me do it until I leave. I promise to train my replacement."

"Michelle, you know you're going to have trouble keeping men honest. I need someone who's not going to hesitate when they need to beat the living daylights out of one of my miners." He glared at her in such a way as to say he doubted she'd manage that.

With some justification.

She couldn't see herself winning a fistfight with a man half-mad with gold fever.

"That's the other thing I've decided, and it's part of letting me run things."

Zane didn't hammer his fists again. Instead, he laid his face straight down on the table with a sigh that sounded like his whole body was deflating. "What now?"

She stared at the crown of his head. The dark swirl of his hair seemed much happier than he was. "I've decided that, for now, we shouldn't hire miners. You should hire a few trusted men as guards and just let me and Jilly mine your gold. We'll find out soon enough if it's a rich vein. If it goes deep, then we can't handle that much mining. But what if that big chunk of quartz is all there is? Jilly and I can quietly mine the gold. We can transport it back here under armed guard, and word won't get out that you found it until you've sold it and used the money to buy half of California. That's your goal, right?"

"Don't act like I'm greedy." He was speaking straight into the tabletop. "Not when you own a whole mountain covered with trees and live in a mansion that'd make a king blush over the excess of it."

"You've never seen it." Michelle paused, then shrugged. "It's huge, though, and beautiful. A king would be lucky to have such a nice house."

"I'm never going to let you run my gold mine. I'm sure you'd be good at it if you didn't have to handle a bunch of rough men who probably have gold fever and might be willing to kill you."

Nodding, Michelle said, "Not too many lumberjacks have any dreams about running off with their pockets full of trees."

One of her brunette curls swung loose from the bun at the

back of her head, and she twisted it in her fingers thoughtfully. "I could handle it, though. I might need a gun. Can I borrow a gun, Zane?"

That lifted his head up at least. She saw him roll his eyes. "You're admitting it's a dangerous job. I can't put you at risk."

"I'm educated enough to manage. And there's no way to get the material in here to work on my gas engine." She gave him a narrow-eyed look. "Is there?"

Zane shook his head. "Forget the engine. We don't need an engine on a ranch."

"It's not for the ranch. It's for, well, for lots of things. But mainly it can be used in the sawmill my family owns and the trains we're going to own. And I also have some ideas for improvement on rolling stock."

"You're not rolling my cows anywhere."

Michelle blinked at him. "Um, not stock like livestock. Rolling stock like the rolling cars the train engine pulls. I want to alter them to load logs onto them more easily and make sure they're strong enough to take the weight. And there are issues with the braking system on a long downhill slope, so I—"

"Stop talking about trains and logs and tell me what you want to manage."

"Well, your gold mining operation, of course. But honestly, I want to manage everything. The whole world would run better if they put me in charge. Don't you like the hot water in your back room? In the kitchen? I could turn one of your upstairs rooms into a proper bathing room with a tub, if you'd just get me a—"

"No. The hot water in the house is a wonder, and I thank you kindly for it. But I'm not letting you run my mine."

"We're alone for the first time. Let me explain again how my papa raised me to—"

"Zane!" Shad, Zane's foreman slammed into the kitchen. "Trouble. Come quick."

Shouting sounded from outside. Screaming.

Zane was on his feet running.

Michelle gritted her teeth. Thwarted again. But as Zane ran for the kitchen door, Michelle got up and ran after. Whoever was shouting really sounded frantic.

Michelle got outside as two horses, galloping as if they were running from wolves, charged into the ranch yard. The first was ridden by a woman with . . . two heads. Michelle squinted. What she was looking at made no sense.

A woman, for sure. Oh, not with two heads, but with a small child in front. Michelle felt better to figure that out despite the madly racing horse.

The woman's dark hair flew wildly behind her as she screamed for help. The child, with her matching dark hair, wailed like a feral creature.

A man rode just behind her, terrible in his silence.

Michelle stopped feeling better. Too much blood. The woman was bleeding, but the man made the blood on her pale blue dress look like a scratch.

"Annie?" Zane's shout could've shaken a roof down.

The woman, Annie, reined her horse frantically, and it skidded to a stop, almost sat on its haunches to do it, but she brought the horse under control. The man didn't even react. He leaned down until the saddle horn had to be poking him in the chest. His horse galloped on until it came up on the barn. It whinnied and tossed its head and reared up higher and higher. Michelle thought it'd go over backward.

Zane ran toward Annie. Four men around the place, drawn by the shouting and galloping hooves, rushed for the rearing horse. The man tumbled off the horse as Shad reached the horse's head, leapt high to catch the bridle, and pulled the horse down with his weight. He led it away so it wouldn't trample the fallen man. The other three cowhands hurried to the rider.

Michelle pivoted toward the house. Jilly was better at this than she was. Then she remembered Jilly was gone. Laura was gone. That left Michelle, almost certainly more educated about anatomy and medicine than anyone else around the place. Nothing even resembling any practice at doctoring, though.

She spun back for the injured man and saw Zane rushing toward him carrying a little girl, with Annie clinging to his arm.

"Todd!" the woman screamed. She let go of Zane and ran faster.

Michelle sprinted, trying to get there, see what she could do.

The horses were taken into the barn.

The little girl began crying, "Pa, my papa. Pa." High and wild and terrified, just like her ma. Michelle didn't blame them.

Annie dropped to her knees beside Todd and tore at his shirt.

Zane, with his hands full of shrieking toddler, wasn't much help. He looked around and saw Michelle and made one brief move to hand the little girl off.

Michelle dodged around him and knelt by Todd as his wife got his shirt open. He was utterly still.

"A bullet into his stomach," Michelle noted. The next words to say were *he can't survive this*, but Michelle had learned a few things about handling people in tough situations, and she kept her prognosis to herself.

"Let's get him inside." She snapped out the order with such command that the two cowhands not busy with the horses picked him up and carried him toward the house.

Michelle helped Annie up. The woman wasn't steady on her feet, and it looked like she was bleeding from at least two wounds. Her arm was bleeding and one leg, but both seemed to be working fine. She'd live.

Todd . . . It would likely be time wasted. But Michelle had plenty of time, and Annie would need to see someone trying to help.

That's when it hit her.

Annie and Todd. And the toddler was . . . was . . . Michelle dug deep. Her memory for names was excellent. Caroline. Annie Lane was Zane's sister. Married to a rancher named Todd Lane. This gutshot man was Zane's brother-in-law. Their picture was up in Zane's office. Zane had mentioned their names once.

The men went inside and headed straight toward the stairs.

"No, bring him back. I want him on the kitchen table." Michelle's voice, again, got action. She turned to Zane. "I need bandages. Needle and thread, any medical supplies."

She turned to Shad, who'd come in right behind them, the horses dealt with. "Get me a basin of water." From the handy boiler she'd installed. But she didn't say that. "And cloths. The rag bag is—"

"I know where it is." Shad leapt into action.

Zane stood across the table from Michelle, Todd's unconscious form between them. Caroline shrieked in his arms.

Michelle pressed two fingers against Todd's neck and

found a steady pulse. Aware of Annie's fear, Michelle spoke of what she'd found. "A very strong pulse. That's a good sign."

Maybe he had a chance, except Michelle only had the most miniscule notion of what to do. She found the bullet wound. The basin of water and a stack of clean rags were there before she could ask again.

Wringing out a wet rag, she wiped the terrible bleeding aside. "Two bullets. He's been shot twice."

She looked at Annie. "Zane, get her a chair. She's been shot twice, too, but I want her to stay close to Todd."

Annie grabbed her husband's hand and pulled it to her lips. "Todd, Todd, can you hear me?"

"Shad, can you handle the chair?" Zane snapped.

Shad moved a chair behind Annie and as good as knocked her into it. Her knees were wobbly, so it wasn't hard.

"Shad, get Jilly and the Hogan sisters back here. All three of them are fine at doctoring." *Fine* was a little strong, but better than her. None of that mattered. Todd would die regardless of the skill of his doctor. Annie would live, regardless of who treated her. And Michelle, for now, was here to do her best for both of them.

Shad cracked an order to the two men who'd carried Todd in, and they left the room at a run. Jilly was riding herd with the Hogan sisters. The Steinmeyer family had ridden to town with some of Zane's hands. Melinda and her baby had gone along. The first time to town for any of them since they'd come to live with Zane two weeks ago.

Shad hustled out of the room and was right back with a good-sized cloth bag. "Here's what we have to treat injuries."

Michelle had Todd's bullet wounds wiped clean. She dug in the bag and found a long, stiff wire.

"I need to find out if the bullet went through. I didn't see his back well enough to be sure."

Bo, one of the steadiest cowhands, came in. "I didn't see any blood on his back. I'm thinking the bullets are still in there."

Michelle's stomach twisted. She was about to operate on a man who had no chance, or maybe just almost no chance. She had to try to help him. And that began with removing the bullets.

Carefully probing the wounds, Michelle felt the wire scrape against something metal almost immediately. She felt a surge of hope. "Not that far in. The bullets may have been spent when they hit him. Maybe they didn't hit anything vital."

Michelle looked up at Zane, who was bouncing little Caroline with surprising skill. "I could use a hand. Unless you've done this enough to want to take over."

"Nope, you're doing fine. How can I help?"

Michelle wondered what people saw when they looked at her. She must appear to be capable and confident. In truth, the sight of those wounds, the smell of the blood, the ashen face of the unconscious man, it all shook her deeply, and she was fighting to keep her hands from trembling.

Shoving her fear aside as best she could, she dug in the bag and was relieved to see long, narrow tweezers. "I need hot water to sterilize these tweezers."

Zane hurried to the stove and dipped water out of the wells into a basin and brought it to Michelle's side. She dropped the tweezers, and a needle in, then stared, wondering how long to leave them.

Or should she hold them over a fire? She'd read about Joseph Lister's sterile operating methods and knew cleaning her tools made everything safer.

Yes, she'd read about it, but she'd never come close to actually doing any of this kind of medical treatment. All she knew was, find the bullet and get it out. Sew the wound shut. If things were damaged inside, as they almost certainly were, she could do nothing. Her minimal knowledge of medicine, which she'd read and studied as part of her science courses, told her no one could do much.

Michelle prayed as Zane eased Annie closer to Todd's head. He stood across from Michelle. Michelle's eyes shifted to the little girl, then to Zane.

Zane seemed to read her mind. "Shad."

Zane's foreman was there before Zane quit uttering his name. He thrust Caroline into Shad's arms.

Shad, a man to keep a cool head, shifted his grip and said quietly, "Do you want a cookie?" He walked away with the little girl, bouncing her, easing her terrible weeping.

Shad left the room, and there was silence.

Michelle pulled the tweezers out of the water and probed. She listened to the sickening sound of a metal tool digging in flesh. The bullet wasn't deep, and the path it'd torn in Todd's body was straight. The tweezers pinched onto the bullet and slipped off. Breathing in and out to calm herself and steady her hands, Michelle tried again. She got hold of the bullet on the third try and pulled firmly. The bullet came out. Shad, toddler still in hand, was somehow back in the room and standing there with a plate.

Michelle hadn't asked for the plate and hadn't thought of what to do with the bullet. Just getting it out was as far as she'd planned. She dropped the bullet on the plate with a dull click of metal on glass.

And went back for the second.

Michelle glanced at Zane. "Get a cloth and put pressure on the wound I've finished with."

The second bullet wasn't as easy to find. A surge of sickness almost stopped her from working when the wire went deep before it clicked against the bullet.

Michelle looked up. Zane was staring at the wire, then his gaze came up and met hers. It was all there in his eyes. In the bleak expression on his face. He knew exactly what happened when a man was gutshot.

Turning back to her surgery, she pressed the tweezers in through blood that nearly boiled out of the wound.

It was too long before she got a solid hold on the bullet and got it out.

"Pressure on this one, too, Zane." Michelle retrieved the needle from the bottom of the basin, then found the thread. She'd never done such a thing as sew someone up before. She'd never seen it done. And she knew . . . without really knowing at all . . . that there were things inside Zane's brother-in-law that needed sewing up, too, and she couldn't begin to handle that.

Remembering whom she was working with, a tough cowboy who lived a long way from a doctor, she asked Zane, "Can you set stitches?"

"I have. Shad's better."

Such a deep sigh of relief came over her that she gasped for air and only then realized she'd quit breathing.

Shad was there. He took over. Michelle got handed the baby. She backed away and realized she had blood on her hands. She went to wash as best she could without dropping little Caroline. Once her hands were clean and with the toddler distracting her from her panic, Michelle turned to Annie.

"Let me have a look at your wounds."

"They're nothing. Wipe the blood off and wrap them up. I have to stay near Todd."

Michelle thought Annie was an admirable woman. To distract her from being so blasted brave, she set Caroline in her lap.

Michelle went and wrung out a cloth, then knelt in front of the valiant woman. Between holding the baby and holding her husband's limp hand, she barely noticed Michelle pulling a bullet out of her calf.

"Not in the muscle." At least not much.

Annie nodded as if Michelle was speaking the obvious.

Michelle didn't tell her it was a long way from a scratch and would need stitches.

Michelle decided to make Shad do that, too. For now, she pressed a pad of cloth to it until the bleeding stopped, then wrapped the pad tight.

She turned to Annie's arm. Her sleeve was soaked in blood.

"Do you have another dress?"

"Y-yes." Annie blinked at Michelle as if she feared why Michelle had asked.

"It will be faster and more modest if I rip your sleeve open rather than make you, um, disrobe. Your dress will be ruined. I just hoped you had something else to wear."

"Rip it up. I have clothes here at Zane's house." Annie's voice was laced with fear, pain, and anger. "I'm never wearing this dress again no matter how careful you are."

Michelle nodded. Since there was a convenient bullet hole in Annie's upper sleeve, Michelle put both fingers in the hole and ripped. The sleeve split without much of a fight.

"This one isn't bad at all. I'm afraid you'll need some stitches on your leg, but this, well, it bled freely, but the cut isn't long nor deep. It's mostly closed. I can wrap it—"

"Just wrap my leg, too. It'll heal."

No, it wouldn't, but Michelle had things to do now. She'd wait and fight later.

She felt good about the tidy bandage on Annie's arm. Stepping back, she turned to wash her hands again, then came right back to pick Caroline up. Done crying, Caroline, with all the strange commotion around her, eagerly watched all the activity.

"How much longer on those stitches, Shad?" Michelle wasn't as good at handling a baby as Zane or Shad.

"I'm done." Shad straightened from his stitching.

"Let me bandage it." After a few minutes' practice on Annie, she felt like she had a reasonable skill with that.

Michelle settled Caroline gently back on poor Annie's lap. She looked over at Zane. "Wash your hands. You're going to need to hold the baby."

Michelle rounded the table as Shad straightened from his stitches. Under her breath, she told Shad, "Right calf. Stitches."

Shad nodded and went to his next patient with his needle and thread. Michelle didn't say anything, but she was impressed to see Shad stop and wash his hands before going to work.

Annie was so fixated on Todd that she didn't seem to notice Shad coming at her with a needle.

Zane went to take Caroline back just as Shad got a firm

grip on Annie's leg. He pressed one hand solidly on Annie's shoulder. "Brace yourself, sister."

Startled, she looked up at Zane, then down at Shad. "What are you doing?"

The needle poked her, and she hollered. She'd've jumped up, but Zane and Shad were ready for that, and she was held utterly still—not counting her mouth.

Caroline started crying.

The toddler crying, the mama shouting, it was loud enough—or maybe Michelle's bandaging hurt bad enough—that Todd's eyes flickered open.

"Annie, Todd's awake." Michelle used her whiplash voice. She'd had plenty of practice bossing people around.

Annie's shouting stopped. Caroline cried on. Zane didn't let his sister go, so Annie leaned forward to grasp Todd's hand.

"Todd, you're going to be all right. Both of us are."

Michelle didn't disabuse her. She was busy with bandaging, so she didn't see if Zane had a grim expression or not.

Shad set the last stitch and started with a rolled bandage. Michelle finished with Todd's wounds. Caroline quit crying.

The Hogan sisters and Jilly came into the kitchen at a run.

"Harriet, Nora, we need to get Todd to a bed down here. I don't want to carry him up the stairs," Michelle said.

"We'll go get it ready for him." Harriet did most of the talking for the two of them.

Nora took a sharp look at the bandages and blood all around. "You get things ready, Harriet. I'll help in here."

Nora came around to slide a supportive arm across Michelle's waist. Quietly, she said, "Sit down before you fall down."

With strong arms and the take-charge nature of a lifelong schoolteacher, she guided Michelle to a chair. Only when Michelle sat and her knees gave out on the way down did she realize how light-headed she was. Dropping the last few inches, she drew in a long breath.

Jilly rushed over with a glass of water and thrust it into Michelle's hands. Then she went around and plucked Caroline out of Zane's arms so deftly he barely realized his niece was being taken away.

Jilly got water for Annie and helped Nora clean the kitchen as best she could one handed. If not for the large man on the kitchen table, the room would be considered restored to order.

Todd and Annie were in their own world, speaking, holding hands. Praying. The world went on without them.

Two cowhands had come back with the Hogans and Jilly. Shad had stopped them at the door. He looked at Zane. "I'll be right outside if you need help, so will a few men. Call us when you need to move him."

Shad's eyes shifted to Todd. Michelle saw the grim truth.

They wouldn't be moving him to the bed. They'd be moving him to a grave.

Michelle's head went dizzy. She caught hold of the edge of the chair, afraid she might topple out. Her hearing went weird. As if a hive of bees were buzzing in her head. Her vision narrowed. At last it eased, and she knew she wasn't going to faint.

She noticed Zane speaking quietly to Shad but was too fuzzy to bother eavesdropping.

When she was sure she wouldn't pass out, she gulped down her water.

Todd and Annie continued to talk softly to each other. Zane joined in once in a while with a solid hand on Todd's shoulder. Then Zane asked Jilly for the little girl and brought her to Annie. Todd looked at the child, who was calm now.

"Hi, baby girl."

"Hi, Papa." She grinned and waved her arms, then tried to climb on the table.

Zane moved to grab her.

"No, let her come, but watch where she lands. Don't let her kick me." Todd smiled weakly. "Let me hold her for just a minute."

That's when Michelle realized Todd knew what his injuries meant. He wanted to say goodbye.

Annie's eyes filled with tears. She carefully held the little girl so she could be tucked in her papa's arms. Annie bore her weight and made sure Caroline didn't bump the bandaged wounds.

Todd pulled the toddler close and spoke gently to her. Spoke of love. Hugged her tight. Then he looked at Annie. Michelle looked away from the raw pain, the loss, the longing that passed between the two of them. It was an intimate moment, and they should have been allowed it without witnesses. But there wasn't time.

He gave a shudder violent enough that Annie lifted Caroline away from him. "She doesn't need to see this, Zane."

Zane took the child. "Jilly, can you take Caroline to the other room?"

Jilly bounced the little girl as she walked out.

Todd's shuddering stopped. He went still. Every bit of tension in his body left him. Michelle couldn't look away, and she saw the moment his hand went limp, slipped through Annie's grip, and dropped to the table.

Annie began to sob. She hugged her husband, and her weeping rose. Zane let it go on a long time. Finally, when the worst of the storm passed, Zane pulled her into his arms and held her tight.

## CHAPTER
# TWO

ZANE HADN'T STARTED OUT THIS DAY with any intention of digging a grave. Burying a man who was as good as a brother to him.

It was a dry year, and while Michelle badgered him about that stupid gold, his thoughts had been for his cattle. His ranch was in a rich place, with heavy grass that grew year-round. His cattle thrived with little work from him, though he put up some hay every year for days with heavy snow cover.

But this year the rain hadn't come. The July grass was turning brown. The springs and ponds he used for water were dry. He needed to move his herds closer to the rivers and creeks. The water in them ran low, but still, they ran.

None of that even touched him now.

"Let's go in, Annie." He rested his arm along her shoulders and urged her away.

Struggling against his hold, Annie shook her head and refused to move.

Zane wished Caleb, the parson who had married Laura,

were here. He would know what to say. But Caleb and Laura had headed back to the Stileses' mountain home.

The older sisters, Michelle and Jilly, along with the mission group that had come west with Caleb, had somehow ended up settling in Zane's house and were apparently in no hurry to leave.

Zane liked them well enough, and after some lonely years since his ma died, he realized he missed having women around the place. But the Stiles sisters had a way about them, smarter'n whips. Liked to manage everything. Michelle had even performed surgery today, though she'd looked about all in after it was done.

The summer had been interesting. For certain a break from normal ranch life and his worry about a drought. And now he faced a grim future with a heartbroken sister and a serious need for revenge against whoever had shot Todd Lane.

Annie gave him a look of such despair Zane wondered if she'd lose her mind.

"We can stay out here as long as you need." He nodded to his cowhands nearby. Shad had sent men to find Todd and Annie's cowhands that had been shot while riding along with them. They'd brought them back, then dug three graves in the family cemetery. Now they began filling them in.

The rest of the mourners had wandered away. Zane noticed his ramrod, Bo, talking quietly with Harriet Hogan, a schoolteacher who'd come into the area as a missionary with Parson Caleb. Her sister, Nora, walked side-by-side with Harriet. At Nora's opposite side walked Jesse Green, another of Zane's cowhands.

He didn't have time to think on that overly while his sister sobbed.

The tears finally eased. Zane saw Jilly come to the back door with little Caroline, assess the situation, and go back in.

Annie lifted her head to look up at Zane with tear-drenched eyes. "Can we send for Beth Ellen? I wish she were here. Your house is so full of strangers, and I know you're busy. If I could just have someone of my own."

"I'll send a rider with a wire before another hour goes by. She'll want to come." Beth Ellen was the youngest of the four Hart children.

"I know she's courting that banker."

"Loyal Kelton." He was the son of a wealthy banker and poised to step into his father's shoes. Zane had ridden all the way to San Francisco to meet him, and he seemed like a fine young man.

"I had hoped she'd come home for the summer, but she's in good hands with Todd's brother and his wife. I'll have to write to them, too." Annie waved her hands as if it was all too much. And it probably was.

"I'll include word to Todd's brother in the wire. You can write later."

"Beth Ellen wanted to be near Loyal, but this will bring her home." Annie looked up at Zane as if she wanted him to assure her of Beth Ellen's presence. She seemed helpless as a child. Wanting him to handle everything. Which he would do.

"Yes, it will. And with the train coming to Lodi, she can be here in a couple of days."

Annie nodded.

Zane went on. "Maybe she'll stay until you're ready to go home. She might even spend the rest of the summer. She can go home with you until you—"

"I've got nowhere to go, Zane."

"Nowhere to go? What about the ranch?" Todd was a very successful young rancher. Not as established as Zane, who'd taken over his pa's place, but he had a good start.

"I haven't even spoken of what happened. We've been pressured to leave our land. The title to it is being disputed. We've got a neighbor who claims every acre of it. Horace Benteen's been telling us we had to get out for a while, but we knew our ownership was fully legal. Then this morning, our ranch was raided."

"What? That's why you were coming here?"

"Yes, we were running for our lives and thought we'd gotten away. It was a land grab, pure and simple."

"I'll gather my men. We'll go down and take that land back. We'll do it today."

Annie shook her head. "There's nothing to go back to, Zane. We saw the house burning and the cattle being driven off."

"That's cattle rustling. We'll go to the law," Zane insisted.

"Benteen is rich and connected to powerful people. Todd has been to Lodi several times with complaints to the sheriff, but he said what happened outside of town wasn't their problem. Benteen owns the sheriff."

Zane drew her back into his arms. He didn't want her to see the fury on his face.

"The hands who were loyal rode with us a long way. Most of the way to your property line. Long after we'd left all pursuit behind. Finally, all but two of them split off, heading for their own destinations. We thought we'd made it. We thought we'd live to fight another day."

Zane looked grimly at the three graves.

"The men who rode with us were cut down first. Then Todd. Benteen must've known we would run here to you. They must've been waiting. Just a mile or so before we reached your land, someone opened fire on us. And me with Caroline riding on my lap. They might've let me live just because they couldn't quite descend into such evil by killing her. But for Todd and the men riding with us, they spared no lead."

"We'll get a lawyer. We'll figure this out. I know that ranch was bought legal. Until it's sorted out, you'll stay here."

Which set him to thinking of his crowded house.

With Laura and Caleb gone, there was an empty bedroom upstairs.

Jilly seemed to like building. Maybe he'd let her add on a couple of rooms.

"Let's go in. I'll send a rider for town to wire Beth Ellen and Todd's brother."

And where was he going to put Beth Ellen? Zane was a little ashamed of himself for worrying about it. He could sleep in the bunkhouse.

"Who are all these strangers in your house, Zane?" Annie's confused voice sounded the littlest bit interested. He hoped that, if only for a moment, she could think of something besides her husband. Zane knew grief would fill her thoughts for a long time to come.

JILLY HAD WITNESSED THE WOMEN PREPARING Todd's body for burial. It was something she'd never seen before, but it seemed to be nothing unusual to the Hogan sisters or

Annie Lane. The three women had covered his bloodstained clothing by wrapping Todd in a blanket. They'd combed his hair and washed his face.

The Hogan sisters, women of strong faith who'd been with Caleb on his mission, were a bulwark to Annie. They'd talked quietly with her, prayed with her, held her when they needed to.

Jilly was in charge of Caroline and was surprised how much she enjoyed the little girl. Annie broke into sobs often, but she'd go on working. The tears would end, then they'd come again. Jilly tried to keep Caroline away from the funeral preparations and her mother's tears.

All the while, Gretel, who'd also come here with the mission group, had worked with Michelle to clean the wreckage in the kitchen.

Jilly would come into the kitchen on her walk through the house bouncing the little one or holding her hand as she toddled along exploring a different house. Caroline couldn't really see her papa after the Hogan sisters and Annie surrounded him. And Caroline seemed to have no idea what was going on.

As much as possible, Jilly let Caroline down to run. The toddler seemed to have taken a liking to her. A pang in Jilly's heart told her it was mutual. She'd been around babies before. She had friends her age in San Francisco who were married and already mothers. But as for being in charge of one for such a long time, it was all new. It twisted Jilly's heart to realize she'd like to have a child. But the only way to get one went through a husband and marriage.

She dreaded the very thought.

She'd kept Caroline inside during the rustic proceedings of

the funeral. Michelle and the Hogans had come back inside. But looking out the kitchen window, Jilly watched Zane and Annie linger at the gravesites. She bounced Caroline in her arms as she wondered about the two other men. Who were they? Who would mourn them?

Jilly gave the little one a gentle kiss on her unruly dark curls. Caroline giggled as if the kiss tickled. The little girl had eyes as blue as her mama's and hair as brown. Of course, her papa had dark hair, too. Jilly hadn't seen the man's eyes. They'd been closed most of the time.

This baby girl would never remember her father. She was too young. It caught hard in Jilly's throat to think of such a loss for one so young. Jilly's mama and papa were the foundation of her life. They'd been her first and strongest support. The faith they'd taught her was the rock she leaned on, grew on, built on.

Losing Papa had devastated Jilly. Well, all of them. But Jilly knew how the grief had torn at her heart. Caroline was spared that, but somehow that seemed like its own terrible tragedy.

Michelle came up beside Jilly at the kitchen window. "We need to leave."

Jilly turned toward Michelle. "Why? What happened?"

Michelle gave Caroline a significant look. "The house is overflowing. I heard one of the hands say Zane's other sister will probably come home and Annie will stay, at least for a while, if not permanently. This house is packed to the rafters. We need to get out of it."

Harriet came up behind Michelle and rested one of her hands, in her usual friendly way, on Michelle's shoulder. "You needn't go anywhere."

Jilly noticed a faint blush on Harriet's cheeks. "What's going on?"

Nora came over just a second later. The two sisters exchanged a smile.

"Two of Zane's men have asked us to marry. Bo Sears—"

"The ramrod? He has his own cabin here."

Harriet smiled. The Hogan sisters were in their thirties. Dedicated schoolteachers who'd always lived together. That they, comfortable spinsters, would be brides clearly surprised and delighted them.

"Yes." Nora blushed a deeper pink. "And Jesse Green proposed to me. He was riding herd with us today, Jilly."

"I remember him." Of course, Jilly remembered everyone. "He's got wild blond curls and smiles a lot."

"They asked us yesterday, and we accepted. We were going to announce it tonight at the supper table, but it's not appropriate after today's grief." Nora rested a hand on Caroline's chubby cheek and managed a generous smile. She was a fine woman with a kind heart, but she had a stern way about her. Jesse would keep her smiling.

Harriet went on. "They're going to ask Zane if they can build two line shacks out near where the Purgatory settlement was. But down in Zane's valley, not on that rocky high ground where we set up the mission group. Zane sends men out that far almost daily to ride herd. He's talked of putting up a cabin out there. Bo said the Steinmeyers could possibly move into his cabin. Gretel might come in and work as a cook and housekeeper if she's willing. Her husband, Rick, is handy enough he can work around the ranch yard. He's no cowboy, but there are plenty of chores for him. And we think two of Zane's men are showing an unusual interest in Sally Jo and Melinda."

Sally Jo and Melinda were the remaining members of the mission group, though they hadn't come west with the group. They'd lived in Purgatory under terrible conditions. They'd asked to join the mission and had been accepted. Melinda had a baby girl named Hannah.

"So is Zane going to build two more cabins?"

Harriet shrugged as if nothing worried her. "It's been wrong of Zane to ask so many men to live this kind of bachelor life. Having married men working for him will make for a better life for everyone. Caleb and Laura probably should have stayed and claimed Zane's ranch as a mission field."

Jilly knew Michelle wanted to stay and work at the gold mine, which was still a secret hidden from most everyone.

"I can build all those cabins if Zane wants me to. With help of course. But I love building." Jilly felt the spark of excitement few things gave. "He needs four more cabins at least. Five if he names someone as ramrod, because Gretel and Rick need a cabin. And we'll make them good-sized, larger than the one-room church I built in Purgatory."

Jilly rested a hand on Nora's shoulder, then looked from her to Harriet. They had long ago chosen life as schoolteachers over marriage and family. But now they had a second chance, and they were taking it. Jilly was delighted for them. "You'll need rooms for the children."

Both women turned so pink Jilly suspected the idea had never occurred to them. But they didn't seem to dislike the idea one bit.

"If you two go," Michelle said, always planning, "and Melinda and Sally Jo move out, maybe Jilly and I could take over the housekeeper's rooms. Then Annie and Caroline could have our room—"

Harriet cleared her throat loud enough to stop Michelle from organizing the whole world. She gave Michelle and Jilly a rather alarmed look. "As for you two being housekeepers, I think we need to do some serious work on the skills required for the job."

Jilly knew Michelle hadn't really considered taking the job of a housekeeper. Only taking the housekeeper's small three-room apartment in the back of Zane's lovely home.

Michelle was a highly educated woman, a woman trained to take a hand in running a huge business, a woman with plans to invent and improve machines. She already had two patents. Jilly was trained to build roads through dense, mountainous forests, bridges across rushing rivers, and trestles across vast gorges, and lay train tracks on all of it. Laura had plans to blast tunnels out of the heart of a mountain, or at least manage a crew of men while they did it.

Yet with all that, the sisters were failures at cooking, cleaning, and sewing.

Zane had been told the truth about the Stiles sisters, but no one else. There was still a danger in being found by their stepfather and forced into marriage. Edgar had lost his chance with Laura, but if he could get Michelle and Jilly handed over to the cronies he hoped to marry them to, he could still control two-thirds of the company. Edgar could hang on to the power and money that went with marrying Margaret Stiles, the fabulously wealthy widow of lumber baron Liam Stiles. And Edgar wanted that badly.

They believed Mama was safe now. But Jilly knew she and Michelle weren't.

Harriet and Nora went back to cleaning the kitchen. As soon as they were out of earshot, Jilly whispered to Michelle,

"How have four of the women in our group rounded up husbands within a month of moving here, but you haven't?"

"Five." Michelle crossed her arms and scowled. "You're not counting Laura. And why me? You're supposed to get married, too."

"I think I'd make a poor wife. I've been trained too well how to manage men. I'd have a wreck of a marriage. If you get married, that'll give us two-thirds interest in Stiles Lumber. We'll kick Edgar out."

"We've solved the problem of him abusing Mama, and as long as he can't find us, he'll be unable to marry us off to those lecherous friends of his," Michelle said, staring into the middle distance, thinking it all through, organizing her thoughts. "But he's doing a terrible job of running the company. He'll run us into ruination if we don't take the company back from him soon."

"Not to mention he has to be searching for us. We were a lot better hidden in Purgatory with the mission group. Neither of us has gone to Dorada Rio or anywhere else. No one save Zane knows our name."

"Except Caleb and Nick. And all the people at Laura's wedding when Caleb had to say her name for the vows."

It was getting to be too many people.

Jilly trusted Caleb, Nick, and Zane, but the circle of people who knew where they were was growing.

"Edgar will still want the marriages he planned for us. And he'll want them more than ever." Jilly glanced out the window. Zane was still talking to his sister, but now they walked slowly toward the house. His arm was wrapped around her.

Jilly lowered her voice and talked fast. "I thought you were going to marry Zane."

Michelle looked out, too. Maybe just a bit too long. "He'd never leave his ranch. What good is a husband who won't come home with me? That's got to be a requirement. And he loves being a rancher. I wouldn't want him to give up his life's work. Nope. Zane is out."

Michelle gave him another long look.

Jilly didn't say anything. Michelle was right. The only trouble was it appeared Michelle had some tender feelings for Zane Hart.

Tender feelings and no idea what to do with them.

LAURA HEARD CALEB GASP BEHIND HER. It was a reaction common enough at the sight of the Stiles mansion.

Caleb rode up beside her. "You said it was beautiful, Laura, but no words can fully capture it."

The home was three stories tall, though the third wasn't a full story. It was a collection of turrets and gables with complex angles to the roof that always struck Laura as fanciful, something out of a fairy tale. The turrets had stairs and rooms where a young girl could hide away and read or look out the high windows at the vast woods and dream. The gables brought light from the sun to keep every corner of the house bright and warm.

A porch wrapped all the way around with sweeping steps on three sides, and a roof over the porch was supported by elaborately turned posts. The railing along the porch was adorned by spiraling oak spindles.

Everything about the house celebrated Papa's love and respect for lumber.

Laura had only a small memory of it being built. For years, the Stiles family had lived out here in a common little house. Nice enough, but nothing like this. The men who tended their stables—the massive Belgian draft horses, the teams of big mules, and a collection of beautiful saddle horses—now lived in that house and in the quarters above the stable.

Beyond the house, there were corrals, a carriage house, and a long line of bunkhouse-type cabins. There was a good-sized kitchen, staffed with a cook. A large dining hall connected to the kitchen. A small corner of the dining hall held an office, and another area held the doctor's office and infirmary. They didn't have a doctor but were fortunate to have a well-trained medic who'd learned enough working with a doctor during the Civil War. Doc Sandy did well serving the men who worked at the rugged, sometimes dangerous job.

The men were well cared for and well paid, out of respect for their importance to Stiles Lumber. But Edgar had done a lot of harm to the morale of their faithful lumberjacks.

Laura was almost frantic to see Mama and make sure she was all right, but she took this moment with Caleb to look at the house and cherish the love that had been in the building.

"I remember Papa used to say, 'We've created something beautiful here, Maggie. Something a man who has wood for his livelihood can respect.' Maggie was his nickname for Mama. Other than Papa, I never heard anyone call her anything other than Margaret."

"Let's go see how your ma is doing, Laura. Let's go home."

Home, a beautiful home. Mama was here.

And yet it struck hard that she'd have to face Edgar.

*I'm safe. I'm safe. I'm safe.*

She knew it. She believed it. She prayed for it.

She saw Pete, the groom in charge of the stables who'd worked for the Stileses all his life, watching her as she approached.

His face broke out in a huge smile. He waved, and she waved back. He jogged over to the front of the house as she reached it.

"Miss Laura, it's a fine thing to see you come home."

"Pete, this is my husband, Caleb. I'm Laura Tillman now."

Laura wanted to ask a dozen questions, first and foremost, how was Mama. And she wanted to ask about Nick Ryder, the young man who'd left Zane's ranch at a gallop to come here and stand between Edgar and Mama. He'd grown up in Michigan in lumber country, and when he'd come west, he'd worked for Stiles Lumber for a time. When he recognized the Stiles sisters and heard their story of running from Edgar's cruel wedding plans and of his harsh treatment of Mama, Nick had ridden off from Zane and his ranch, straight for Mama to protect her.

Letters had since arrived from Mama, warning them off of their hasty plans to marry quickly to gain control of their inheritance. She'd insisted she was safe and urged them to take their time and marry wisely, for fear of ending up in the hands of a man like Edgar.

By then Laura had already been married, but although Caleb had some bad things in his past, including a prison term, he'd made his peace with the Lord and felt the calling to be a parson. He was a good and decent man. Laura loved and trusted him.

She swung down off her horse and handed her reins to Pete with her thanks. She and Caleb ran together up the broad front steps. The door was unlocked, and Laura hurried inside.

"Mama! Mama, I'm home." The grand entrance was three stories, peaking in a turret. Stairs led up to the right, then a second set of stairs led to the turret with a balcony, where a person could stand looking out at the grand landscape of mountains and forest.

Stepping inside was glorious—and frightening.

Seconds later, Mama came running from the morning room, where they ate breakfast. It wasn't that early, but Mama sometimes wrote letters or read in the beautiful, sunlit room.

"Laura? Laura, you're home." Mama ran toward her, looking joyful and best of all unharmed.

Laura met her halfway, and they clung to each other.

The feel of those strong arms! Laura never felt so safe as when she was in her mother's arms. Except now she had Caleb's arms. His strength and decency were her haven, and a dearly loved one.

Nick followed Mama at a distance. He managed to be a protective presence while, at the same time, he didn't inject himself into the reunion. Tears came to Laura's eyes to see him here, standing as a sentinel for Mama.

The hug went on for several minutes, and even then, it was all Laura could do to ease back, smile at her precious mother, and say with a grin she knew took over her face, "Mama, meet my husband, Parson Caleb Tillman."

Caleb came up at Laura's right side. He rested one strong hand on Mama's arm. "It's a pleasure to meet you, ma'am. Laura has told me so much about you. I'm glad we could come and see that you are all right."

"Home, are you, Laura?" The cold voice rang with a sneering anger as Edgar stepped out of the office her papa had furnished with such care. "High time." Boot heels clicked on the hallway tiles. "You're finished, then, with your childish stunt of running away? I'll send a wire to Myron Gibbons, the man who has agreed to take you off my hands. I'll finally get at least one of you wretched girls settled."

A chill went down Laura's spine. She'd seen Myron Gibbons at social events in San Francisco. He was huge with thick, slack lips, and he'd come up to her once or twice when he shouldn't have. She'd read the hunger in his eyes when he looked at her.

*I'm safe. I'm safe. I'm safe.*

It ran through her head as a simple prayer. And yet to see the arrogant cruelty in her foul stepfather's eyes, she couldn't quite believe she was safe.

Caleb deliberately moved to stand with his shoulder in front of Laura, between her and her stepfather.

Nick came up behind Mama to face Edgar with his arms crossed.

Edgar could do nothing to her or Mama. A curl of savage pleasure awakened in Laura, and she said with quiet satisfaction, "Edgar, I'm no longer available to marry a man of your choosing. I'm now Mrs. Caleb Tillman."

With Caleb in front of her, it was easy to rest one hand on his shoulder. "This is my husband, Parson Tillman."

Edgar's eyes narrowed, and his jaw went so tight she expected his teeth to crack.

She'd never be so fortunate, of course. Edgar was a handsome man. Part of the reason Mama had become involved with him was his tall, dark good looks.

"You know, Edgar, you really are a fool." Laura felt almost giddy to speak to Edgar this way. She'd wanted to so many times, but fear had ruled her.

*I'm safe. I'm safe. I'm safe.*

She was starting to believe it.

"You are obviously capable of being kind and charming. Mama wouldn't have married you if she hadn't seen that in you. Why didn't you continue behaving like that? You could have had a good life with Mama and my sisters and me. Instead, you couldn't contain your true nature. And now you are surrounded by a family that holds you in contempt. That's the life you chose with your ugly behavior."

Nick extended his hand to Caleb. "Congratulations. You've managed to marry one of the finest young women in the world."

Every word rang with sincerity. For a moment, Mama looked at him with affection, then turned to Edgar. "Your presence is not welcome here."

Then she turned away to address Caleb. "A parson? What a wonderful calling. I trust you're planning to stay here permanently?"

"Laura and I have come to live in her home."

Mama linked her hand through Caleb's elbow. "It's early for luncheon, but you must be hungry after your ride. Would you like something to eat? Coffee and cake maybe? We could have bread and cheese, maybe some cold meat, made up quickly. Or do you and Laura want a bit of time to settle in?"

Caleb smiled that wonderful smile at Mama. His hazel eyes glowed with kindness. His dark blond hair, unruly from the long ride, curled around his ears. He patted Mama's hand where it rested at his elbow. "I am starving, ma'am. I'm sure we're covered in trail dust, but Laura doesn't want to go tidy up when she's been so anxious to see you. If you can bear our grime, food would be very welcome."

Mama smiled right back, and Laura fell a little more in love with him. "Come along, then." She linked her hand through Laura's arm, too. "And, Nick, you too. I'll ask the kitchen to send us some food, and we can all talk."

When they faced back toward the morning room, Edgar still stood near the office, glowering. His eyes calculating as he studied them.

*I'm safe. I'm safe. I'm safe.*

Laura now owned one-third of Papa's lumber business. Edgar looked to be trying to figure out how to put a stop to any interference, especially interference with the flow of money he'd taken possession of. Could the calculation be removing her husband from the picture?

Horrified, Laura knew rationally that even if Edgar arranged something awful for Caleb, she'd still own the company. Of course, there were ways a woman could be forced into marriage, including at the muzzle of a gun. Her little chant of *I'm safe, I'm safe, I'm safe* rang hollow.

Laura hoped the day would come when she believed it.

## CHAPTER
# THREE

LIFE WAS MELANCHOLY AT THE RANCH, though Michelle was grateful for all the little ones. They brought cheer to the household.

Michelle was sitting on the settee in Zane's office tending the three babies. Hannah, Melinda's baby, was only a few months old, so she was in Michelle's arms. The baby liked to lie on the floor kicking her feet, but Caroline tended to dance around, and falling onto a baby was a bad idea. Willa, the daughter of Heinrich and Gretel Steinmeyer, was crawling now and pulling herself up on anything she could reach. She held her own with Caroline, under close supervision, but Hannah didn't stand a chance.

So Caroline danced, Willa crawled, and Hannah chewed on Michelle's fingers. No teeth, so except for the soggy drool, Michelle didn't mind. Michelle wasn't as good at caring for the babies as Jilly. But Jilly was busy building cabins.

Harriet and Nora had announced their engagements, then promptly rode to town with their cowboys and came home as married women. Caught up in the romance of it all, Sally

Jo married just as quickly, and Melinda had confided to Michelle that she expected a proposal any day.

In addition to the line shacks at the far end of his ranch, Zane was building two cabins near his own home. Jilly was wrangling around for a fifth, and Zane didn't seem overly opposed, just harassed at the sudden building boom.

"I'm starting my own town," Zane muttered.

Michelle rolled her eyes. "You can afford it. Besides, it's going to be better here for your hands, and for your own life, to have women about." Michelle knew he was increasingly worried about the drought. Rain would make him a much more cheerful man.

"It's all talk so far. I haven't dug a single"—he glanced at the empty door—"ounce out of that rock."

Michelle whispered, "If you'd let me manage your you-know-what, that would get me and Jilly out of the house. You'd have plenty of room in here."

With Caroline toddling around the room, Michelle especially didn't dare say the word *gold*. The little girl repeated every word she heard.

"You're not getting that job," Zane said.

"You haven't given it to anyone else yet."

"I'm trying to find the right person."

"Me."

Zane glared at her.

He'd kissed her exactly once. And that had been weeks ago. The day she'd told him about the gold. He was excited and not in his right mind exactly, so she didn't take it seriously. But she thought of it. Now and then, and now.

"At least the house has settled down some. I suppose Sally Jo and the Steinmeyers will move out soon, too." As soon as those houses were up. And the work was going fast. They might well be gone by the weekend.

Michelle felt a sudden weight on her shoulders. "Jilly and I should go, too. If you want us out now, we'll go."

"Where would you go?"

Michelle shrugged. She had no idea. "We had no plans when we set out, so we're no worse off than we were before. We'll just go. We'll . . . we'll . . . move to . . . to . . ." She shrugged again. "San Francisco, I suppose."

Except people knew them there. But if they rented humble rooms and lived quietly in a neighborhood far from where they'd grown up, they'd almost certainly not run into any friends they had in San Francisco.

Probably.

Not as much fun as running a gold mine, but maybe she could rent two humble rooms and turn one into a space for her inventions. Or, better yet, one humble room and one small warehouse where she could work on her inventions.

She had ideas for making train travel down steep mountains with tons of logs safer. She also had a keen interest in building a new kind of engine that had been written about but was still just a theory. Whoever perfected the theory would change the world.

Michelle kind of liked the idea of doing that.

She wasn't sure what Jilly would do. No construction company in San Francisco would hire a woman. Maybe Jilly could find a library and read, study, and, oh yes, find a husband.

Laura had liked the idea of a husband.

Jilly dreaded it.

Michelle kept forgetting she needed to find one.

"We'll go now if you wish. Otherwise, we can wait until Jilly's done with the cabins."

"My men know how to build a cabin."

Michelle frowned at him. "You know hers will be better. And done faster. You helped build that church with her giving directions."

Jilly was excited about the two new cabins for the Hogan sisters and two more for Sally Jo and Melinda, all of which Zane had approved. She'd kicked off the building for the Hogans in that distant meadow where Zane wanted a line shack—now he was getting two line shacks. Once that project was running, Jilly had come back and laid out the foundations for the cabins here at the ranch. Now she rode out every day with a group of Zane's cowhands and the Hogan sisters to build. Sally Jo went along to help with the building and to cook a noon meal. Annie and Melinda, along with Gretel, had taken over running the house. Michelle was mostly tending the babies, though Caroline hardly counted as a baby anymore.

"Jilly's a top hand as a carpenter," Zane said, "and even if she weren't, I'm not letting two women traipse off alone to San Francisco."

"As if you have any say about what Jilly and I do."

Zane, sitting behind his desk, shoved to his feet and jabbed his finger at her. "I forbid you to—"

The kitchen door slammed open so hard Michelle jumped to her feet, clutching Hannah too tightly, and Hannah started crying.

Caroline hurtled herself at Michelle's legs and hit with enough force that Michelle staggered. Willa, standing up beside the couch, plopped onto her well-padded bottom and stared in the direction of the racket.

Then a scream came from the kitchen. "Annie!" The newcomer's voice broke, and sobs echoed through the house. "I'm so sorry!"

"Beth Ellen is home." Zane sounded exhausted.

He walked out of the room, forgetting all about scolding her. Or forbidding her. Or whatever else he'd been doing.

Michelle followed much more slowly with a baby in her arms, Caroline clinging to her, and Willa crawling along behind. Michelle didn't trust the crawler to keep coming, so she took a step, then waited, then took another step.

Michelle eased her way out of the room, glad Zane hadn't gone on with his forbidding because she might've just snapped his jabbing finger off. Apparently, she was a surgeon now, so once she'd made her point, she could sew it back on—if she was in a good mood.

She got to the kitchen in time to see Zane head straight for Annie, who was being hugged by the prettiest little blond woman Michelle had ever seen. And she'd seen a lot of people in San Francisco.

Michelle recognized stylish clothes, too. Beth Ellen had a dark red dress with the proper petticoats and underpinnings. The skirts were draped and gathered in beautiful layers. One of the underskirts was a soft cream color, making the red skirts over and under it stand out. And was she wearing a bustle? Michelle had worn the finest clothes when she lived in San Francisco, but fashions changed like the tide. There had been talk of bustles, and she'd seen a few, but she hadn't worn one.

Beth Ellen wore a bonnet, too. Michelle subconsciously touched her hair, bedraggled after a long day of chasing children. Beth Ellen's bonnet was a feminine version of a top hat in the same color as her dress. She wore it well forward on her head with a large bow wrapped around the crown and wide ribbons hanging down to drape among her blond curls.

Annie wore pretty clothes, too. But she was a rancher's wife and a young mother. Her dresses leaned toward comfort and practicality. Even so, both of them put Michelle to shame. She wasn't proud of the pang of envy.

Beth Ellen was the youngest Hart sibling. She held Annie as if she could keep her big sister from flying into pieces. And yet Annie, though she was crying and hugging Beth Ellen back, was much calmer, much more mature, and honestly, it looked like she was doing the comforting.

Michelle stuck it in her memory that whenever she saw someone who was grieving, she needed to remember who was supposed to be the saddest.

Zane spread his arms wide and wrapped them around both his sisters. Caroline yelped and let go of Michelle to run for her mother. Willa used Michelle's skirt to pull herself up to standing.

All Michelle could think was that they needed another bedroom.

And construction was going full steam ahead. Still, Beth Ellen needed a room now, and as a daughter of the house, she should have the room she grew up in. Michelle knew that was the room she and Jilly were sleeping in.

There wasn't space for everyone.

Michelle thought of a bright side. Beth Ellen would only be here for a few days. She was visiting, but she'd soon be back in San Francisco.

"Who are these women, Zane?" Beth Ellen paused her crying long enough to give Michelle a resentful look. Then her eyes slid to Melinda and Gretel, who were pressed back against the sink, where they'd finished cleaning up after the meal.

Beth Ellen looked at them like they were intruding.

Michelle couldn't blame her.

"Melinda, come and get Hannah. Gretel, fetch Willa. I'll leave Caroline here with you, Annie, but if you wish it, you can bring her in, and we'll tend her while you have your . . . reunion. We'll go into the office. Give you some privacy."

Michelle turned and hurried out with Hannah still in her arms. If Melinda wanted her baby, she'd have to catch her.

They'd barely reached the office when Michelle heard Beth Ellen break down in sobs again. Even from this distance, Michelle heard her shout, "He didn't come with me. I'm through with Loyal Kelton forever." Her crying grew louder. "He had a mistress the whole time he was courting me. I'm done with San Francisco. Oh, Zane, I want to come home."

Michelle handed the baby off to Melinda and considered finding Jilly, wherever she was building. Michelle could help with that project. This house was packed to the rafters.

In fact, Michelle thought the roof was about to blow all the way off.

# CHAPTER FOUR

ZANE STARED AT THE CEILING while he tried to fall asleep. He was surprised his house didn't burst at the seams. It was a wonder, really, that he didn't have both his sisters in his bed while he slept on the floor.

At least his brother hadn't come home. But Josh loved the seafaring life and only came by every year or two for a few days.

It was nice to have his sisters home. Zane loved them dearly. But they were both distraught. He'd've never wished them back under such circumstances. One with her husband murdered, and the other betrayed by her cheating beau.

Zane felt terrible for his sisters. At the same time, he felt helpless.

It seemed like Michelle should handle all this. Jilly was busy building. He had to give her credit, that woman didn't settle for a boring square of logs. The cabins she was working on were simple, but they had three rooms, besides an entrance, plus a pantry and two closets. And they really were well constructed. Jilly had a flair for somehow making them nicer than most cabins.

Though she was working hard at it, Gretel couldn't speak enough English to help with Annie's and Beth Ellen's grief, and the rest of the females around here were either married or on their way to it. That left those women with little time to supply a shoulder to a pair of women who seemed prone to breaking into tears with little notice. Except for taking care of three babies, Michelle wasn't doing anything.

As Zane awoke the next morning, still pondering his troubles, he decided Michelle was the answer. She had few if any womanly skills in the kitchen or anywhere in the house. She was doing a decent job chasing babies, but she was often confused about just what was necessary to care for them. He suspected her skills were being grossly underused.

He shoved back the covers and dressed quickly, determined to make Michelle handle all weeping women from now on. He was giving her a roof over her head, so she oughta pay him back somehow.

He strode out of his room and down the stairs to find Michelle slipping out the back door, dressed for a long ride judging by the bedroll and sack of food.

"Stop right there."

She glanced back with a grimace, then went on out.

Zane was after her quick as a flash. "Where are you going? Not San Francisco. I'll lock you in the cellar before I let you do that."

"No. Jilly, the Hogans, and some of your men already rode out to the cabins they are building over by—" she glanced around—"you-know-what."

He knew. He just didn't know how he was ever going

to gather up that gold without causing a huge problem. Considering all the building going on around here and the fact that he'd bought two houses in the nearby mining town of Dorada Rio for the two remaining families that had been settled in Purgatory, he probably oughta round up that gold.

Purgatory was where Caleb's mission group had been, and Laura had found gold in a deep part of the forest near the ramshackle settlement. Before they could even tell Zane about the vein, a mob had stormed through Purgatory. They'd burned down Jilly's newly built church and nearly killed Caleb. Had been bent on it, in fact, when Laura, who turned out to be a highly trained chemical engineer, had used her handy supply of dynamite with great precision to knock out most of the mob.

Then Zane had come and rounded up the rest of the rabble. The sisters eventually told him of his gold. So he'd bought houses in town for the two remaining families who were down on their luck. Afterward, he'd burned down the shanties so no newcomers, looking for shelter in times of dire need, would come onto his property.

"Ride along with me," Michelle said. "I think I've figured out how to solve your gold problem."

She was so sure. So organized. So convincing that he found himself saddling his horse and riding out with her.

"Tell me what we're going to do." He noticed she had a large, carefully wrapped packet behind her saddle.

"It's simple. One of the reasons it's hard to go forward with any plans for the gold is because we really don't know what we're dealing with. If it is a deep vein of gold, it's going to have to be properly mined. It'll take machinery and men and maybe years to get it all. That's a big job and a big headache, but a lot of wealth.

"If it's only a pocket of gold, we can gather it up and be done with the whole thing ourselves. No miners to hire. No gold rush because there's no gold. With the men so close out there building already, I can slip up to Purgatory and do a day's worth of mining, and no one will realize I'm up there instead of working on the cabins or surveying the nearby land for other buildings. Since you're coming along, you can help me."

"I can?" Zane gave up hope that Michelle would be good for his sisters. She wasn't even babysitting anymore.

"We'll spend a day digging. We'll know a lot more when we're done. Honestly, it'd be best if it was a pocket of gold. You could get it all out, then take it to Sacramento, or maybe San Francisco. Word would probably get out that you'd found gold. But if at the same time, you could say this was the lot, then maybe no gold rush would start."

"I have nightmares about a gold rush. A crowd shoving me, pushing past me, overrunning my land, eating my cows, all while wielding pickaxes. In the end, I get trampled, and I wake up swinging my fists. Fighting for my land as I get crushed, along with you and my sisters. Oh, everyone's wandering into that dream."

"Today will tell us more. We'll get what gold we can in a long day's work and hide it somewhere."

"Hard to hide gold."

"We'll put it in the saddlebags."

Zane frowned. "Men in gold country notice things like bags that hang heavy or hoof marks that sink in deep."

Frowning, Michelle said, "We'll make sure not to overload our saddlebags."

"Saddlebags full of gold. Who'd've ever imagined it? It's gonna play havoc with my ranch and my life. But it's hard to resist the call of gold." Zane shook his head in wonder. "You're right. We need to find out what we're dealing with."

They rode at a good pace through the pastures and mountains of Zane's land. It was about two hours in the saddle when they came upon the cabin construction.

The cabins were nearly complete. The Hogan sisters would be gone by the weekend. They could probably start sleeping in the cabins right now. The chimneys were up. The roof on each was enclosed. Doors hung. The windows still gaped open, so they needed shutters. Zane wondered how furniture building was progressing.

Jilly had told him last night she was splitting logs for a wooden floor. Many log cabins didn't have floors, so that was a luxury.

The cabins weren't far from each other, fifty paces or so. Far enough for privacy, close enough for safety. They were close to the trees for shade and a windbreak. It was a beautiful setting with the wooded mountain rising up behind the buildings. A small stream trickled behind the cabins. With Michelle's help, they'd piped water into the cabins and arranged a drain so they had running water at hand. Homes with modern conveniences.

Jilly didn't have to see it all through to the very end. And she had two cabins to build closer to Zane's house, though they were going up fast, too. She'd soon be done and looking for something to do. Like mining gold. A two-person crew. Three if Zane insisted on coming every day.

"Is there a way to circle around this meadow so they won't see us coming?" Michelle asked. "We can act like it's some routine thing for one day, but if we come over and over, that'll make them wonder."

"I've got a ranch to run, Michelle. I can't just ride off every day and expect my men not to notice. Bo and Jesse are two of my best hands. Shad will take charge, but I'm going to have to have someone ramrodding the outfit if Bo is over here. And I don't *act* like anything." He glared hard at her. "Two Harts is my spread. I go where I want, when I want, and offer no excuse nor explanation unless I choose to."

She smiled. "Does that mean no? There is no way to slip past without being seen?"

"There's a way."

She didn't ask for more.

"Getting past these cabins isn't the only problem. Both of us will be missed. My men aren't stupid. Neither are the women at the Two Harts. They're all going to wonder."

The valley had a nice herd of Zane's Hereford cattle. With their red coats and white faces, Zane thought they were about the prettiest critters in the world.

"You know, your brand is almost an infinity symbol," Michelle said.

"A what?" His eyes went to the brand he was so proud of. "It's shaped like two hearts lying on their sides with the tips touching. It's registered as the Two Harts Ranch. Pa chose the brand with himself and Ma in mind." But folks thought it looked like a sideways eight. Zane had heard it called the Lazy Eight. He didn't like it, but he kept his mouth shut.

"The tops of the hearts have that little dip in them, of course, but to just look at it, an infinity symbol is the first thing that comes to mind."

"Since I've never heard of such a thing, it doesn't come to my mind. What is it?"

"Picture an eight lying on its side. If you put your finger on the line at any point, you could trace it around and around. No beginning, no end. It strikes me as a very Christian symbol, like how God has no beginning and no end."

"Then a number eight is an infinity symbol, too."

"It is, but the mathematical symbol for infinity is always on its side. It's a sign for a number too large to ever count. The number of stars in the sky is infinite. God talks of the children of Abraham being as many as the sands that are upon the seashore. That's infinity. There are uses for it in mathematical calculations, but to me it's a beautiful concept. And here you are with infinity as your cattle brand."

"My cattle marked with infinity." Shaking his head, Zane smiled. "I like it."

He waved at Harriet when she stepped out of her cabin. The trail to Purgatory, or what was left of it, didn't wind close to the cabins, so it was easy to keep well away to not encourage any delays. Or to have to answer any questions.

They took the narrow trail into the heavy, rock-strewn forest and wound up a steep mountain slope.

When they arrived, Zane took in the ashy remains of what had been a wretched little community where people came when they were as far down on their luck as they could be.

Caleb had hoped to reach people here for the Lord. Instead, his dream was in ashes. He hadn't let it concern him long. With Purgatory gone, he and Laura had ridden back to the logging camp. Zane figured they would need a parson there just as much as a mining town did.

CALEB AND NICK TALKED long and hard about what was going on at Stiles Lumber.

Caleb didn't know much about lumber, but Nick did. And he could tell things were going badly. Very badly.

Too many men had quit or been fired. Those still here mostly stayed out of loyalty to Mrs. Stiles, whom they seemed to revere, despite being mistreated. Underpaid, overworked. They weren't even being fed well because the men who had cooked for them quit, and the new cooks were incompetent but loyal to the man who had given them their jobs: Edgar Beaumont.

"The men live in bunkhouses, not exactly like the ones at the Two Harts," Nick said. "There are three lines of cabins, and each is built for two men to live in. There's also a dining hall where they gather to eat. But the roof leaks on about half of the cabins, and Beaumont won't have them repaired. I also talked with Old Tom, the man who amounts to the foreman out here. He can't fire the new cooks. He tried. They tattled to Beaumont, who overruled Old Tom."

"Why wouldn't Beaumont want the lumberjacks well fed and comfortable?" Caleb asked.

"All I can think is cutting corners gives him more money to spend. But I also think part of it is just pure contempt for laboring men. He doesn't respect them, because they get dirt under their fingernails."

Caleb shook his head, then shook it harder. "He won't have any money if they all quit."

"Nope, and when a man does quit, Beaumont hires a new one, but the new man isn't here to work. He's here to spy, bully, and report any disgruntled comments to Beaumont, at which time, Beaumont fires anyone who speaks poorly of him. The new men make better wages, too, so they're not going to quit."

"Can Laura wield enough clout as one-third owner to give the rest of the men raises?" Caleb looked toward Laura, sitting beside her ma on a little couch they called a love seat in front of the fireplace.

The love seat was upholstered in a rich gold fabric that complemented a pair of wingback chairs in gold and black fabric, one a bit smaller, as if made for a husband and wife, while three daughters took up the love seat.

Caleb studied the two women. Their delight at being reunited seemed to overflow. The two of them were talking quietly, intently, holding hands, heads together. Caleb guessed Laura was giving a full report on what she and her sisters had done while they were away.

Nick leaned back in the chair he sat in facing Caleb. They were across the room. When Nick picked these chairs, Caleb had thought they were giving Laura and her ma time and space. Now it was clear that Nick had his own story to tell.

"As I understand it," Caleb said, "Laura owns a third of the company. But does she own a third of the inseparable whole? Or can she rip one-third away and run that part herself? Hire the lumberjacks, pay the wages, make the money? If her income is enough, maybe she can pay for better food for all who work for her—better food for everyone. Fix each and every leaky roof."

"I think someone said two of the sisters needed to marry to own two-thirds and have controlling interest." Nick's two-colored eyes glinted with the new idea. He had one blue eye and one green. It was quite unusual, but they gleamed with honor and intelligence.

"But why couldn't Laura take over a third? We're so short-handed most of the skilled lumberjacks could come to her third of the property. Work solely for her and for much better wages."

Nodding, Nick said, "I think that would work."

"How about you? Do you get paid?"

Nick snorted. "Not since I rode away from Zane. But I don't need much, and the roof in here doesn't leak."

"With me here, the men taking turns watching over Mrs. Stiles can get back to work." Caleb considered the situation.

"I can't leave here. I *won't* leave because I don't have enough hours as it is to keep an eye on Mrs. Stiles. But now that you're here, at least I can—" Nick glanced at the women, leaned close, and whispered—"run to the outhouse without worrying."

"I thought there were some lumberjacks helping you?"

"There are, but it's a mean situation. Beaumont threatens to fire them. He's cut the wages to the bone of anyone who stands between him and his wife. He hasn't fired them yet because he's shorthanded. Most of those two-man cabins only have one man living in them. And Mrs. Stiles feeds them better here in the house than the cooks at the camp do, so we've been rocking along. But one of these days Beaumont will explode and fire them all. I think some of them still might stay. They care that much about her safety."

Caleb heard a door open and saw Beaumont enter the room. "You might get that explosion sooner than you think."

The women were between Caleb and Beaumont. He and Nick stood and walked to stand near the women before Beaumont could do something stupid that'd make the explosion come right here and now.

## CHAPTER FIVE

"LET'S NOT LEAVE THE HORSES IN THE CORRAL." Michelle looked around at the sad little remnants of their mission field. The corral was one of the few things still standing in Purgatory.

They walked into the woods, Michelle leading. The woods swallowed them up. Tall oaks and spreading firs. The ground heavy with scrub brush and centuries of fallen limbs.

"The ground is dry up here, too," Zane said.

They'd ridden miles today, and signs of dried-up ponds and withered grass were everywhere. She had some ideas about that, but she hadn't had time to work them out, let alone convince Zane to try them. That should have probably come before gold mining.

She'd talk with him about it on their ride home.

Michelle tethered her mare. She'd brought a halter along so the horse could graze without the bit in its mouth. She stripped the saddle off and plunked it and the saddlebags on the ground.

Zane rode his big buckskin stallion and got him settled in

for a day of grazing just like Michelle had done. Michelle knew he saw her handling the heavy saddle as men's work. But if he wanted to take over, he was going to have to move faster.

Michelle unpacked a pickax, hammer, and chisel. She should have added more tools once he decided to come along.

She handed the pickax to him and pointed to a spot a few paces away from her. The better not to accidentally ax her.

"Get to work, cowboy. We don't want to spend all day on this."

She set her chisel in place and struck it. A rock the size of her fist flew off. She picked it up and hammered on it.

Zane swung his ax.

The quartz seemed eager to shatter. When it did, Michelle saw gold. Rich and heavy. Wonderful and worrisome.

Zane didn't seem too interested in cleaning up the gold he chopped loose. Instead, he just kept hacking.

A couple of hours later, Michelle looked at the mountain of rocks Zane had scattered all around. All veined with gold.

"Time for a break."

Zane, ready for another swing, relaxed and straightened away. He looked at the pile he'd made. "I just wanted to see how deep the gold goes."

He met her eyes.

She grinned. "It goes really deep."

She got bread and cheese out of her saddlebags. She'd brought apples and cookies, too. When Zane announced his plans to come along, she'd gone back and doubled the food. She'd thrown in a good supply of beef jerky, too, which they kept on hand at Zane's house. There was enough to feed them both a meal right now and one later if they worked through supper.

She set it out as he came over with his canteen.

"What are we going to do, Zane?" Michelle sat on a downed log with her back to the gold they'd dug.

Zane settled in beside her and began eating. He chewed thoughtfully, and she didn't rush him. She liked when people were thoughtful.

He finished a whole slice of bread and half the slice of cheese she'd handed him. After a long drink from his canteen, he said, "I want you to understand that I respect your ability to run this for me. My objection to it is that I think the men who come to work this gold will be dangerous. Even if they don't run mad and turn thieves and killers, you'd be subjected to foul language and unsavory approaches by men with no decent thoughts in their minds. I can hire the best men I can find. But you remember that man from Caleb's mission group who hit his wife when he was drunk?"

"I saw that happen to a couple of women." It still shocked her, and she wished she'd never seen such a thing. She suspected Edgar had struck her mother in private, but it was a different experience to actually see it happen.

"Well, I talked with him later. So did Caleb. He seemed like a decent enough man. When his head was clear, he was nice to his wife, and he spent time paying attention to his children." Zane shrugged one shoulder. "That man, behaving as he was when I talked to him, was one I'd've hired. Between gold and whiskey, add in poverty and stress when you've come home with no food for your family and your paycheck drunk away . . . you can't just look at a man, talk to him, and judge how he'll behave once he's faced hard times or when he's got gold within his grasp."

Michelle twisted around to stare at the rock pile they'd

made. Michelle had hammered hers up and stripped the gold from the quartz. She had a pile of nuggets that might equal two or three pounds of gold. Zane had a knee-deep pile of gold-veined quartz around him but had yet to hammer out the gold.

"Assuming the quantity of rock you've loosened contains an amount of gold equal to what I've been knocking away, I'd say we have nearly seven pounds of gold. Possibly ten. That's one hundred and sixty ounces of gold at twenty dollars an ounce. That's three thousand two hundred dollars' worth of gold."

Zane blew out hard, almost as if someone had punched him in the stomach. "In one morning?"

"Well, I'm estimating, and the work is by no means done, so no, not in one morning. I'd say what's in that pile you made is all afternoon's work. I'm going to quit digging and get the gold free of the quartz you knocked loose. That'll fill the rest of my day. You can keep going with the pickax."

"My pa's been out here a long time. He came out for the gold rush and was smart enough to decide there was more gold on the hoof than there was in the ground."

"My papa did the same thing." Papa, how she missed him. The greatest loss in what had been her greatly blessed life. "He made a good, not great, strike and saw that the shopkeepers were going to take most of it when he bought supplies. He had left Mama and us girls back east. He wanted to build a home for us, and lumber was at a price, as he said, that only a madman would pay. Instead of buying supplies and making himself penniless, he decided there was more gold in the trees than there was in the ground."

Zane smiled. It did something to her. Lifted her heart a bit. When thinking about Papa usually made her sad.

Zane's smile remained, and his eyes lingered on her.

She remembered their one and only kiss when he was excited about the gold discovery.

"Pa had some really rich years once he got the herd started. Prices were crazy. He drove twenty head of three-year-old calves to San Francisco one year and made one hundred dollars per head. Two thousand dollars for a year's work. Now I'm going to make more money from a day's work. All for gold."

He looked with some distaste at the gold.

"I could handle it," Michelle said. "I know how to shoot a gun."

"I'm just afraid you'd have to use it, Michelle. That's the problem. And I don't want that for you."

"That's the life I've been raised for, educated for."

"But is it right? I can see you're organized and smart—no, brilliant. Very capable. But what will you do when a burly, hungover man comes busting into your office up here shouting that it isn't fair a rich man like Zane Hart gets the lion's share of the gold while he does all the work?"

"What would a man do? Are you going to hire a fighter? What if he can't win a fistfight with a burly, hungover man any more than I can? Are you going to post guards? And how will you choose those guards? How can you be sure you can trust them?"

Zane gave her a long, solemn look. "I don't know."

Michelle didn't really know, either.

# CHAPTER SIX

A LOUD RUSTLING IN THE TREES made Zane surge to his feet and draw his pistol.

"Don't shoot. It's me," Jilly said.

Zane almost fell over backward. Almost shooting a woman shook him badly enough he missed his holster when he tried to shove his pistol into it.

"I made noise deliberately, afraid you'd be jumpy." Jilly came in. Her red hair glowed against the green leaves. Her eyes were so green it was like the trees had shared their color.

She led the pinto gelding she seemed partial to.

"What are you doing up here?" Zane heard the snap in his voice. That wasn't fair.

"Wow, that's a rich vein of gold." Jilly barely glanced at Michelle or Zane. He noticed she only had eyes for the gold, and who could blame her?

Michelle gave Zane one very sassy glance, then went to walk with Jilly to study the gold.

"I estimate we've found around three thousand dollars' worth of gold this morning."

Jilly picked up one of the rocks Zane had busted the quartz off of. She studied it, turning it in her hand. "I'd say more like four thousand five hundred."

Michelle picked up a rock. "Really? What makes you say that?"

"It's just a guess."

Zane snorted.

Jilly and Michelle both turned to look, then they grinned at him.

"Jilly is the mathematician in the family," Michelle said. "If she says four thousand five hundred, I'd bet she's right to within a hundred dollars."

"You can't know that."

"Well, I don't know." Jilly grinned again. "But I can estimate, deduce, round to the next highest factor, multiply by the price of gold, which is steady on the commodity market as a rule, and, you know, guess."

Zane held back the next snort.

Barely.

"By the way," Jilly continued, "you have ten thousand seven hundred and, oh, I'd say about fifty head of cattle."

Zane arched a brow, but neither woman looked at him this time. "I keep a tally book. You must've seen it."

"No, but I've ridden out to two of your meadows. The largest and one your cowhand called a regular-sized one. I counted the number of cows in one section of the large meadow. They were spread quite evenly, so I felt able to extrapolate the number of cattle. Then I judged the size of the meadow and multiplied to get a total. Your hand said you have five regular-sized meadows, the big one, and three small ones. I assumed—and that can be dangerous in mathematics—you spread your cattle evenly between the pastures. So beyond extrapolating, I multiplied, corrected for meadow acreage, rounded down to the nearest fifty, and so on."

"And so on? There's more to it?"

"Well, what I really did was take into consideration some geographical anomalies in your pastures, assumed the land was generally the same, and then I created an equation, solved for the nearest—"

"Stop." Zane cut her off. "You don't need to tell me how you did it. You're within ten of the number I have in my tally book." He tugged it out of his breast pocket so she could see the book but shoved it back in. "I get this number by actually counting the cattle."

"You count to ten thousand? Every day?"

"Not every day. But we don't ride out to each pasture every day."

"I honestly figured about ten higher, but to be so exact is just showing off."

Zane closed his eyes, then they popped open. "So, girl geniuses, what am I supposed to do with all this gold without causing mayhem?"

Michelle and Jilly shared a long look. They seemed to be communicating without words . . . sister magic or something. But he knew what they were both doing was thinking while they stared through each other.

"I wanted to see what we were dealing with," Michelle said. "Is this a huge strike that's going to require years, possibly a lifetime, of managing? Or is it a pocket that could be dug out, and Zane could be done with it?"

Nodding, Jilly said, "No way to be sure of that yet. If it's a pocket, you're not to the end of it. It'll be a nice pocket. Tens of thousands of dollars, Zane. You already seem like a prosperous man, but now you're going to be rich."

"I've got enough cattle to last a lifetime. Enough money, too. What am I going to do? Buy more land and more cows? Buy fancier guns and horses? Hire more servants and cowhands?" Avenge his sister's husband?

That was in his head day and night.

"I guess you could build a bigger house." Jilly grinned mischievously. "I'd be glad to help you."

He surprised himself by smiling back, then looking at Michelle, probably for a little too long. A man who didn't need a thing, who'd soon fill his pockets full of gold. He probably could marry Michelle.

Tearing his thoughts away from that, he looked at the gold. "We'll dig awhile. A few more days, but I can't come every day." He glowered at Michelle. "If I could be sure you'd be safe, you could come out alone. There is a trail you can ride that no one in the cabins would see."

Michelle almost wiggled with pleasure.

"I said *if* I could be sure you were safe. I'll have to think more about that. After a few more days digging, we'll know if it's a big strike or not."

Frowning, he added, "I need to do something about Annie. She's willing to just walk away from her ranch, give it all up. But that's her grief talking. I can't let a land grab and the murder of three men stand and call myself an honorable man."

Michelle said quietly, "Don't start a fight you can't win, Zane. You can take care of Annie and Caroline here. I heard your sister say powerful men are siding with the tyrant who is behind the land grab and murders."

He looked right in her eyes. Dark, lively blue. Her hair pulled back into a bun, but after a morning of gold mining, curls had escaped and danced around her neck and over her ears.

"Aren't you and your sisters involved in a plot to take on a tyrant? Weren't you all willing to risk everything by jumping in a flume and riding down it to escape him?"

"You're right. Look into it, then, but be careful. Don't just go charging down there, guns blazing. Find out what you're up against first."

Nodding, Zane said, "Jilly, you've got to go back to the cabins, or one of those builders will be up here wondering where you've gone. Michelle, it's time for us to get back to gold mining."

Jilly looked mutinous for a few long moments.

"You want to dig for gold, too, don't you?" Zane asked.

She gave a sullen shrug. "Sure I do."

"How long until the cabins are done?"

"Three days."

"And you ladies can both handle a gun?"

They both smiled.

"You two really resemble each other."

Michelle looked at Jilly. "We are as different as can be. We have completely different hair and eye color."

Jilly piped up. "I'm taller. And smarter."

Michelle whacked her in the arm with the back of her hand. "Jilly's got those dreadful freckles while my skin is pure as cream."

Jilly laughed.

"Those smiles," Zane said. "Especially when you're getting your own way."

"We should always get our own way." Jilly plunked her hands on her hips. "We're very smart."

Zane snorted. "So I've been told and told. When you smile at the same time, you're alike as two raindrops. Now let's get back to work."

"WHAT IS IT, EDGAR?" Margaret, her voice dripping with disdain, stood from the love seat. Laura stood at her mother's side.

Caleb was a little surprised Beaumont had the nerve to follow them into the morning room when he knew he'd be the main topic of conversation.

Caleb had heard all about how Mrs. Stiles . . . or no, Mrs. Beaumont . . . maybe he oughta call her Mama—or Margaret —Marge maybe. Maggie. It was early yet. He'd figure it out.

She'd told them about her trusty fireplace poker. Caleb wished Laura had it at hand now.

Instead, the women had Nick and Caleb. And sadly, Caleb knew from his misspent youth that he would be up to the task of protecting them.

Caleb had seen the cold, angry side of the man in the front entrance. There was none of that now. Yet something about Beaumont struck Caleb as . . . wrong.

Caleb's misspent youth included reading people very well, and he was still good at it. Reading Beaumont, Caleb braced himself for a pack of lies.

Beaumont, with none of the angry stiffness from earlier, came around the sofa where Laura had sat with her mother. He settled into a chair at an angle to the sofa, his right side to the unlit fireplace.

Caleb saw Laura stiffen. Margaret bristled. Caleb didn't have to be told that Beaumont was sitting in Laura's pa's chair, and neither woman liked it.

"Having Laura come home has opened my eyes to how awful I've been, Margaret." Beaumont's voice was calm, kind, etched with regret.

He was good. Caleb would give him that. But not good enough to fool anyone, least of all Caleb with his experience with swindling.

"Please sit down. Please let me have my say."

Margaret frowned, but she retook her seat. Laura sat beside her.

Caleb glanced at Nick and saw no dawning trust, which was what Beaumont was aiming for.

Deciding not to waste time with a scheme, Caleb rounded the sofa and took the chair that most likely belonged to Laura's ma.

"Beaumont." Caleb heard the hostility lacing his voice and fought it down. He started again as Beaumont, all genial good nature, turned his attention to Caleb.

"Yes, what is it?" Before Caleb could speak, Beaumont raised one hand to halt him. "But before you tell me, I want to apologize. I saw Laura with a husband of her own choosing and realized I had run mad." Shaking his head, Beaumont went on. "I hope someday to earn your forgiveness, Laura, and the forgiveness of your sisters. But for now, I've come in here to tell you I've seen the error of my ways. I'm leaving.

I can only believe it will be a relief to you all. I will write to you, Margaret, and spell out how I let myself get so far beyond any bounds of decency. Maybe in time, with plenty of people around you to make sure I stand by my pledge, you will give me another chance."

Then with a gracious gesture—which looked good but struck Caleb as a king giving his lowly subject a chance to speak—Beaumont said, "Go ahead."

Caleb forced himself to relax, to pray, to search for the right words. Because before anything, he was a man of faith. "Edgar, Laura and I plan to make our home here for as long as God leads us to do that."

"Welcome. Having one of her daughters back will be a comfort to Margaret."

"Listen to me, Edgar, for just a few minutes."

"Of course." Again, the king granting the subject a few words.

Caleb had to fight to keep from clenching his teeth. "I wasn't always a man of God. I had a stretch in my life when I was a man very much like you."

Margaret gasped and clutched Laura's hand.

Laura patted the tight grasp and smiled.

She knew what he was doing. He was trying to lead a man to God.

"Because of those years, I can recognize a liar when I hear one, and I'm hearing one now. Not that Margaret would ever trust you anyway."

Reading a man by how taut his jawline was, whether his knuckles were white when they were supposed to be resting on an overstuffed chair arm, whether a vein pulsed in his neck, was all part of Caleb's skill set.

"She won't trust you because you put your hands on her in violence. She most especially won't trust you after you threatened her daughters."

Edgar kept a serene, remorseful expression on his face, but some of the color heightened in his cheeks. The man's temper was under tenuous control.

But Caleb honestly didn't want to make the man erupt in fury. "You ruined your marriage, and I'd say you've ruined any chance you'll ever have to make it right, but you haven't ruined your chance to change how things are between you and God."

Edgar's eye twitched. Something calculating shifted in his genial gaze. Caleb wondered if the man would lie, pretend to turn to God.

Or maybe he really would. Caleb prayed with every word he spoke. A glance at Laura told him she was praying, too. And she hated Edgar. That stopped his thoughts. *Did* Laura hate him? It was a terrible thing to hate.

Feared him, absolutely. Was furious at him for what he'd done to her mother.

And yet now she prayed. He saw her eyes closed. Her head just slightly bowed. She wasn't putting on a grand show of it, just praying for a man who'd been terrible to her, or maybe for Caleb to say the right things, but that amounted to praying for Edgar, too.

Caleb would have said he couldn't have possibly loved his wife more. And yet he felt himself slide even deeper. His own prayers included thanking God for bringing Laura into his life.

He went back to talking to Edgar. Praying God would give him the right words. Knowing he was casting his seeds on thorny soil.

Nick moved around the sofa slowly until he was standing slightly behind Edgar. Caleb hoped he wasn't preparing to pounce. That wouldn't go well with his ministry.

"Like I said, I don't think there's much of a chance Margaret will ever trust you again."

Temper flashed in Edgar's eyes, but he blinked and regained his serene expression quickly.

"But she might forgive you."

Margaret made a small protesting humph.

Caleb turned to her and smiled. "Those things are different. I can forgive someone who's done me a terrible wrong and is unrepentant. But that's mainly so I don't carry the ugliness of unforgiveness inside me—not after God has forgiven me so much."

Her scowl eased a bit.

"You can forgive without trusting. I don't believe God asks us to trust someone who has hurt us and clearly intends to do it again. Trust has to be earned through true signs of regret and a change of behavior. Even then, with a violent man, I'd be very wary." He turned back to Edgar. "But *God* will forgive you. He will know if your repentance is genuine because He knows what's in your heart. So He'd know if He could trust you or not. If you sincerely believe that Jesus came here and died for your sins, if you repent of those sins, God will forgive you and save your soul."

Edgar's shoulder jerked, and he clasped the chair arms tightly.

Caleb was silent, watching the man who thought he was such a talented liar. He really wasn't all that good. What had Margaret and her daughters been thinking?

"I appreciate you taking the time to talk to me, Parson Tillman."

"Call me Caleb. I'm your son-in-law now. Maybe I should call you Papa." He couldn't quite control the little jab because he didn't want Edgar to believe his act was working. He was focused on Edgar, but he felt Margaret and Laura flinch at the word *papa*.

He saw Nick roll his eyes.

Caleb almost smiled. "If you want to talk about your faith, if you're truly sorry for how badly things have gone with your marriage, I'd love to talk with you about it and help you find a path that leads you to God. I am living proof that God can use a flawed man, save a lost soul. God writes the truth of salvation on every person's heart, and He loves us all enough to give us a chance to turn to Him."

He watched and prayed and waited.

Then the shift in Edgar's eyes. The fake sincerity. It was all there.

"I've handled things terribly with my marriage, that's true."

And Caleb knew he'd lost. But then, he hadn't lost, had he? He'd laid the truth before the man. It was Edgar who had lost. Who *was* lost.

Edgar rose from his chair and turned to Margaret. "I do ask you to forgive me, Margaret. And I hope our marriage can be healed. I need time away to think things over, to . . . to *pray* over all I've done."

"You're leaving?" Margaret failed to keep the hope out of her voice. She wanted this man to go away, no doubt about it.

"Yes, but only until I've searched my heart for why I've turned to such wrongdoing. I'm going to be a better man. I'll write to you." With a slight tip of his head to Caleb, Edgar strode from the room.

Nick had moved to the door and held it open for him, then swung it shut with a sharp bang.

"I failed with him." Caleb felt a wash of grief for the man's soul. "But then, it was my job to set truth before him, and I didn't fail at that. Whether he accepted that truth was up to him. But still, it hurts me to see a man so lost."

"You may have failed with him, Caleb, but you're right about forgiveness. I have no trust in that man, but I am going to do my best to cast the unforgiveness from my heart." Margaret stood from the sofa and came to take Caleb's hand. "And you can call me Mama."

She turned to Nick. "You can call me that, too."

Nick scratched his head and didn't call her anything.

# CHAPTER SEVEN

THE DAY FINALLY CAME when Sally Jo and the Hogan sisters—who were no longer named Hogan—moved out, and the Steinmeyers moved into the newly vacated ramrod cabin.

Melinda announced at breakfast that she was getting married that very day, and she'd move into the second new cabin built near the ranch house this afternoon.

Michelle and Jilly moved into the housekeeper's apartment, and each had her own bedroom. But giving them the housekeeper's rooms wasn't exactly right because they did very little housekeeping. They probably oughta change the name of the room.

The upstairs, with its five bedrooms, was now occupied by Zane's family.

And Michelle hadn't gotten back to her gold mine all week.

She was spending hours every day helping people move and settle in, chasing the three children. And not digging gold.

She was slowly dying from impatience, though she had smuggled the gold they'd brought home into the housekeeper's apartment. With Jilly's help, working quietly at night, they'd cleaned the gold of every crumbling speck of quartz, and Jilly estimated the gold was valued at . . . exactly what she'd estimated when she'd seen it still veined through rock.

Today was Sunday, everyone was settled, and Michelle vowed that tomorrow she and Jilly would spend the day digging.

She had to find a way to tell Zane.

And get him to say yes.

Gretel headed to the house she now lived in, taking a portion of the meal she'd helped cook, to eat dinner with Rick and Willa. Gretel had agreed to take on the job of housekeeper for Zane. Rick was now permanently hired to do ranch chores.

Both the Steinmeyers were working hard, and all of it with baby Willa to handle . . . which seemed to mostly be Michelle's job.

Annie brought a platter to the table with roast beef on it, and Beth Ellen came with a bowl of carrots and another of potatoes. Michelle and Jilly added gravy, a platter of bread, dishes of butter, jelly, and a glass of milk for everyone.

The Hart family and the Stiles sisters sat down to dinner.

"It's so quiet in here." Zane looked around like he expected people to come storming in.

"I think it's mainly the two babies being gone." Michelle thought they were all enjoying the quiet. Even Caroline ate in contented silence.

When the meal was eaten, Annie rose to pull a baking dish of peach cobbler out of the oven and brought it to the table, then added a pitcher of sweetened cream and a stack of smaller plates.

"I'm planning to become a better cook," Michelle said, scooping up a serving of cobbler. "I've been chasing after the babies. But now with them in their own homes, I'll try harder."

"And I've been busy building." Jilly looked at Zane. "Do you have anything else to build around here?"

Zane rolled his eyes. "As if four cabins in a matter of weeks isn't enough. But with the Steinmeyers in the ramrod's cabin, we could probably use one more cabin for a new ramrod."

Jilly grinned.

"I've been wondering about running some irrigation lines to water your grass and adding windmills to fill ponds for the cattle to drink from. You need at least one per pasture." Michelle munched on the sweet dessert.

Zane's head whipped around. "Irrigation?"

"Yes, irrigation is when you—"

"I know what irrigation is." Zane waved an impatient hand. "But I've never done such a thing. As a rule, the rain is dependable on my land."

"Well, it's a lot of work, but there's nothing hard about it. We could get a paddle wheel in here and use the energy from the river to power an engine that would pump—"

"My cattle are thirsty, and my grass is drying up. When can we start?"

Michelle looked at Jilly.

"I can draw up plans tonight," Jilly said. "If you use the waterpower to run an engine, the irrigation wouldn't be hard to set up. The windmills will take a little longer, and you'd need to order some parts."

"Do it." He turned to his sisters. "I have money set aside from the ranch's profits for you and Josh. I'd need to spend some of that. But irrigation and windmills are ranch expenses, and they'd pay for themselves over time."

Annie and Beth Ellen shared a look. Then Annie shrugged. "It's fine with me."

"Me too. We can't have the cows thirsty." Beth Ellen smiled at Michelle and Jilly. "You two can set up an irrigation system and windmills and . . . what else did you say? A water-powered engine?"

"Yes, it's the same theory as the windmills, but that's wind power used to pump water," Michelle explained. "We can use waterpower to pump water, too."

Then Zane gave Annie a kind look. Michelle braced herself for something bad.

"Before we start on any irrigation, I'm going to ride down toward Lodi tomorrow."

"Oh, Zane. No, please don't do that."

"I'm going to be careful. I'm not going to charge in and demand your ranch back. But I want to know what happened. If you're right and the man who stole it has powerful connections, then I'll back off without causing trouble."

Annie burst into tears. Caroline sat beside her, boosted up by a little wooden box Zane had found in the barn. She burst into tears right along with her mother.

"You know, Annie, I happen to know a few powerful people, too," Zane said. "I know our state senator well enough to have had dinner in his home. I'm acquainted with the mayor of Sacramento. I've got enough connections that I can get some answers without risking my life."

"How about a US Marshal?" Jilly asked. "You could find

out if there's one in the area and make your accusations to him."

"And check with the district attorney for Sacramento. Stealing someone's land isn't a quiet little crime. It might be hard to prove a murder under the circumstances, but—" Michelle straightened and snapped her fingers. "We know the governor. Uncle Newt came to the house regularly when Papa was alive."

Zane said quietly, "Uncle Newt?"

"And the state attorney general." Jilly tapped on the table. "And the man who was mayor of San Francisco at one time. He didn't run for the last election. His wife and our mama had tea frequently, and there were some other ladies there with plenty of connections. I'm not sure being well connected in San Francisco helps, but the statewide offices do."

Michelle rested a hand on Jilly's shoulder. "We'd have to ride to Sacramento, talk to the people we know. Um . . ." She glanced from Annie to Beth Ellen. "Our whereabouts would be revealed."

Jilly subsided.

Michelle looked at Zane. "We'll help. But it will be a delicate thing. Let me write a few letters tonight. I don't know if Mama's friends, nor Papa's, quite realize our situation. We left for the mountains as usual, but we spent the whole winter up there. I have no idea if anyone has noticed or wondered about us yet."

"And you don't want your whereabouts to be revealed?" Beth Ellen asked.

Michelle looked at Jilly. Jilly was thinking, Michelle too. All the pros and cons. All the consequences of their actions.

Telling Annie and Beth Ellen what was going on. Did that include the gold? Did that mean their real names, or did it mean coming out of hiding to try to regain control of Annie's ranch?

She thought of one thing that would make a difference. She turned to Zane and said firmly, "I'll tell them everything and use all the influence I can gather, if you'll marry me."

ANNIE GASPED SO LOUD, so deep, she must've inhaled something because she started coughing.

"What?" Beth Ellen shouted and stood so fast she knocked her chair over behind her.

Startled, Caroline knocked over her milk.

Zane gave Michelle a narrow-eyed look and got up to pat Annie on the back.

Jilly grabbed a towel and stopped the milk before it flowed onto Caroline or the floor.

"What is going on here?" Beth Ellen demanded. "Who are you really, and what are you trying to do with my brother?"

"Why do I have to marry you as part of this?" Zane flinched a little at his tone of voice. "Let's just tell them the truth."

"Once I go out, make my presence known in Sacramento, Edgar will come after me. If Jilly and I do it together, he'll come for both of us. As a single woman, I'm worth a fortune to him, and I'm not one bit sure I can avoid the plans he has for me."

"But as a married woman . . ." Zane's jaw tightened as the silence stretched. "The thing is, Michelle, I'm not that opposed to marrying you. You're a beautiful, brilliant, likeable, even lovable woman. But I'm not interested in lumber."

"I guess then we tell them our names and . . ." Michelle slumped back in her chair as Annie quit coughing. Beth Ellen righted her own chair and sat down. Jilly returned to the table with a new cup of milk for Caroline, with very little milk in it.

"And?" Zane prompted her.

"And . . . and it's the right thing to do to try and get justice for Annie. So . . ." Michelle reached out to Jilly, and they joined hands.

"So we'll go," Michelle said. "We've known it's wrong to stay here with you. It was not part of our plan to just move in with someone who was too nice to kick us out. We'll go to Sacramento, make our appeal to the governor and others, and send the information we gather back to you with any help we can gain."

Nodding, Jilly finally said, "It's our own responsibility to care for ourselves. It's not yours, Zane."

"We've imposed long enough." Michelle looked at Annie. "We'll need all the information you can give us about who stole your land and any threats beforehand. Jilly and I, along with our sister Laura, who has married and gone back to our home, ran away from our stepfather. He had plans to force us into marriage with his horrid friends who were paying well for us. But when we marry, we inherit one-third each of the lumber dynasty our father built. We've been living quietly. To our knowledge, our stepfather has no idea where we are. But I have no doubt he's searching for us."

She turned to Zane. "I apologize for that proposal. It was rude of me." Then she smiled. "You really are the most appealing man I've ever met. Marriage to you would be no hardship. If things were normal, I might pursue you, and if I could catch you, I might be content to stay here and be a proper ranch wife. But I have to go home, and you love your ranch. And that's that."

She pushed back from the table. "You decide what details you want to share with your sisters about all of this. I'm going to bed."

Michelle walked out. Jilly, after a quick good-night, followed her.

Zane stared after Michelle long after she was gone from the room. His heart pounded too hard and not quite evenly. She thought he was appealing. The most appealing man she'd ever met.

It was something he'd always remember. Always cherish. Fine words from a fine woman.

He gathered his thoughts and studied his sisters. His instinct was to protect them. And yet here he was with the brilliant Stiles sisters planning to strike out on their own, care for themselves. He needed to give his sisters more credit.

"Let's go into my office where we can get comfortable. I've got a few troubles, and maybe you can help me figure out what to do."

Once they were settled in the office, he didn't go over the Stiles sisters' troubles again. Instead, he dived into his own.

"I found gold on my ranch—*our* ranch."

Both of them gasped. He watched them closely to see if their eyes shone with greed. Or if they seemed to have a fever. Annie was startled but calm. Beth Ellen might have the littlest bit of avarice in her gaze.

"Where?" Annie asked.

He told them everything. Most especially his worries about what a gold strike might do to the ranch.

The three of them sat in silence as they all mulled over the gold. Caroline scampered around the room. She seemed to mainly be intent on climbing, the higher the better, but they could keep ahead of her here. And there wasn't much fragile. The room's lanterns were in sconces on the walls. There was no fire in the fireplace.

"You need to put in a few more days like the one you've already put in." Annie watched Caroline trying to climb the sofa. "See how much gold you can dig out of there. It would be nice to just get all of it and be done."

"And you bought two houses in Dorada Rio?" Beth Ellen asked.

"Yes, but it was right after the mines closed in the latest panic. The houses were sitting empty. They're solid but not fancy. They didn't cost much."

"Have you built anything else here but the cabins?" Annie asked.

"That mostly just took time. We cut our own lumber. Jilly and the hired men did the building." It occurred to Zane that maybe he ought to offer to pay Jilly. Seemed unnecessary when she'd wanted to do it so badly he'd've had to lasso her to get her to stop. And besides, he was feeding her, clothing her, and giving her shelter. That was close to good enough.

"And the gold you've dug is here in the house?" Annie glanced at Caroline, looking uneasy at the thought.

"Jilly and Michelle have been working on it in their spare time, breaking the nuggets out of the quartz, getting it ready to sell."

"And you're sure you can trust them?" Annie's eyes narrowed. She looked to the door of the office as if she could see all the way to the housekeeper's rooms.

"They're rich, Annie. My hired man Nick had heard of them, and he rode out to make sure their ma wasn't in danger. He wrote back here and said it was all as he'd remembered. So sure, a body can go mad over gold. I know that. But these Stiles sisters don't seem apt to steal my gold. My real problem is once I ride out of here with gold to sell, then I'm going to lead a parade of madmen back with me. I can't see avoiding that. If all the gold is mined and gone, there will still be a gold rush. I just don't know how to avoid it. But I hope the ones who come will hunt awhile, then leave."

"You could ride far afield. Could you ride to Virginia City to sell it? Sneak in, hope they don't pressure you to tell them where your claim is. Tell them it's a secret. Which it is. Then slip out of town with your money and come back here. No one would know where the gold came from."

Zane perked up. "That could work. Though maybe Virginia City is too close. With the train running, I could go even farther. Denver maybe."

"Are there big enough banks in Denver that you could just put your money in a bank and leave it? Wait for some time to pass?" Beth Ellen asked. "Do banks get robbed in a big city like Denver? Do trains get robbed?"

Zane was afraid everything got robbed now and then.

"These are good ideas," he said. "I'm sorry I didn't talk with you about this earlier. I think I'll handle it just that way, though I'm not sure if Denver is the best place to go. Maybe Carson City. But in the meantime, Annie, what do we do about your ranch and Michelle's offer to run interference for you? The governor would be a powerful ally. Better than anything the men who ran you off could match."

"While we're talking about offers, what about Michelle offering to marry you? For her own safety."

Yes, what about that? "I have some thinking to do. Maybe for now we can set aside the fight to regain your ranch and just mine gold. By the time we have a hefty load to sell, I'll have figured it out. The gold is secret. Your land can't get any more stolen. Michelle is safe without needing a hasty marriage. There's no rush."

CHAPTER

# EIGHT

MICHELLE'S EYES POPPED OPEN in the dark room, and a chill rushed down her spine that almost sent her screaming from the bed.

But a year of living with Edgar had taught her caution.

What woke her up?

A dream?

A noise?

A cry for help?

Without moving, she opened her eyes just a slit and studied the room. Luckily for her, she slept on her side. The window was open, and something moved in that window. A black shape, but it was a night with a bright moon.

A man slipped in the window.

Silent as the grave.

*Think. Think. Think.*

Scream? Leap from bed? Run? Grab something . . . her bedside book? Fight?

Remaining silent wasn't a choice. If he was sneaking in here, he had evil intentions, and if they weren't for her, they were for someone else.

He stepped one leg down on the floor to a slight creak. Then the other leg came through. In that second, she could see he was a big man and knew in a fight, she'd lose.

All the possibilities coalesced. She did it all—except the quiet parts.

She flung back her blanket, leapt to her feet, and screamed.

Grabbed her heavy book and ran, screaming every step. "Help! Help! Jilly! Zane!"

With an open window, her voice might even alert the bunkhouse.

The man hissed out an awful word, and his feet thundered as he stormed at her. She wrenched open her door just as the vicious brute slammed her to the floor with all his weight.

"Help!" Her cry broke off as the air rushed from her lungs, but she sucked in another chestful and went back to screaming for help. It was enough to shred eardrums. Lying flat on her belly under a massive weight, she swung the book behind her, as high and hard as she could, and caught his head.

His grunt of pain turned to a vicious growl, as if he were an animal attacking her.

Something else hit.

Michelle, her face pressed to the floor, couldn't see, but she heard Jilly yell as she dove at the man.

"Zane!" They both hollered and struggled.

Michelle was free as the man rolled off under Jilly's assault. She scrambled to her feet to face the man. He and Jilly were tumbling, Jilly wailing, but her words were threats not fear.

Michelle, still shrieking with all her might, couldn't hit anyone in the dark, afraid she'd hurt her sister. Holding the massive book in both hands, she rushed at the two of them. She felt around long enough to be sure it was Jilly now crushed to the floor with the man on top of her. Michelle hit the man with the book, glad it was a heavy tome. She struck again and again, pummeling him. She swung down, the sideways book hammering him in the face, then she hit the back of his head so hard he let out a thick grunt.

While she swung her only weapon, she never let up the noise. Jilly was still shouting threats. They both knew noise would be their salvation.

He broke off his attack on Jilly to lunge up at Michelle just as she was bringing the book around again. She clobbered him hard enough he staggered back, tripped over Jilly, and went down. He was back on his feet with a roar of anger. If Zane didn't hear her or Jilly, he'd hear this fool.

The housekeeper's door slammed open. Michelle didn't have time to look, but she knew Zane was here.

Having a cavalry division arrive wouldn't have made her feel any better.

The man must have realized he was badly outnumbered. He whirled away to run for the open window.

Jilly was on her feet again, and she went in low, hit him on the back of his knees, and took the man's legs out from under him.

"Zane. Get him." Michelle realized as she spoke that Zane didn't need any orders.

Grabbing at the wrestling pair on the ground, Zane came up with Jilly and tossed her toward Michelle. Then he swung a fist, made hard as iron by a lifetime of wrestling thousand-pound steers and breaking wild horses.

The man went down in a heap.

A second later, a light came on. Beth Ellen had joined the fray, carrying a lantern.

Zane lifted the man off the floor. No one Michelle had ever seen before. Zane slammed a fist into the man's jaw, and he groaned, all the fight gone out of him.

Annie arrived then, looked at what had happened, and rushed away.

Michelle had seen the determination in Annie's eyes and knew the woman, who'd mostly ignored being shot twice not that long ago, wasn't running.

She was back in a trice with rope.

Zane bound the man so fast Michelle was a little dizzy. Then he flipped the man onto his back. "Bring that lantern up here."

Beth Ellen came close but not too close. Wise woman. For all her city ways, she'd been raised a rancher's daughter and had a lot of common sense.

"Who is he? Anyone know?" Zane's question was met with utter silence.

At last, Jilly, breathing hard, said, "I've never seen him before."

Coming from Jilly with her memory, that was saying something.

"Do you think our dear stepfather sent him?" Michelle asked.

Jilly's head snapped around. "You think he came for us?"

There was a long stretch of silence as Michelle considered it all.

The kitchen door banged open. Shad shouted, "What's going on in here?"

He came straight to the housekeeper's rooms. Apparently,

he'd heard enough from the bunkhouse to be sure of where the trouble was coming from.

Zane turned to his foreman. "This man broke into the house and attacked Michelle and Jilly. Lock him in the root cellar. Post a double guard. When he comes around, I want to talk to him. Then we'll escort him to the sheriff."

Shad grabbed the man. Two more cowhands were pressing into the room, eager to assist. Michelle thought she heard a crowd behind them.

The cowhands dragged the man to his feet and out of the room.

"Are you all right, Michelle?" Annie asked.

"Yes, he didn't hurt me. Knocked me down is all. Jilly got him off me."

"You're both going to be sore in the morning," Zane said. He looked closer at the book Michelle held. "You were pounding on him with . . ." He read the title. "*War and Peace*? I'm guessing you picked war."

"I got it from your library."

"A passing trader gave it to us to get the weight off his wagon. I only kept it because it's too big to have much hope of getting it to burn." He scratched his head. "The trader told me it was in Russian."

"Russian and some French." Michelle looked at the book and set it aside. Time to disarm herself. "There are quite a few Russians and Frenchmen in San Francisco, including among the lumberjacks we employed. Mama and Papa thought it wise to learn their languages."

"We know several other languages, too," Jilly added.

"That man made a serious mistake in taking you two on."

"Taking on us and Tolstoy."

Zane turned up a lantern seated on a wall sconce in the sitting room of the housekeeper's apartment. It had two bedrooms and a sitting room, left from the days when Zane's ma had been alive. The housekeeper had been a married woman with a couple of youngsters. Her husband had worked on the ranch. When she and her husband, their children grown, had moved on, Zane hadn't replaced her until Sally Jo needed to escape her parents in Purgatory.

Zane turned to Michelle and Jilly. "Do you really think he was sent here by Edgar?"

Michelle looked at Jilly. "It's possible, and if he was, then our secret is out, and we must leave. We've brought danger to your doorstep."

"I-I wondered if it could be the man who sh-shot Todd." Annie's arms were nearly wrapped around herself. "Could he want to make sure I didn't go to the sheriff? I might well have taken the housekeeper's rooms because of the two bedrooms and Caroline."

"Or is it about gold?" Zane asked with grim anger.

"Well, I didn't do anything wrong," Beth Ellen said. "He didn't come for me."

NICK SPRINTED INTO THE DINING ROOM, where Laura and her family were eating breakfast. "Beaumont sent men after Michelle and Jilly."

Laura shoved her chair back. Caleb leapt to his feet. Mama cried out and clenched her fists.

"We have to go." Laura turned to Caleb. "Right now. We have to warn my sisters."

Laura was around the table, heading for the door when she shouted, "Wait!"

Everyone skidded to a stop. Caleb was just behind Nick, going out the door. They whirled to see what was wrong.

Laura turned to see Mama standing up at the table, watching them go. "We can't just leave you alone."

Caleb came to her side.

Laura was silent, analyzing the situation.

"Come with us," Caleb said. "You're a good rider, aren't you?"

Mama, wringing her hands, suddenly straightened, and her eyes flashed with determination. "I am an *excellent* rider."

She grabbed a napkin off the table and shoved every piece of bread from a serving plate they hadn't gotten to yet into the napkin and rolled it up.

"Food for the journey. It'll save us time not to stop and eat. Let's go."

"I've got Old Tom filling my saddlebags and a couple of canteens. I rode like a madman to get here from the Purgatory settlement, and it took three days. I expect it will take us longer but not much." Nick turned away and went back to running. Laura, following Caleb, ran hard after him.

They rushed out of the house to find Old Tom with six horses saddled. One for each of them and two for himself and another lumberjack named Carl.

Laura, not mindful of her skirts at all, swung up on the horse. Mama was only a second behind, and that only because she took time to shove the bread in her saddlebags.

Laura saw the horses were all carrying plenty of supplies. Old Tom had been thinking fast.

They galloped hard until the trail, a stupid, slow trail, grew steep and narrow. They picked their way along, single file. The trail was wide enough for a wagon to come up, but still steep enough that it was best for a rider to keep to the center and have some elbow room.

Many years ago, they'd packed wagonloads of supplies up this mountain to build the house. And wagons still came and went. But the flume had been built specifically because of this wretched trail. Someday it would be wide enough, straight enough, and solid enough to carry train tracks.

Now that the horses were slowed to a walk, Caleb said, "Talk, Nick. What did you hear?"

"I had a few of the men follow Beaumont when he left. Men good enough on a trail not to be noticed. In fact, while Beaumont was packing, I sent Carl ahead."

Laura glanced behind her at the man bringing up the rear behind Old Tom.

"There's only one way down the mountain, and no forks in the road for most of the way. There was a slim chance he'd turn off, but he didn't. Carl picked him up at the bottom."

"Why didn't you tell us about doing this?" Mama rode behind Laura, who rode behind Caleb, who rode behind Nick.

Nick looked back to meet Mama's eyes. "Because there are folks in your home who eavesdrop, ma'am. And there's a telegraph wire. Careful as we are, I was afraid someone would hear what I was up to. As it was, I feared confederates of Beaumont's would notice that men had ridden off ahead and behind him."

"So your men followed Beaumont to Zane's ranch?" Caleb got the questioning back on track.

"He hadn't left San Francisco yet, but Carl watched close.

Two others helped him. Men Old Tom knew were loyal. They took turns following him. He and a good-sized group of henchmen found where I'd been working—the Two Harts Ranch." Nick punched himself on the thigh. "I was in San Francisco earlier this year. I'm not sure how he found out about me, but I didn't make any secret of my name or my presence there. And someone knew I worked for Zane. I expect Beaumont to be heading for Zane's ranch right now."

"We should have wired Zane."

"No telegraph on his ranch, but there's one in the nearest town, which is none too near. But someone in Dorada Rio could ride out with the message." Nick frowned. "We'll ride past Hatcher's Creek." It was the closest town at the bottom of the mountain. "We can wire Zane then. It'll be a while reaching him."

"Include in the wire," Mama said, "that I'll pay a man handsomely to rush the message to him."

Nick nodded. "Good idea."

The trail widened a bit and grew somewhat less steep. Nick picked up the pace, and there was no more talk. Only urgency.

# CHAPTER NINE

"SHAD, BRING IN THE MAN WE CAUGHT," Zane ordered.

Shad was none too gentle when he brought the man in.

Zane grabbed the intruder by the arm and sat him down hard at his kitchen table. He was huge. He had an ugly scar down the left side of his face. His nose was red and bulbous, possibly broken by Michelle and her book.

Zane remembered how Michelle and Jilly had beaten on him last night. It stirred a strange kind of pride in his heart for these two tough women.

All four of them, plus Annie, stared hard at the intruder.

"What's your name?" Zane finally asked.

"It's Jarvis Smith, Boss," Shad said. "He told me when I bribed him with breakfast."

"Smith? A pretty common name."

"Ain't no way to treat a man to withhold food like that. You get food even in prison."

"Which is where you're going when we're done here," Zane said.

The man snorted. "Not likely."

Zane studied him. He would have been good-looking if not for the ugly scar and the bruises. His hair was neatly trimmed. He was well dressed in a western manner. Little wear on his blue jeans. Boots that looked like they were shined regularly. No tattered shirt collar. A well-paid hired hand was Zane's guess. But hired by whom? And for what?

"You think you can break into a woman's bedroom, attack and assault two women, and not spend time in prison?" Zane said.

"I won't spend a single night in jail. I've got friends."

"And I'm friends with the sheriff." Zane scowled. "Stockwood is a good man. If your friends intend to bribe him, they're out of luck, and if they try a jailbreak, they'll end up in the cell right alongside you."

Zane didn't see the man squirm even a little. "Who hired you?"

"Don't know what you mean. I had a little too much to drink. Fell off my horse and walked awhile. I stumbled on your place. Didn't know where I was when I climbed through that window. I don't even remember doing it. These women attacked me. I'm sure I scared them, and I'm sorry for that. But I didn't mean any harm."

Zane thought of all the stupid things a man could do and blame it on drink. He didn't believe it. He'd helped knock this man down last night. Not a whiff of whiskey on his breath. Any staggering he'd done was due to the beating he'd taken.

"I shouted when you came in." Michelle's voice was cold, sharp, and direct. "I screamed for help and ran. You came after me and tackled me. There was nothing uncoordinated about your movements. You were steady and fit and sober as a judge. When the trial comes, I'll be glad to testify to that."

She said it without hesitation. Complete assurance. Zane saw the first trickle of sweat appear on Smith's brow.

"I was there, too." Jilly came around the table and stood beside her sister, hands on her hips, green eyes bright. "You didn't climb in a window looking for shelter. You came in quietly. I was in the next room and didn't hear you until the screaming started. When I knocked you sideways off the woman you were attacking, you fell, but then you spun around, steady and capable. Very deliberate. You knocked me down and held me down until my sister came after you. And even with both of us struggling and crying for help, you didn't break off the attack until Zane came into the room and dragged you off both of us."

Zane noticed that Jilly was very careful not to say her or Michelle's names. But if they testified at a trial, they'd have to identify themselves.

Another trickle of sweat followed the trail left by the nasty scar on Jarvis's face. There was something about these two women. A solid, confident way of talking that knocked him loose from his story.

"Who hired you?" Zane repeated. "If you talk, the judge will take it into consideration when he passes the sentence when you're found guilty. If you don't, it's a rough country around here, Smith. A mostly male country. A woman is a rare and fine thing, and men in the West protect their women and judge harshly a man who would harm one. Attacking a woman will get you hanged. And well it should."

Smith gave Zane a wide smile, which didn't match the sweat and the tension around his jaw. But he did a good job of faking a confident smile. "They were scared. They misjudged the situation. It could happen to anyone."

When he smiled a gold tooth flashed. Not front and center but close.

Into the quiet, Annie spoke. "I recognize you. That smile. That tooth. Yes, and the scar. You're one of the men who attacked my ranch. Your name isn't Smith. It's Benteen. You're Horace Benteen's son."

Michelle gasped so hard she started to cough. Jilly turned away from their prisoner and patted Michelle firmly on the back.

Zane looked at the Stiles sisters, careful not to pull his attention all the way off Jarvis.

"Is that right? Are you Horace Benteen's son?" Zane's stomach twisted. He knew very well why Annie didn't want Zane involved with this. Benteen was a wealthy, ruthless, greedy industrialist with one of the biggest cattle ranches in the state. His reputation was brutal. He had powerful friends, and he was well-known for taking what he wanted.

But what did this have to do with Michelle and Jilly Stiles?

"Swallowed wrong. Excuse us." Michelle grabbed Jilly's hand and tugged her out of the room. Jarvis watched them go, his brow knit as he studied them.

"Did you find his horse?" Annie asked.

Shad shook his head. "We haven't hunted around."

"Do it. I think you'll find he rides a beautiful blood-red bay stallion with black mane and tail. A horse with my husband's brand on it. Jarvis here is probably so smug he hasn't even bothered to try and hide the brand."

"I bought that horse all right and legal. I've got a bill of sale I can show anyone who wonders. You're Mrs. Lane?

You had to know your husband sold that bay. I bought it from him."

"The only thing anyone will wonder is who did the forgery." Annie's hands settled on her hips. "My husband never sold that stallion. It was the cornerstone of the breeding at his ranch. He sold stud fees as recently as two months ago for good money. No one will believe you bought that horse from him."

"They'll believe what they've been told to believe." Jarvis's arrogant smile was pulled out of shape by the scar until his face was a mask of cruelty.

"I know how connected your father is, but he's still worried, isn't he?" Annie said. "He knows I might challenge his claim to the land he stole. You were sent here to kill me."

Color faded from Benteen's face.

"The two women you assaulted will testify that you attacked them. I will testify that you helped burn down my home, then rode hard along with others to drive my husband and me from our ranch."

"Are you sure, Annie?" Zane studied the man in front of him.

"Yes. He was one of a crowd, but yes, I am very sure." She glared at their prisoner. Zane saw her hands drop from her hips and clench into fists. For a long second, he thought she'd swing. And he'd've let her. She owed Benteen a fist in the face. She owed him a whole lot more.

"Lock him up again, Shad. We'll ride in to the sheriff within the hour. I want four men riding with me. I'll be taking Annie, Beth Ellen, and . . . two others with me."

He didn't say Michelle's and Jilly's names. Something was wrong with Michelle. She'd left at a near run on a feeble excuse.

Zane needed time to talk to her. See if she had changed her mind about testifying before a judge.

"WHAT ARE WE GOING TO DO?" Jilly had led the way to their rooms.

Michelle closed the door firmly and turned a key in the lock. The key was always there, just sticking out of that lock like it was part of the doorknob. But they'd never locked it. They'd felt safe here.

"You recognized the name?" she asked Jilly.

"The second I heard Benteen. It's his father that you were supposed to marry."

"Mama said his wife was never seen in public. By all accounts, they had this one single son, and Benteen wanted more. Mama overheard ugly, cutting remarks about his wife failing him. Meanwhile, Horace Benteen was known to carouse in San Francisco. He had a house where he installed a mistress, but there were rumors that he had more women besides the mistress, and he was known for leaving a woman battered. He's been married three times. All his wives died unexpectedly. Word is he's desperate for another son. His third wife died a year ago from a fall down a flight of stairs."

"He killed them all." Jilly rubbed her hands up and down her arms. "Now he's looking for a new wife."

"And he's the one Edgar had picked out for me." Chills ran like icy fingers down Michelle's spine. "If we testify against Jarvis, we'll have to identify ourselves. His father might even show up. Zane wouldn't let the man drag me out of town, but Benteen would tell Edgar right where we are, and he'd come. There would be little we could legally do to stop our stepfather from dragging us home."

A short, sharp knock sounded.

Michelle whirled to face the door. A slash of fear almost made her scream.

"Michelle, let me in."

Zane. She realized she was expecting Edgar, with Horace right behind him and a parson to perform a wedding ceremony. She wondered if, should it ever happen, Benteen would hand over cash to Edgar right in front of her.

She exchanged a look with Jilly, who shrugged and waved a hand at the door.

Michelle let him in.

Zane didn't speak for a long moment. He studied them as he stepped in, quietly closing the door. "You knew the name Benteen."

It wasn't a question. Michelle considered herself smarter than most everyone she met. But she needed to admit that there were different kinds of smart. She doubted Zane could beat her in a test about advanced mathematics. But he might outthink her and read her expressions like the written word.

Hesitating, she looked at Jilly, who said, "There's no way we can keep this from him."

Zane's eyes narrowed, and his arms crossed. He seemed annoyed that they even had to decide.

That's when Michelle realized something.

She trusted him. She even counted on him. Zane's knowing about this was the very best thing that could happen.

"We told you our stepfather—"

"Edgar Beaumont, the man you ran from," Zane interjected.

"Yes. He had plans to marry us to men of his choosing. We have a lot of connections that would be very valuable. Edgar has profited greatly from marrying Mama. So these men paid Edgar a high price to marry the Stiles sisters. Horace Benteen was one of the men. I've seen him at social gatherings in San Francisco, but I don't really know him. Mama called him lecherous and cruel. She said he and the other men Edgar chose for us, well, marriage to them would be a living death. A nightmare. She said the risk of riding down that flume and floating down a river, hiding somehow until we were safely married, was safer than marriage to the men Edgar chose."

"We took that risk," Jilly said quietly. "And now it sounds like a trial for Jarvis Benteen will reveal us to a man who will immediately betray us to Edgar. And whether Jarvis is here for us or Annie, we will probably never know. I think, based on him not seeming to know us, he must have come for Annie, which makes his coming here an attempt at premeditated murder. But to stop him with our testimony puts us in deadly danger. We're pretty sure Horace Benteen killed his wife a year ago. Possibly he's killed three wives now. He was meant for Michelle."

"I wouldn't let him take you, Michelle. Nor you, Jilly."

Michelle shook her head. "A father—even a stepfather—has rights over his daughters. Legally, you couldn't stop him."

Michelle looked at Jilly. "If we testify, and I believe we have to, we'll need to run again."

Jilly nodded her head with a terse little movement. "So be it. We do have to testify."

"Both of you stop." Zane began pacing through the sitting room of the housekeeper's apartment. It wasn't large, but it was big enough he could pick up some speed.

He made it through the room, then wheeled back to face them. "A simple solution is for Michelle to marry me."

Michelle froze. Her eyes locked on his. No words came to mind.

"Jilly, can you leave us alone for just a moment?" Zane asked.

Jilly stepped into the bedroom she slept in rather than go out into the main part of the house. Her door clicked shut. Michelle wished she'd gone a bit farther away. At the same time, some small part of her wanted Jilly to still be close.

Zane walked up to face Michelle. "I'm not giving up my ranch. If we marry, we live here."

"I-I . . . um . . ."

"But you'll be safe. And as I understand it, you and Laura will hold majority ownership of the company. You can kick Edgar out. You can stay here with me, and Jilly can stay here or go back to your home, whichever she chooses. We'll make sure she gets there safely. Caleb and Nick can then look out for her. Under her mother's care, with Caleb and Nick close, Edgar won't be able to take her. With your permission as one-third owner, she and Laura can get on with building and blasting. Maybe you can be involved through the mail, do bookwork, work on your inventions, and do other organizing, but I won't give up my ranch."

His hands came up to grip her shoulders. "I can't, Michelle. I don't belong up there on your mountain." His hands moved on her shoulders. He was offering to save her. "Can you live with that?"

Michelle was glad he talked for a while. It gave her a chance to organize her thoughts. "Can I go visit? Can *we* go visit?"

Zane nodded. "There are slow spells on the ranch. I'll put Shad in charge, and we can go spend a month with your family, maybe a couple of times a year."

Michelle thought of Benteen and shuddered. She could tell Zane felt it.

"Do you dread being married to me? Do you hate the idea of giving up on your lumber company dream?"

"I was thinking of what Horace might do to me." She turned her thoughts from that vile man. "But you don't deserve to have me thinking of him when you propose. You're an honorable man, Zane."

"Our life might be complicated," Zane warned her.

Michelle's arms slid around his neck. "It might. But I admire and respect you. I think I'd be marrying a man I'd like to share my life with. Yes, I'll marry you. I'll join my life with yours here at Two Harts Ranch."

He held her gaze. "Let's get Jarvis to town and find us a preacher man, Miss Stiles."

He hooked his arm through hers, and they headed out. As they stepped through the door to leave the housekeeper's apartment, Michelle stopped so suddenly she almost stumbled.

She looked back into the room and said, "Come on out, Jilly."

Jilly had the door open before Michelle finished telling her to come. "Is the wedding on?"

Michelle noticed Jilly had spent the time changing her clothes and was now wearing a riding skirt. She'd also combed her hair. Michelle, the bride, should probably do that, too, but she was already wearing a riding skirt, and as for the rest, the ride would just mess her up again.

"The wedding is on. We're heading to town."

Jilly grinned, and it was such a happy expression Michelle could only believe her little sister thought now she'd never have to marry.

What had happened to Jilly that she'd kept hidden from everyone? Michelle admitted to herself as she left the room on Zane's arm that she was afraid to press her sister for an answer.

# CHAPTER TEN

DORADA RIO WASN'T WHAT MICHELLE HAD THOUGHT OF when she heard it called a mining town. It had a settled look with a broad main street and two rows of buildings with tidy boardwalks in front of them.

The group had ridden into Dorada Rio along a street with dozens of tightly squeezed, miserable-looking houses. These gave way to nicer houses, larger ones with room for backyards and pretty front porches.

Finally, they rode down a street with regal houses, many favoring the Victorian style Michelle's papa had used to build his own house. Though none of these was as pretty and whimsical as the Stiles mansion.

"This town is long past the gold boom," Zane said quietly as they left the beautiful row of houses behind and came toward the business section of town. Dozens of businesses, built close enough to share walls, ran down each side of Main Street, each store with its own false front. Façades that squared off the otherwise peaked roofs, to make the buildings appear to be a full two stories.

"Men have their own claims, but they're poor yielding things," Zane said. "So they sign on with the mining businesses and make a decent living, if they aren't fools with their money. Many live a solid existence, though the work is hard.

"Prices are high for most things here, so there isn't much left after food, clothing, and coal for the stove. We usually drive our cattle into Sacramento. We get good money for them there, though it pays even better to take them to San Francisco, so some years we do that. But I always drive a hundred head or so into Dorada Rio. I get decent money, but with only a thousand people living here, they can't use much more of a herd. Not all at once."

"Do you have that list of parts Jilly and I made up last night?" Michelle asked.

"Yep, I'll talk with the general store, lumberyard, and blacksmith, get it all headed our way fast."

Satisfied, Michelle watched as people strolled down the boardwalks. They'd been built up just a step above ground level. It would keep feet out of the mud that must plague the area during wet seasons.

Jilly rode beside Michelle on her right while Annie rode beside Zane on his left and on past her, Beth Ellen. The five of them rode abreast on the wide, dirt street of Dorada Rio. Several men, including Jarvis Benteen, formed a second row.

Annie had come along to testify. Beth Ellen insisted on coming for the wedding. They'd left Caroline behind with Gretel Steinmeyer. A jail was no place for a child.

Zane pointed to the end of the block, and they went around the corner to find the sheriff's office in a building standing off just a bit from the others. Zane rode up, dismounted, and led the women inside. Shad and Rick dragged Jarvis along between them.

Michelle followed Zane in the door, looking at everything with keen interest. She'd never been in a jail before.

The sheriff, a tall, slim man with short dark hair and a clean-shaven face, rose from the desk and gave a nod. "Zane."

"Sheriff Stockwood, this man broke into my home last night and assaulted two women. I got to them before terrible harm was done."

Hugo Stockwood had sharp eyes. They flickered to Michelle and Jilly, then to Annie and Beth Ellen. Michelle could see he recognized Zane's sisters. Then the sheriff's eyes went to Jarvis Benteen and narrowed, turning hard as stone.

"Jarvis, you broke into Zane's house?"

"I was drinking, Sheriff. I didn't know what I was doing. I frightened these women, and I'm sorry about—"

"Save the lies, Benteen. No reason to be out around Zane's place that late at night. And drinking might work as an excuse between two drunks in a bar, but it's no excuse to assault a woman in her own bedroom, you coyote."

Benteen, smug and arrogant to the end, flushed with anger. Evil flashed in his eyes. Michelle was afraid they'd made a bad enemy. She hoped they kept him locked up tight.

The sheriff turned to snag a key hanging on a nail behind his desk. He went to a wooden door to the side of where he sat, swung it open, and led the way toward a cell. Shad and Rick followed with Jarvis. Zane went in with them, and Michelle went to the door. Zane swung the door shut, but she stopped it in time. She and Jilly wanted to see the jail.

She glanced back to see Annie, unusually somber and pale, coming in behind Jilly. Beth Ellen stayed behind. Maybe she'd seen a jail before.

With a metallic clink, the sheriff turned the key in the cell's lock. Shad and Rick escorted Jarvis in, then stepped back. All of them watched carefully as Sheriff Stockwood slammed the door with a loud bang and twisted the key. All of them trooped back to the front of the sheriff's office.

They gave the sheriff all the details about Annie's ranch being stolen, her husband and two cowpokes killed. The sheriff knew exactly who Horace Benteen was, knew him well enough to take threats very seriously.

He stepped out and sent someone running for his deputy. "I'm going to pick a few men I know I can trust and have them stay close. We'll have the trial later today, and if he's found guilty, I'll have him transported right away to the state prison."

San Quentin. A fairly new prison near San Francisco. The sheriff went on. "I want him out of this town."

"Horace has to know he's in trouble," Zane said. "He'd've wanted a report, and Jarvis hasn't shown up with one."

"Horace Benteen hired murder. Sure as can be he did it. I'm going to throw him in that cell right along with his son on the smallest charge. And showing up here, threatening a jailbreak, is plenty."

Once the questioning was done, Zane shook the sheriff's hand, and they all left. Standing outside on the tidy boardwalk, Zane hooked an arm through Michelle's, smiled, and said, "Let's go get hitched."

She smiled back. Being this close to him helped her keep a sturdy backbone. It was strange to depend on a man like this. She'd always depended on her father. But somehow, she'd expected any man she married to let her take charge. This imagined husband might even depend on her. It didn't look like it was going to work out that way with Zane. She couldn't feel overly upset about that.

MICHELLE LOOKED DOWN at the bright orange flowers in her hands.

Annie had found them. And Dorada Rio didn't seem like the kind of town that would have greenhouses full of flowers. But it was summer in California. These grew wild around here. Michelle had studied botany. These were poppies, and their vivid color and large floppy heads made her smile.

Annie had found a ring at the general store. Plain gold but more than Michelle had expected. It fit too. Right now, it was safely tucked in Zane's pocket.

Annie would have put Michelle in a white dress and veil, and had her hair done up fancy, but Dorada Rio didn't stretch to such things. There was a nice little dress shop in town, and at Annie's nagging, they'd gone in, and Michelle had found a pretty blue dress that fit quite well.

Everything she had at the ranch had been hand sewn for her, mostly by Nora and Harriet, though Gretel had made her a decent black riding skirt and pink calico top, which she'd worn to town. Good, well-made clothes, and she was very grateful to have them.

This dress was fussy and finely made. It had lace at the collar and cuffs and wasn't burdened with the foolishness of a corset or bustle or, heaven forbid, hoops. Putting it on had fed a—oh, she'd probably just as well admit it—a feminine part of her heart that was lonely for pretty dresses. The dressmaker also found a straw bonnet with a ring of blue flowers on the brim.

Michelle felt well turned out for her wedding.

She'd been to fine weddings in San Francisco among the social group her parents were part of. Very beautiful, elaborate affairs with flowing white dresses and intricate veils. Michelle knew what a formal wedding looked like.

Under the circumstances, she was more than a little stunned to find herself even having this wedding, and she'd certainly not expected this pretty dress and a bouquet. Yet here she stood at the back of the church, facing Zane at the front, with orange flowers clutched in her hands.

She even had guests. Jilly and Zane's sisters and the cowhands that had helped them haul Jarvis to town.

The church had a center aisle. Pretty stained-glass windows lined the walls and cast colorful light into the sanctuary. Before she'd come inside, she'd seen a large brass bell hanging in the steeple.

And the altar was a thing of beauty. Shining oak with a high varnish and elaborate carvings on the front. The top was draped in a white altar cloth, embroidered with golden threads. Behind the altar hung a cross, carved with designs that matched the altar.

Parson Lewis stood beside Zane, who had turned to watch her walk toward him. No Papa to walk the aisle with her. No Mama to smile and sniffle.

No, not the wedding of a girl's dreams . . . and that had nothing to do with the lack of a white dress and veil.

The parson was a slender man with a shock of white hair.

His wife was as skinny as he was. They looked like people who worked hard every day of their lives. Mrs. Lewis played beautiful music on a nice little piano while Michelle walked toward a future she'd never foreseen.

Toward Zane.

She was going to be a cowboy's wife.

He stood there in his regular cowboy clothes. As she drew near, his solemn expression changed, and he gave her a smile fit to shine right out the windows.

She wondered if the folks outside noticed a light beaming through the stained glass.

Jilly, sitting alone in the front row, rose and came to Michelle's side, to stand as witness.

Michelle glanced at her and smiled, then turned back to Zane, that bright smile on his face drawing her like he was magnetized and she was a Euclidean vector field.

Only when the parson cleared his throat did Michelle realize she was staring at Zane. Flushing, she turned to face the parson, who had a benevolent expression on his face.

"Dearly beloved . . ."

The service was simple and direct. Love, honor, and obey.

Since she was right in the middle of risking her life to convict the man who'd broken into Zane's home, she figured that "greater love hath no man than this, that a man lay down his life for his friends" covered her so far as "loving" Zane. She thought it was fair to check that one off.

Honor, yes. Not a problem.

As for obey, he had gold, and she wanted to manage the mining. So far she'd obeyed his wishes that she not do that. But then, it was hard to get around him.

The wedding vows didn't say you had to like it.

She'd checked off all three boxes, and she thought she was fully able to take these vows.

And then the sickness and health. Richer or poorer. Better or worse vows.

Michelle considered those vows unnecessarily dire, promises written by a pessimist somewhere along the line. With no expectation of being poor, hoping to put off sickness until dotage, and considering last night she'd been attacked by a man in her bedroom—that had to be the worst, so things were bound to go up from here—she duly promised with a firm "I do."

There was no mention of abusive stepfathers and vile men who wanted to buy her. Nor men who attacked in the night with terrible intentions. And certainly no one brought up gold.

All those probably fit under the "for worse" section. She decided what the parson didn't know wouldn't hurt him. No sense starting a discussion with the cheery man that neither of them wanted to have.

She heard the same grim vows asked of Zane and heard his firm "I do."

Michelle looked at Zane as he said it. He smiled into her eyes. Fully, with bright white teeth. She really hadn't noticed him smiling all that much before. He seemed to be all for this wedding business, whereas Michelle had a few misgivings. But that didn't make her hold back a smile as the parson talked on.

"I ask God to fully and richly bless this marriage." Parson Lewis raised his hands high and wide and finished with quite a flourish. "I now pronounce you husband and wife. You may kiss the bride."

Which Zane did with considerable enthusiasm.

Michelle returned the kiss in full measure.

The church door banged open. "Stop the wedding!"

Michelle gasped and whirled to see her mother rushing down the aisle, Caleb and Laura only a pace behind. Nick Ryder, Zane's cowhand, brought up the rear.

"Mama." Michelle ran toward her.

Jilly was half a step behind her. They ran to their mother at the same time and wrapped their arms around her. Jilly squealed with joy. Michelle laughed out loud.

Laura threw her arms around all three of them and started to cry.

"Mama. You're safe. You're here," Michelle said, but her sisters were chattering such things at the same time.

Michelle couldn't remember a deeper pleasure than holding her mother and seeing Laura again. The Stiles women reunited at last.

## CHAPTER ELEVEN

ZANE HAD SOME BAD NEWS for Mama Stiles. He crossed his arms and watched the women laugh and cry and squeal.

No sense telling her the wedding was over until the din died down.

Then he realized he was watching Michelle with such rapt fondness, it wasn't exactly normal. Not for a man who was marrying a woman just to protect her.

He tore his eyes away and looked at Caleb, who stood on the far side of the knot of Stiles women halfway down the church aisle.

Nick took up the aisle space next to Caleb. Shad and Rick stood by one of the church pews. Two men Zane didn't know stood in the church doorway. Every one of them was watching those pretty women.

Zane turned to the parson, pointed out Michelle's mother, sister, and brother-in-law, slipped a twenty-dollar gold piece into his hand with his sincere thanks, then went down the side aisle to come down a row of pews to stand with Nick and Caleb. He reached them just in time to see Parson and Mrs. Lewis go out a door at the side of the church.

"We'll post a watch outside, Zane." Shad led the way out and started talking to the men at the door. They appeared to be with Nick.

"Mama, I'm already married." Michelle's voice came through above the general chatter.

Mrs. Stiles, or Beaumont or whatever her name was, broke down and cried.

Not the way a man wanted to be welcomed to the family.

Michelle looked over her mother's bowed head, grinned at Zane, shrugged, then pulled her ma into her arms again.

"What're you doing here?" Zane didn't figure it was for a friendly visit.

"Nick got bad news." Caleb tugged on Zane's arm.

They moved to the back of the church.

"What happened, Ryder?" Zane faced his hired man. He was young but a solid, intelligent, hardworking cowpoke. Nick was a man Zane always paid attention to, and he wasn't sure why. It might be that those odd, two-colored eyes gave him the appearance of intensity. Or maybe he just had intensity.

"Beaumont tried to pretend he was sorry. Caleb did some preaching to him. Beaumont said he needed time to think, time to mend his ways. Then he left."

"He left the Stiles mansion?" Zane's senses went on high alert. He thought of Benteen and how there was a connection to Edgar and a history with the Stiles family.

"Yes, we had some warning while he packed. I sent men to follow his trail. He went to San Francisco and stayed at the house the Stiles family owns there. My men kept close but on the sly. Beaumont didn't spend much time in prayer that any of them could see. He did a lot of talking to a group of hired men who spread out asking questions. They were trying to backtrack Caleb and me. They found someone that knew me from the cattle drive last fall. I've got these strange eyes, and folks tend to remember me. I'd made no secret of my name, neither at the Stiles home nor in San Francisco. Once Beaumont knew I'd been on the drive with you—"

"You knew he'd check to see if you ran across the Stiles sisters at my place. Then he'd come right straight here." Zane nodded and wondered if Jarvis had been in his house hunting Michelle after all. Maybe Jarvis was just a boy looking for his runaway stepmother-to-be.

"Laura was insistent she come." Caleb picked up the story. "And we couldn't leave Mama Stiles behind."

"You call her Mama?"

"I don't call her much of anything, honestly."

"So she came along." Zane turned to study the little female crowd. "Why'd she yell stop?"

"She didn't want Michelle to get married just to save the lumber company," Nick said. "I recognized your horse at the church hitching post, and Mrs. Stiles jumped to a conclusion. A correct one as it turned out. She's afraid she's put her daughters in danger by letting them cook up this plan to round up husbands and hurry home. She's afraid they'll end up with scoundrels and brutes."

Zane's eyes narrowed, and he crossed his arms. "I'm neither of those."

"Me neither. But you're going to have to convince Margaret." Caleb shrugged. "I don't really call her that, either. And I sure as certain don't call her Mrs. Beaumont."

"I call her Mrs. Stiles," Nick said.

"And now I have four more people to crowd into my house."

"That big house is empty, Boss," Nick said. "I'd think you'd like a little company."

Then Nick looked closer at the crowd. "Is that your sister Annie?"

Zane gave Caleb and Nick a quick rundown of all that had happened since they'd left. The theft of Annie's ranch and her husband's murder. Beth Ellen's return, the weddings of Caleb's mission group members, the houses built, the womenfolk springing up at his home like wildflowers.

Nick filled in some details about his trip to protect Margaret and what he'd found. Caleb added in his share of the tale. By the time the women dried their tears and joined the men, everyone was caught up.

Margaret, looking shaky, her eyes still shining with tears, came to Zane with both hands outstretched. Zane caught her hands, and she squeezed them.

"I'm sorry to come in shouting like that." She sniffled and let go of one of his hands to find a handkerchief and swipe at her eyes. "It's no reflection on you. Michelle, as well as Jilly and Laura, assure me you're a fine man. But I had wanted Michelle to know she didn't have to marry in haste."

"Yes, she did, ma'am." Zane didn't see himself calling her Mama.

"Michelle explained about that awful Horace Benteen's son finding her. And she said she's happy to be married to you."

Michelle, standing just behind her mother, with her hand

resting on the woman's shoulder, wrinkled her nose at him and grinned.

He fought to keep his face straight and focus on Margaret. Shoving from his mind just how beautiful and interesting his new wife was. It wasn't a proper thought to allow to show while facing your new mother-in-law.

"I'm right happy to be married to her, too, ma'am. And I'm glad you're here. I think you're safer here with me. We have a trial to attend this afternoon, then we'll head out to the ranch, and you can stay until Laura and Jilly are ready to go back and wrest control of Stiles Lumber from Beaumont."

Margaret's expression darkened. "He's ruining the company my husband and I built. How could I have been such a fool to marry him?"

"Hush now." Zane, still holding one of her hands, squeezed it tightly. "He's a man who cheats and lies for a living. He has a talent for seeing exactly what you want and giving it to you."

Caleb came up beside Zane. "I've told you about my past, Margaret. I know how he thinks. He has a talent for reading people, watching how they respond to him. Teasing out the exact feelings he wants from you. You're an honest woman, and you trusted the wrong man. It doesn't make you a fool, only too pure of heart to be suspicious of an apparently kind man. There's no shame in that, and it's best you don't waste time wrapping yourself in those bad feelings. I've said you need to forgive Beaumont. Well, you need to forgive yourself, too."

"I know." Margaret squared her shoulders and nodded. Her chin lifted just a fraction of an inch. Her eyes flashed with the same bright intelligence Zane saw in the three Stiles sisters. They didn't get all their smarts from their father. Plenty of it came from this woman right here.

"And kicking myself for mistakes that now have to be dealt with is exactly that—a waste of time. So what do we do? How exactly is Horace Benteen involved with this mess?"

"His son, Jarvis, is locked up," Zane said. "He broke into Michelle's room last night, and she beat him with a copy of *War and Peace*."

"That's a heavy book." Margaret gave Michelle an approving nod.

Michelle shrugged. "It was just volume one, but it did the trick."

"Horace Benteen is behind stealing my sister's ranch and killing three men, including Annie's husband."

Margaret gasped and turned to Annie, drawing her into her arms. Zane saw Annie respond. Then Margaret reached out and drew Beth Ellen close. How long since either of them had been hugged by a mother? Their ma had been gone a long time.

"We aren't sure if Jarvis was looking for Michelle, because of his pa's thwarted wedding plans, or Annie, to end any witness to their land grab. Either way, he assaulted two women after breaking into my home. And during the trial, it'll come out that Michelle and Jilly are the Stiles sisters. Once that happens, Horace will know Michelle is hiding at my ranch, if he doesn't know already."

Margaret released Annie and Beth Ellen, gave Michelle and Jilly a worried look, then turned back to Zane. "We'll attend the trial. I can add my own voice to some of Horace's evils. Though I doubt that will come up in a trial of his son."

"Let's go eat a noon meal." Zane gave a look around the

room to include everyone. "Then it'll be time for the trial. I hope Jarvis is locked up for good, and we can go home to wait for the next attack."

Michelle sighed, then came to take his hand. "Lunch sounds good."

He laced his finger through hers, then turned to offer his arm to his brand-new mama. Maybe, if he worked at it, he could call her that.

They all left the church, and Zane led them to the finest restaurant in town. Also the only restaurant in town: Fatty's Diner.

# CHAPTER TWELVE

"HE'S GONE, ZANE. I COULDN'T HOLD HIM." Stockwood's face was taut with anger. "He had the judge with him who would oversee the trial. It was next thing to a jailbreak, but they had the right paperwork and the force of law on their side."

Mrs. Stiles gasped so loud it was almost a scream.

Michelle went to her side and hugged her. Jilly came near, her red hair such a contrast to her mother's. Laura, all blond prettiness, threw her arms around all three of them.

"Edgar could be here any minute." After that first gasp, Mrs. Stiles's chin firmed, and her shoulders squared. "He might not have controlling interest in Stiles Lumber, but he still has patriarchal power over Jilly."

"She can come back home with me," Michelle said. "We'll post a guard so no more nighttime intruders get inside."

"Jilly can stay, and Mrs. . . . uh . . . Mama, you can stay here, too," Zane said.

"Laura and I need to get to work removing Edgar's name from the company records," Caleb said. "We can ride to

Sacramento right away with proxy voting rights from Michelle." He turned to Zane. "Is there a lawyer in town who could draw up such papers?"

"Yes, we'll go there before we head home."

"We can block his ability to take money out of the accounts," Caleb said. "Banish him from your San Francisco house, then ride to your mountain home and fire all his cohorts."

Laura nodded. "But if Edgar knows where Jilly is, no matter how well you guard her, Zane, she's not safe. If we shut down his access to the accounts, he'll have all the more reason to move fast to marry her to someone."

Jilly, with her flashing eyes, gritted her teeth. "He really does have a fair amount of power over me, as far as pushing me into a marriage with his awful companions."

"I'm going with you to Sacramento," Margaret said. "I plan to talk to a lawyer and see what can be done about barring Edgar from my property."

"You could see about a divorce," Nick said uncertainly. "It's not easy, ma'am."

Zane wondered how he knew such a thing.

"So I've heard," Margaret said. "My understanding is he has to agree to it. We both do. He can't be forced to accept a divorce. And I doubt he will. I once knew a woman who had to chase down the man who'd abandoned her and run off with another woman. When she found him, he laughed in her face and refused to sign, and there was nothing she could do. She's still legally married to him, and it's been years. No doubt she'll remain married to him for the rest of her life."

Then Margaret added with a hint of shame, "And I took vows before God. I took them fully and sincerely. To break those vows, even though he's broken them dozens of times, is still an awful thing."

Caleb rested a hand on Margaret's shoulder. "The Bible allows a divorce. In Corinthians, it says, 'If the unbelieving depart, let him depart. A brother or a sister is not under bondage in such cases: but God hath called us to peace.' God doesn't call you to live in bondage with an unbeliever if he wants to go. And chances are," Caleb said with grim certainty, "if you can block him from all the money and keep him away from your homes, he might seek out a divorce just so he can find some new woman to cheat. Maybe at the end of this, somehow we can lock him away in prison so he won't harm anyone else."

"For all that he's a horrid beast, I'm not sure if anything he's done is really a crime. Is hitting your wife illegal anywhere? Arranging marriages for your stepdaughters, however abhorrent the grooms? Draining funds from the business your wife brought into the marriage? No, I doubt he's committed a crime."

"This isn't over yet, ma'am," Zane said. "We're about to give a good hard yank on the devil's tail. Then we'll see how he acts. Let's go to the lawyer's office and get those papers. You can't head for Sacramento today. The evening will be on us before we get those proxy papers in hand. Let's spend the night here in Dorada Rio. You can have the evening and morning with your daughters. It would give me great pleasure to have you to my ranch for a stay, but right now, there's no time. At least tonight will give the Stiles family a chance to spend time together before we get back to fighting Beaumont."

Caleb looked at Laura, who nodded and said, "We've already ridden miles today. I'm about ready to drop."

"So am I." Then Caleb looked at Margaret. "You look exhausted, Mama Stiles. Are you sure you want to come to Sacramento and San Francisco? You could stay here with Michelle and Jilly."

Margaret hesitated, then nodded. "I think I have to. I can do a few things in Sacramento none of you can. The governor will act if I tell him about the judge who helped a man escape from jail, a man who attacked two of my daughters and stole a ranch from . . . my daughter-in-law, Annie."

Annie arched one eyebrow as if surprised to find herself adopted into the Stiles family. But she didn't look upset about it.

Margaret went on. "No local judge"—she slammed one fist into her other palm—"not anywhere in the state of California"—she punched her palm again with a loud smack—"is going to take the law into his own corrupt hands. He's been bribed or is being blackmailed. However it's been done, he's definitely acting under the orders of Horace Benteen. That is going to stop, and I think I'm the woman to stop it. I want this judge's name before I go. He'll soon find out he's not as powerful as he imagines himself to be."

She slammed that fist into her palm one more time.

Fierce woman. Zane decided to never make her angry.

"Let's go talk to the lawyer." Zane started for the door.

"You're sure he's trustworthy?" Margaret asked.

Zane grinned at her. "He's only a part-time lawyer. He's also the parson who performed our wedding service. The church was his second calling. He's a good lawyer but without a ruthless bone in his body. Anyway, he's too poor to be corrupt. In gold country, corruption pays very well."

They headed for the lawyer, Parson Lewis. Caleb seemed especially eager to meet him.

Zane led the parade, and as he approached the parsonage, he spent some time fretting about all the trouble swirling around him. The women needed to be guarded. If they stayed in a hotel, the men needed to take turns outside a door with the women inside.

He wondered if he'd even manage to get his wife to share a room with him. If she wasn't in the mood for that, or if he decided he didn't dare be . . . distracted . . . he might find himself sleeping on the cold floor of the hotel hallway, his body stretched across Michelle's door. It would be a disappointing way to spend a wedding night.

# CHAPTER THIRTEEN

THE DAYS WERE LONG IN CALIFORNIA IN JULY. The sun was still high in the sky when they left the lawyer's office, which was also the office of his parsonage, with the proxy papers in hand.

Michelle handed them to Laura. Jilly came up to stand with them and said, "We now have controlling interest in Stiles Lumber."

Laura nodded and took the papers. "Jilly, I think it's important that you stay hidden somewhere until this is all settled."

"Or you could marry . . . someone," Michelle added.

Jilly turned to walk toward Fatty's. They were lucky he stayed open fairly late because, full daylight or not, the supper hour was long past.

The three sisters walked side by side. Laura closest to the storefronts, Jilly in the middle, Michelle nearest the street.

The men walked behind talking quietly, no doubt planning how to solve all their problems. It bothered Michelle a bit because she'd been raised to believe she could solve her own problems, but right now, her problems seemed to need a man with iron fists and a gun on his hip.

She considered getting a gun, but until she did, she'd always have Tolstoy.

Mama came up beside them on Michelle's right, in time to hear her tell Jilly to get married.

"I don't want another hasty wedding. Please." Mama reached across Michelle to hold Jilly's hand for just a moment. "We have enough power now to run the company. Jilly, I want you to choose a husband in an orderly fashion. Your sisters have found good men, but that seems to be more good luck than a thoughtful choice."

"I knew Zane well enough to be sure he was an honorable man, Mama."

"And I certainly believed Caleb was trustworthy." Laura glanced back and smiled.

No doubt at Caleb.

"Or I might not choose one at all." Jilly shrugged.

Jilly dreaded marriage. The reason was never spoken of, and Michelle's concern for her sister was only second to honoring Jilly's refusal to talk about it. Michelle's gaze met Laura's, and she saw the same concern in Laura's eyes.

"When you know what's going on, send a wire to Zane's ranch, Mama. We'll tell them at the telegraph office we'd pay well for someone to ride out to his place to deliver it." Jilly sounded like her usual fiery self. But there was something there. Something had happened to her middle sister.

"When you believe you've got things in order to stop Edgar from having access to the family homes and accounts, and when you've found a way to rescind the rights a stepfather has over his unmarried daughters, I'll come home and get to work building a railroad."

Laura's expression remained solemn. "And I can start blowing holes in mountains."

"You'll need to come and do the surveying, Michelle." Jilly frowned at her. "Can you do that? Can you get to our forest in time to get that done before winter?"

"And have you done any more work on the braking system for the log cars?" Laura looked around Dorada Rio. "But where would you get the parts you need?"

"I'll come, but I'm not sure how soon. Zane has said we can make long visits during slow times at the ranch. And I'll have to set up a room for my experiments at the Two Harts. I've already done some surveying for the rail line, but I want to make sure we do it right."

Jilly elbowed her. "It would be a shame to blast a hole in a mountain and not come out the other end where you hoped to appear."

"Not a problem. I can easily handle that. I've done a lot of studying on it for the passes we're going to build."

"I know how to survey. I can double-check your figures."

"You could. I'd prefer to do it, but I know you can handle it. Usually, you do the blasting from both ends of the mountain and work toward the center. With two crews going it's much faster. And it's a simple surveying analysis that will ensure the tunnels meet in the middle."

"It's simple because you are brilliant, Michelle," Mama said. "It's far beyond the ability of most people."

Michelle gave Mama a one-armed hug as they walked toward the diner. Mama really was her favorite person in the world.

And then she thought of her husband. He probably ought to occupy that space.

Well, give them time. They'd get there. Someday. Maybe.

She heard the heavy boots thudding along behind them and wondered where Zane expected to sleep tonight.

FATTY'S HAD SURPRISINGLY GOOD FOOD.

After they'd eaten fried chicken, mashed potatoes and gravy, corn on the cob, and custard, Zane walked along to the hotel with Caleb and Nick. The other hands from Zane's ranch had headed home. Rick didn't like being gone overnight from his wife. Shad needed to run the place.

Old Tom and Carl reunited with Michelle and Jilly with almost as much affection as they'd shown to Laura and Margaret. They'd gone ahead to eat rather than wait at the lawyer's office and had rooms in the hotel. They were probably already asleep.

Annie hadn't wanted to leave Caroline at home overnight without her. She'd headed to the ranch with Beth Ellen and Zane's cowhands.

"I'm going to quit, Boss." Nick had his eyes open, looking around, a man on guard.

"Going back to being a lumberjack?"

"Yes. It was a good feeling to stand between Mrs. Stiles and her husband. When I told Old Tom what was going on with Beaumont and Mrs. Stiles, he was furious. I didn't have to even ask him to help me. He went charging to find men he trusted, and a large group gathered ready to rain terror down on Beaumont's head. I think a woman gets into a tight spot with her husband, and a lot of them don't turn to anyone for help. I'm not sure why she didn't call in Old Tom right from the start."

Zane had no answer for that. "She went to great lengths to save her daughters. Why didn't she do the same for herself right from the minute she realized Beaumont was a bad bargain?"

The women were a few good paces ahead of them, and the men were speaking quietly while the women talked between themselves. But they must've heard because Margaret stopped and whirled around to face them. Anger darkened her face, but it slowly faded away to hurt.

"At first, I was so happy with him. The whole time we were in San Francisco, which was just the first few months of our marriage, he treated me decently, though I couldn't exactly get used to him. It's hard to explain, but he wasn't my Liam, and everything about him felt strange. I let him have a husband's . . . prerogatives, but I felt like it betrayed Liam." A vivid pink blush bloomed on Margaret's face to speak of such intimacies. "Edgar seemed hurt by how I acted. Though I felt like I treated him decently. He accused me of . . . of comparing him to a ghost. Of not giving him a chance because he didn't measure up. There was truth in that, and I felt guilty. When he treated me coolly or criticized me, I blamed myself. Then we moved to the mountains, and it was much worse."

She looked at her daughters and frowned. "Th-the first time he shoved me, he apologized and managed to blame me for it at the same time. That was his way. And I felt at least partly that I *was* to blame because by then I knew I didn't love him. His handling of me was rougher each time.

A shove, then a slap, then a fist. I tried each time to be better. It's not right, but he wore me down, made me feel like if I was just *better* to him, more loving, he wouldn't be so upset. He wouldn't hurt me."

She shook her head. "I knew my marriage was never going to be a happy one, but I saw no choice but to endure. Then I overheard him planning my girls' weddings. He was discussing it with one of the men he'd brought into the house to act as his own henchmen. I recognized the names of the men he'd chosen for my girls. They were notorious in San Francisco. Wealthy and cruel. Men just barely accepted into the fringes of decent society. That's when I knew the true caliber of the man I'd married. Even then, I couldn't think of a way to stop the weddings. A man has a lot of power over his wife and children, even stepchildren. And the way Edgar fired people, as ruthless as a tyrant ordering the guillotine, I was afraid to turn to men I trusted for help because they'd be fired. All I could think of was to find a way for my girls to escape."

Nick strode the few feet to Margaret and took her into his arms. He held her gently, like a loving son. Margaret's arms came around him and the two of them stood silently.

When Nick stepped back, he said, "Nothing I said was meant as a criticism of you, Mrs. Stiles. You are the finest woman I've known since my own ma. It's been the greatest honor of my life to protect you."

"You're a good man, Nick. I would like very much for you to come back to Stiles Lumber and work with me there."

"I plan to. Old Tom has talked about taking me on as second-in-command. Training me to be foreman, with your permission, of course. I'm possibly a bit young, but Tom said he's not ready to quit for a time, and even when that time comes, he'd stay on and advise me when it's needed. He thinks of Stiles Lumber and that mountain as his home."

"I'm glad to hear it."

"Let's get on to the hotel. I'm going to sleep on the floor, stretched across your door. No one will harm you while I'm alive."

Zane looked at Caleb, who shrugged. Then his eyes met Michelle's. He said, "The hotel is just ahead."

"Why, it's brand-new," Margaret exclaimed. "It's grand in comparison to most of the town."

She went to the door and held it open for her daughters until Caleb got there. Then he swept his arm to send her in. She smiled, patted him on the arm, and went in.

Zane had his work cut out for him if he wanted to be the favorite son-in-law.

As he stepped inside, Zane hoped they hadn't rented out all the rooms to others already. He wanted their group to be able to spread out a little. If he could do it without risking anyone's safety, he'd sure enough like to get his wife alone.

## CHAPTER
# FOURTEEN

MICHELLE WASN'T A WOMAN TO BE OVERLY EMOTIONAL. She didn't cry much. The same was true for happy emotions. She was more likely to grin than laugh out loud. And she never, ever blushed.

Except right now.

There was a very good chance her face was the color of a ripe apple.

Entering the room with Zane just behind her, she turned to face him in time to see him close and firmly lock the door.

"I-I don't know if—if—"

Zane held up a halting hand. "I know we haven't had what might be considered a normal courtship. We haven't spent weeks or even months deciding to marry. I'm not going to put any pressure on you to do . . . wifely things with me tonight, Michelle."

The heat in her face went up a few degrees. Shocked that he'd speak of such intimacies. But relieved, too, that he didn't expect anything of her.

"I did like the idea of spending time alone with you, though. Time to talk and . . . well, I'd like to hold you in the night, just hold you. Sleep next to you. I would never ask for more until you're fully willing. But maybe a good-night kiss wouldn't be amiss under the circumstances."

Michelle managed to grin. "Thank you, Zane. I admit I've worried you, that is that we, uh, might . . . might . . ."

"You really aren't finishing your sentences at all well."

Her grin widened, and she slapped him on the chest far more gently than he probably deserved.

"I will step out into the hall and give you a few moments to change into your nightgown."

It occurred to Michelle that he might be finishing his sentences a little *too* well. His own formal little talk was as laced with nerves as her stammering. It made her feel steadier.

"I'd like to talk with Nick anyway, and see if he wants me to spell him with guard duty."

Nodding, and still blushing if the temperature of her face was any way to judge, Michelle said, "Thank you."

Zane's hand slipped on the doorknob, then he fumbled with the lock for a moment, wrenched the door wide, and stepped out.

Smiling at his awkward effort to be a perfect gentleman, she kept looking at the door, admiring the man who'd gone through it. Then she remembered she had to put her nightgown on and stay in the same room as that man.

Granted he was her husband, but it was still a shocking business, and her smile was nowhere to be found.

There was a mirror in the room. She stepped up to look at herself, and her cheeks were vivid red. With no time to ponder how to get over her embarrassment, she swiftly changed into her nightgown. She was covered in white cotton from neck to wrist to toe, and still she felt ridiculously . . . unclothed.

Afraid he'd come back too soon, or run away, she went to the door, cracked it open, and peeked out.

He stood facing her, with Nick's back to her. Zane noticed the door open, nodded, and she shut it again with a bit more of a creak than she'd intended.

"I NEED TO GO NOW." Zane couldn't hold a single thought in his head anyway. This conversation was over whether he wanted it to be or not.

Nick smiled. "Congratulations, Boss. You've got yourself a fine woman."

Zane went to his room and slipped in, not wanting to chance anyone getting a look at his wife. His very own, sworn-before-God-and-man wife. The woman he was going to share a room with and a bed with for as long as they both shall live.

Zane was innocent of women, having lived his life in a mostly male world. He rarely saw them and didn't spend his time thinking about them . . . well, not much time. Once in a while a man had himself some thoughts.

Frozen just inside the door, he studied Michelle, lying on the far side of the bed, on her side, facing away from him. Her whole body rigid as if she were a small creature hoping she didn't draw the attention of the big bad wolf.

The bed was on his right. It was a good-sized room, but no hotel rooms were ever exactly large. He noticed she seemed to be breathing with an unnatural steadiness as if she was pretending to sleep. She had the covers pulled up to her ears.

It was very unlikely she'd fallen asleep in the two seconds it'd taken him to enter the room after she'd looked out the door.

"I'm going to change into my nightshirt now." He wanted to add something. *Don't look.* Or *Beware . . . if you look you might wish you hadn't.* Or better yet, maybe he should say, *I don't mind if you look.*

He almost turned and banged his head on the bedroom door. He might've if it wouldn't have drawn Nick's attention.

Nothing seemed at all right, so he just hurried to his small satchel. They had planned to stay in town overnight regardless, between the arrest, the trial, and the wedding, so they had packed a few things.

His temper flared when he thought of Jarvis being gone, but Michelle didn't need a cranky man in the room with her.

He stripped out of his clothes and quickly donned a nightshirt. It was more common for him to sleep in his longhandles, though on warm summer nights, this nightshirt made sleep more comfortable.

He moved slowly to the bed, hoping for silence, which was stupid. He didn't want to sneak up on her, but still, he tiptoed, then slid into the bed with a living, breathing wife. She was bound to notice.

He was glad he was lying down, or he might've toppled over from the sudden wave of dizziness.

The bedside lantern was still burning. Before he extinguished it, he turned to her, and doing his best to act like this was a normal and natural moment, when in truth it ranked up near the strangest and most wonderful moments of his life, he reached out a hand, hesitantly but wanting to say something before they went to sleep, and he rested his palm on the graceful curve of her shoulder.

"Good-night, sweet wife."

She rolled onto her back and gave him a sheepish grin. "Good-night, husband."

He remembered that they'd agreed to a kiss. "May I have my good-night kiss now?"

"You may."

Leaning slowly, an inch at a time, so he could remember every moment, he pressed his lips to hers. Felt them warm and tender beneath his. The kiss deepened by the second. His arm came around her waist and pulled her close. She curled a hand behind his neck.

The kiss was perfect. The woman was perfect. Then what was sweet and warm caught fire. He wrenched away from her. Their eyes met and held.

With a startling suddenness, Michelle dove back toward his lips and kissed him with an enthusiasm that woke up all sorts of ideas in Zane's muddled head.

Before long, Zane had another way to define perfection.

And his willing wife hadn't hesitated over the intimacies for one heartbeat.

Being married was the best thing that had ever happened to him.

## CHAPTER FIFTEEN

WE GAINED NOTHING FROM THE LAST COUPLE OF DAYS." Jilly was storming aloud as they rode toward the Two Harts.

"Mama will talk to Governor Booth. Zane will post a sentry every night. I got married. Those are gains." Michelle glanced at Zane, felt the blush when his eyes met hers, and looked away.

Michelle wasn't about to discuss anything else that had been gained.

They'd been pushing hard toward home. Odd to think of a ranch as home. Michelle mentally shook the oddness away. She had to get used to it.

Jilly rode on Michelle's left. Zane on her right. Mama, Caleb, Laura, and Nick had left for Sacramento that morning, so it was just the three of them.

Michelle noticed Zane was watchful as they rode. He probably should have kept his men in town last night, but Annie had thought she needed to be home for Caroline, and she couldn't go alone.

"Jarvis being released adds to the danger, but we won't let that stand," Zane said. "The sheriff obeyed the papers given to him by the judge. But Margaret will go to the governor, and before the week is out, that judge will be kicked out of his office and a new man named. Stockwood will arrest Jarvis again."

That was the part of this that wasn't going to be easy. They'd had him. Now they had to get him again, and his father, Horace Benteen, wasn't going to be nice about allowing it.

"And we'll see him locked away. Old Man Benteen will be kicked out of Annie's ranch, and she should sell it and move back here and live with us, Michelle."

"What are we going to do about the gold, Zane?" Michelle asked.

She saw his shoulders square, and his jaw tightened as he prepared to argue about it with her again.

"I think you should set the two men who married the Hogan sisters and maybe Shad to running it," Michelle said.

Zane jerked as if his saddle had sprung up a nail. He turned to look at her in amazement.

She shrugged. "I could run it, and run it well, and Jilly with me." She looked at her sister, and Jilly jerked her chin down in one hard nod of agreement.

"But it's just not safe." Michelle frowned as she said it.

"No, no, I mean, yes! Yes, you're right. It's not safe. But I've been telling you for a long time it wasn't safe."

"I'm not stupid, Zane. Believe it or not, I'm really smart."

That got a grin out of him. "So I've been told and told and told."

"Before, when we were worried about another mob like

the one that came to Purgatory when our mission group was working there, well, I just didn't think that would happen again. Surely word got around that none of those shacks were still standing, which were what brought people up there. I didn't think that was a real danger. But I can't do it with men on the prowl from Benteen's crowd."

Nodding, Zane said, "Shad could maybe do it. And Bo and Jesse. Bo and Jesse even live out there. The Hogan sisters seem very sensible. They would probably keep the men from going mad with gold fever." He looked intently at Michelle. "There are plenty of ways for you to help with the mining operation, though. There is a lot of managing that doesn't require you to be out there. I'd appreciate having your organizational skills."

Michelle bobbed her chin. "I could do that. I'd be great at that."

Zane frowned back at Dorada Rio, now far in the distance.

"What's the matter?" Michelle twisted in the saddle but saw nothing. "Did you forget something you wanted from town?"

"I didn't exactly forget. I just didn't know I'd needed something."

"Needed what?"

"More cowhands."

"Can you trust anyone in town not to be on Benteen's payroll?"

Zane was quiet for a moment. "I wonder what happened to all Annie's hired men. Maybe we can get the word out that they'd be welcome here. I suppose I need to send another rider to town. But I'm not sure just how I'd reach the right men. Chances are they split up, rode away hunting a new job."

They rode along quietly while Michelle figured how to organize a gold mining business from the ground up. Or rather, organize the blank account book. She found herself eager to begin.

ZANE RODE UP TO HIS RANCH to see a strange horse, along with a loaded packhorse, hitched to the rail at the back of his house.

It'd been a long ride, and he hadn't slept much last night. A thought that put a smile on his face. He was tired to the bone. But the horses put him on edge, though no henchman working for Benteen would come riding onto the place with a packhorse.

His hand resting on his gun, he kept his eyes open, looking all around, as they rode toward the hitching post.

Riding in slow ended on a scream.

Zane threw himself off his horse and charged the back door. He slammed inside to find—

"Josh?"

Annie and Beth Ellen were hugging him. Caroline must've decided she liked having another uncle because she was the one screaming.

Just as Zane and Annie matched with their dark hair, the two blonds in the family were a match, except Beth Ellen was a little thing and Josh a great strapping man.

Zane's heart slowed until it was close to normal. Then

he charged at his brother. "Josh, great to see you. It's been what? Two years?"

"At least." His baby brother, who was every inch Zane's height and built solid as any schooner, grinned and let go of his sisters to give Zane a hug that nearly crushed him. Years on a ship had turned Josh's muscles to iron.

"My ship went all the way around Cape Horn—that's what they call the southern tip of South America—up to New York, then, for the first time ever, I signed on to go to London. Shipped around there awhile, went to Paris and Rome and Cairo. And on around Africa, all the way to India. Then we sailed on across the Pacific to San Francisco. I hopped off to come and visit you instead of setting out again."

"Wow, London. Paris. India. Josh, you've traveled the world. I want to hear all about it."

"I can talk for days with all the stories I've got saved up. But what I most need to say is, after traveling far and wide, I finally realized I was searching for a life I wanted more than home, and there wasn't any such thing. I'm home to stay, Zane."

Zane hugged him hard enough to break a rib. Then Annie was crying and shoving Zane out of the way.

All four of them together. And here to stay. Zane watched Josh swing Annie in a circle, and it put a smile on Zane's face that was big enough it hurt a little.

Michelle and Jilly came in last. Jilly with a grin on her face. Michelle shaking her head at the chaos.

Zane reached out a hand to Michelle. She came on in and took it, Jilly just a step behind her. "It's a good thing we've had so many people move out of the house."

"Move out?" Josh's brow furrowed. "And who are these two women?"

"I've got plenty to tell you, too, I reckon." Zane raised the hand he had joined with Michelle's. "This is my wife, Michelle. Next to her is her sister Jilly."

"Pretty." Josh looked from Michelle to Jilly and back. "Welcome to the family, ladies."

Michelle grinned like she was apt to do and said, "Welcome back to the family, Josh."

"Just so you know," Zane added with a wink, "they're both smart, really smart. Or so I've been told."

Gretel had a hot meal waiting. They washed up and sat at the table. The Hart family was beaming.

Michelle and Jilly seemed happy enough listening to the Hart siblings chatter, though Zane figured it would be hard for them to keep up.

But then Josh started talking about India, and Jilly knew more about it than he did. And when he talked about Paris, Michelle started speaking French.

MICHELLE FELL INTO BED EXHAUSTED that night. The long ride, the long night before, the hectic but lovely reunion with Zane's brother . . . She was having trouble keeping her eyes open.

She was in the same room she'd occupied when Jarvis had broken in. Jilly slept next door to Michelle as she always had in the housekeeper's apartment.

Josh had been fully alerted to the trouble.

All three of Zane's siblings had taken over the upstairs, along with Annie's daughter, Caroline.

And then Zane came into Michelle's room.

She'd sort of forgotten about him.

Now, with him standing there in her bedroom, the lantern light glinting off his brown hair, his blue eyes looking right at her as a husband might, she couldn't think of much else.

Michelle saw him reach for the front buttons of his shirt and quickly rolled to her side, away from him.

Silly after last night, but she reacted first and thought about it second—which wasn't how she normally acted.

And now, on second thought, she just stayed right where she was.

The bed shifted, and the covers rose and fell. Then and only then did she roll onto her back to see her husband smiling down at her. The lantern still on. His shoulders as bare as a baby's backside.

"I'm glad your brother came home. You looked so happy to see him." Michelle reached up and touched Zane's bottom lip. She'd become very fond of his lips.

"It'll be good to have him home. We need people around to help run the place."

Michelle gasped and sat up. The blanket dropped to her waist, and when she realized her nightgown showed, she grabbed the edges and pulled it to her chin.

Zane smiled and arched one brow. "Think of something?"

"Yes, of course. Josh can run the mine."

The teasing smile vanished from Zane's face. "Do you think he'd be inclined to gold fever?"

Michelle sat there, the covers still up to her chin. "Would it be different if the gold was a fourth his? Would he control any greed since he'd be getting a good share of what he dug up with his own hands?"

Zane was quiet a long time. "Josh is an honorable man.

He's always been that way. I think I can trust him. I-I guess if I can't, and he runs off with all the gold, well, it hurts to think of that. I'll trust him until he starts showing me I can't."

Zane shifted closer to her. "Maybe at first I'll go along with him and take you and Jilly. We can even finish the building Jilly started after the church burned down. Josh can live there if he wants or just stay there if the day gets long. And if it's a big strike, I'll pay the miners so well they won't even be interested in robbing me."

Rolling onto his side, he said, "You can still manage things from here, Michelle. I haven't really spent time with Josh for years. He was always a good man. But having you going over the books and minding the expenses and payroll might help keep him, oh, from . . ." He fell silent as he looked into her eyes.

"From temptation?" Michelle asked.

Zane smiled. "When the word *temptation* came into my head while I was looking right at you, I kinda forgot what I was talking about and only remembered that you are a tempting woman. And it's not even a sin to be tempted by my wife. In fact, I believe it's encouraged, even blessed by God."

His smile widened. He reached a hand around her waist and pulled her to lie on her side facing him. Then he lowered his head and tasted her.

Michelle had no interest in continuing their conversation about his brother. Her husband was the only man on Michelle's mind.

# CHAPTER
# SIXTEEN

"YOU FOUND GOLD ON OUR RANCH?" Josh ran both hands deep into his hair. It was the same straw color as Beth Ellen's but curlier, in a coarse way. Cut short as if the curl bothered him, or maybe it'd been long when he disembarked, and he'd gotten it cut when he came ashore.

Zane had waited until after breakfast this morning to tell him the last bit of family news. Josh's eyes flashed, and Michelle watched him closely for signs of madness. The Hart family was prosperous. By many standards, they were flat-out wealthy.

Michelle remembered well those poor folks who'd lived in Purgatory. Lean until they looked like skeletons. People who had nothing.

By comparison, yes, the Hart family was rich. But that didn't always make a difference when it came to gold.

"I want you to run the mining operation, Josh." Zane lifted his coffee cup and took a long drink. Beth Ellen rose from the table to pour more for everyone.

The whole family was there. Annie was washing breakfast dishes. Jilly was trying to help. It took no great skill to use a towel, after all. And Michelle sat at the table bouncing Caroline on her knee and trying to keep her happy until her mother's hands were free.

"Let's go see it." Josh shoved himself to his feet.

"Wait a minute." Zane glanced around the room. "It's not safe to go off and leave the women alone."

Zane had explained most of what had gone on to Josh last night, saving the gold story for now. Michelle realized he'd wanted to talk it over with her first. It warmed her heart to think of it.

"Uh," Josh looked at his sisters, then at the rest of the room. "Can we all go?"

"Bring Caroline." Zane smiled at the little sweetie. "She can ride with me."

Shad swung the back door open with a bang. "We got a cow down, Zane. Need help."

Then Shad was gone, and Zane right after him, Josh hard on his heels.

Michelle looked at Jilly. "Maybe we can head out later, after the cow."

Annie scrubbed a skillet and said with a patient sigh, "There's always another cow."

So Annie spent the day trying to teach Michelle how to peel potatoes. Beth Ellen insisted Jilly help with the laundry. Life on a ranch wasn't as exciting as blowing up mountains.

"YOU REALLY KNOW THE GOVERNOR." Caleb sounded wildly impressed as they walked away from the meeting they'd just sat through while Mama talked to Uncle Newt.

Nick had only gone in with them under threat of force. Mama had ended up latching onto his arm, and he'd've had to knock her down to escape. He'd been utterly silent before the mighty governor.

Laura gave Caleb a one-armed hug for the awestruck tone in his voice. She said, "Uncle Newt ran a wholesale grocery store before he became governor. A very successful one. Papa knew him quite well. Mama, too, well, all of us."

"Uncle Newt?" Caleb sounded a little dazed.

"Yes, he came to the house for dinner now and then. Uncle . . . um, that is, I need to learn to call him Governor Booth, is a bachelor, and I think he enjoyed the company."

"Up to a point," Margaret said. "I think he liked a woman and children around for the length of an evening and then was glad to go home. He was always an ambitious, hard-working man, highly educated and a lawyer . . . but he loved running a business more than working at the law. He never took the time to marry. When his attention turned to politics, Liam supported him, and we were glad to speak up for his campaign. He is an honest and honorable man."

"This is the fanciest building I've ever been in." Nick hadn't spoken since he was dragged into the governor's beautiful office.

"It was built in the same style as the Capitol in Washington, DC." Mama sounded like a tour guide.

"And the governor's office is the fanciest room I've ever been in."

Mama, with her arm through Nick's, patted him. "It is beautiful. The building isn't finished yet but very close. They've made something majestic here."

Their voices echoed as they walked through the rotunda with the high overhead dome.

As they reached the exit doors, a tall, lean man wearing a sharp black suit with a shiny badge pinned on his left lapel stepped forward. He tugged on the front brim of his black Stetson. "You must be Mrs. Beaumont."

"I am, to my everlasting shame. My next chore is speaking with a lawyer about how to protect myself from my husband and stop what he's threatened to do to my girls."

Laura thought of Jilly and her profound resistance to marriage. Had Edgar done more to her than threaten? Or were his threats just really good ones? Or was it something else?

"I'm Trey Irving, the US Marshal assigned to your case." He had a full mustache, and his hair was as dark as his eyes. His suit looked clean and was of good quality. A successful man to Laura's way of thinking. That had to be a good thing in a lawman—unless he took bribes.

He led them into an office in the capitol building. Much more humble than the governor's, but still an impressive room. He sat behind a desk and gestured for the four of them to sit in chairs he had drawn up in a semicircle in front of his desk.

"I always get my man. The governor calls for me when he wants things handled just right. He sent a message down here to me with instructions to listen to your story."

"Horace Benteen is a powerful man in this state and a fierce adversary of the governor." Mama took charge. "He believes he's above the law, and he fears no one."

"I've heard of Benteen." Nodding, Irving said, "There is no question that we need to handle his son just right. I'd like to spend time with you first so I know what I'm facing, then I'll go and get Jarvis and bring him back to Sacramento. And the governor ordered me to fire the judge who's running things in Dorada Rio while I'm down there. The governor is already appointing a new judge. If a man wants to be on Horace's payroll, he's going to work right at his side and not from behind a judge's bench." The man's dark eyes glinted. "I may do more than fire him. If I can find enough evidence, I may arrest him, too. A corrupt judge makes everybody's life harder."

"Not Benteen's life," Margaret said with cold anger.

"Maybe Benteen's life will be harder than he expects. Bribing a judge is against the law. If the judge testifies against him—and he might to lessen his own sentence—Horace might go to prison."

Then Marshal Irving asked all the questions they'd already answered to the sheriff in Dorada Rio and to the governor. They knew the story by heart. But Marshal Irving was good. He drew out information they hadn't thought to provide before. And they explained more about Annie's ranch and her husband's death.

The marshal looked grim when they talked of murder. And angry when they talked of Jarvis attacking Jilly and Michelle.

"It'll be hard to get a murder charge to stick to Horace Benteen, but if we could, it'd be a hanging offense."

"I wouldn't be surprised if he killed his wife. She was a young woman, Horace's third wife. The other two died unexpectedly. The third was next thing to a hermit, and I wonder about abuse." Mama hadn't spared herself the details of Edgar's cruelty.

Laura's tension worsened with every word her mama

spoke of Edgar's abuse. She felt like a clock wound too tightly. She hadn't heard most of this before. Caleb sat next to her in a matching oak chair with a smooth, satiny finish and sturdy, flat armrests. He reached across the space between them, his left hand to her right, and laced his fingers through hers. She glanced at him and closed her hand tightly around his. Some of the tension eased, replaced with sadness.

"The brazen way he stole Annie's ranch is very telling." Mama was a different woman now. Laura hadn't really noticed how she'd changed over the year of her second marriage. But this woman, this brilliant, confident woman, had gone into hiding.

Laura's spirits lifted. Whatever Edgar had put Mama through, she wasn't crushed. She was still Laura's lively, feisty mother.

Laura thought of how she'd grown to dread taking over the onerous duties of helping run Stiles Lumber. Made more onerous now with Michelle's abandoning Laura to marry Zane.

For the first time, it popped into Laura's head that Michelle had given it up quite easily. Was it possible that Laura wasn't the only one who didn't want to be a titan of industry?

But Mama. Maybe the weight of running a business hadn't been overwhelming to her. Maybe she liked it. Right now, she seemed energized by the fight to defeat Edgar, bring Benteen to justice, and wrestle back control of Stiles Lumber.

Marshal Irving finally seemed to have exhausted all his questions. "Thank you for taking time to help me see all the aspects of this case." He rose, and they all followed suit. He went to the door and held it open for them. "You can get on with your own activities. And I'll get this investigation up and running."

Mama reached out and clutched the man's arm. "Two of my daughters are still at the Two Harts Ranch by Dorada Rio. Be careful that my girls don't end up in the crossfire when things come down to a fight."

"No harm will come to your girls, ma'am. I swear it." He stood at the door as they left. Then he followed them out and left the capitol building with determined speed.

Laura had to fight the almost giddy hope that was blooming in her heart. Between Uncle Newt's outrage and his obvious hatred of Benteen and now Marshal Irving's vow, Laura felt more optimistic than she had in a long time.

Their next stop was to see a lawyer about severing Edgar's rights over them.

The lawyer, recommended by Uncle Newt, read Michelle's proxy papers and wrote up legal papers to support the girls' having majority ownership of Stiles Lumber, sole access to the accounts, and veto power over any decision Edgar made.

Preventing Edgar from having any power over Jilly was the hardest to figure out.

When Mama explained things, the lawyer was blunt in his explanation of what lay ahead of her and the limits of the law when it came to a husband and wife.

"I'd recommend divorce, ma'am."

Mama's shoulders sagged from the weight of what she was attempting, and by the end, her teeth were clenched to keep from berating herself for getting into such a mess.

Caleb had helped Mama feel less dreadful about asking for the divorce, but she couldn't seem to go ahead and just say it was what she wanted to do.

"It feels wrong, sinful. I took those vows."

"It's a slow process, Mrs. Beaumont. But filing the papers, well, it would show your intent, it would give me some legal legs to stand on to sever your husband's parental rights over your remaining unmarried daughter."

When Mama agreed, the lawyer removed Edgar from any paternal rights over his adult stepdaughter. But the papers were only as good as the lawmen and judges brought in to enforce them. If Jilly fell into Edgar's hands, she would be in danger.

"The proxy papers are in order. I've got your list of banks and supporting industries here in Sacramento. It also gives Mrs. Tillman the right to sit on all boards that you're a part of."

With Papa's and Mama's sharp investing skills, Stiles Lumber was involved in many of the biggest companies in Sacramento and San Francisco.

"I could handle the San Francisco businesses for you, too," the lawyer went on. "But you'll handle things faster there on your own. I'll file the papers for divorce and guardianship. That will make your intent clear to the law, though it will have no real power." He pursed his lips.

"I'll remember." Mama shook his hand, and they left the law office.

"Now we ride to San Francisco." Mama adjusted her bonnet and pulled on her gloves. She clutched her reticule to her chest as if she needed to hang on to something while her world teetered. "Based on our San Francisco house and mountain home being owned by the company, we can bar Edgar from both places and put a stop to his use of the company bank accounts."

Laura thought she saw a grayish tint to Mama's skin and dark circles under her eyes. Only then did she realize how exhausting this all was for Mama. She worried about the long ride on horseback. Laura and Caleb seemed to have been walking or riding almost since they met. The few weeks in Purgatory were almost the only time they'd stopped moving. She was getting used to sitting a horse. But Mama had been as good as a prisoner for most of a year. She certainly hadn't gone riding. She must be at the end of her strength.

"Mama, let's take the train. It goes back and forth between Sacramento and San Francisco so often now. We can stable the horses here and use the streetcars there. I'm tired of riding."

"That sounds like a good idea. I think there is a train running at least once a day." Mama's face brightened.

Laura decided that while they were in San Francisco, they'd make a few calls that were purely for fun. Mama was so hurt by her marriage and now the possibility of divorce.

Laura knew divorce was a scandalous thing. If such a choice was the only way to keep Jilly safe, Laura knew her mama would have to go through with it. She hoped Mama's old friends wouldn't shun her.

Prayerfully, Laura wondered how God really felt about such a thing. She repeated in her head the words Caleb had spoken about it. But breaking vows spoken before Him was a terrible thing.

But surely Mama needed to escape the pain and nightmarish fear of her marriage.

Laura caught hold of Caleb's hand, and he turned to smile at her. She'd found a good man. And for that she truly, deeply thanked God.

# CHAPTER SEVENTEEN

"AND THEN A WAVE HIT SO HARD the boat nearly laid on its side. We were mighty lucky that—"

"I think I hear a cow bawling." Zane stood and quickly headed for the door.

He just plain ran. The big dummy.

Michelle noticed that Josh hardly broke from his story. Though she'd been distracted, she wasn't sure Josh had ever stopped talking. She wondered if he talked in his sleep.

She decided if Zane could do it, so could she. "I'm going to fetch my mending."

She stood up and just plain ran. Now she was thinking Zane was smart as a whip, and *she* was the one learning from him.

Of course, she didn't have any mending. And for a fact, she didn't know how to mend. But it didn't matter. She wasn't going back.

The days were spent in hard work, and Josh had turned out to have excellent cowboy skills. But the evenings were stretching out in boredom. How could a man make a life on the sea, traveling the world, sound so dull?

Tomorrow, though, they'd go to the gold mine. And Michelle would get to go along.

Jilly too.

Maybe tomorrow night, if they brought gold home, Michelle could stand to listen to Josh's seafaring tales while she chipped the gold out of the quartz rocks.

She got her nightgown on and went to bed, wondering how long Jilly would last listening to Josh. And when Zane would come back from the barn.

She fell asleep wondering.

JOSH SCRATCHED HIS HEAD AS HE STARED AT THE PILE OF ROCKS. "I don't know much about gold. I wouldn't have recognized this as being a gold strike."

"Not sure I would have, either." Zane nudged a rock with his boot. "This isn't a part of the ranch I come to often. Building a church for the mission group took Michelle and her sisters into the woods, and they recognized it."

"Laura found it." Michelle felt like she should give credit where it was due. But she was sure she'd have recognized it, too.

"Let's get to work." Jilly pulled her hammer and chisel out of her saddlebag. They'd added to their supply of digging tools in Dorada Rio. But not overly, not wishing to draw attention to their interest in chiseling in a town very knowledgeable about gold.

The day took up a rhythm of hammering and working

over the gold. They'd do more work on it at the house, but the more stone they could separate from the gold here, the less they'd need to haul.

Beth Ellen and Annie had come, too. So they had a good crew, though Annie had to chase after Caroline most of the time. Beth Ellen took turns with Annie, giving their soft and ladylike hands a break from the harsh mining work.

Michelle and Jilly just wore gloves.

"I think the quartz plays out." Michelle pointed to the end of the thick slab. It went plenty far, but it didn't go on forever. "The gold vein may go down into the ground, but if not, then we'll have a few weeks' work here and that will be the end of the gold."

Michelle came to Zane's side and patted his arm. "You're not going to have to hire miners or worry about a gold rush. Unless we scout up more gold around here, but I've already done a lot of looking. I didn't see another rock formation similar to this. We'll simply harvest all this gold, take it all at once to sell, make sure to announce loud and long that this is all there is, and hope you don't lead a parade of desperate men back to your ranch."

Zane shuddered. "That's all I need."

The day stretched long. They'd ridden over on a side trail so the Hogan sisters and Zane's men wouldn't notice them. They'd made a comment to Shad about a family picnic to celebrate Josh coming home, and they'd ridden off with plenty of food. They'd also hammered as quietly as they could and hoped the Hogan sisters down through the trees in Zane's meadow didn't hear them.

Mining for gold was a complicated business.

Josh said he'd take over and do the mining quietly. Michelle and Jilly offered to come along and help. Zane didn't like that, but he didn't do much growling, and Josh really did need the help, or he'd be all summer on this.

At home that night, Michelle and Jilly taught the family how to split the gold off from the quartz, and by week's end, they had a tidy pile of gold to haul to town.

Except they didn't dare take it.

AT BREAKFAST A WEEK LATER, Josh said, "I think the vein has almost played out. I hope to finish today. Though I could dig deeper. There might be more gold to find."

Michelle saw something flash in Josh's eyes.

"I'd hate to have the vein seem to end, then just a few more inches of digging, find a whole 'nother supply," he said.

"We have around seventy thousand dollars' worth of gold under my bed." Jilly did her mental mathematics.

Michelle could follow the figuring in her head. "That's enough for this ranch to put a windmill in every pasture and a waterwheel in every river and creek and buy a traction engine and threshing machine. You can buy another zillion acres and that many cattle. Or you can do like my father did. You can invest in a dozen businesses under the banner of Two Harts. You can own shares in railroads, construction companies, factories, and banks."

"He did?" Zane asked Michelle.

"And a lot more." Michelle shrugged one shoulder as she drank her coffee.

Jilly went on, sounding disdainful, "He started his lumber

company with about one fifth of what's under my bed. You don't need to hunt gold anymore."

Michelle had wondered a few times if Jilly and Josh might make a go of a marriage, but they'd been working together all week, and Jilly's tone didn't bode well for any romance to develop.

Even without a proclamation of love between Michelle and Zane, she had affection for him, desire, and definitely respect. She heard absolutely no respect in Jilly's tone.

And Josh had a light flush on his cheeks that might be embarrassment, might be anger, or might be a fever. Gold fever.

All of those were bad signs as far as a budding romance. Especially now that Jilly didn't really need to get married.

As for Michelle and Zane . . . love, well, there were sparks between her and her husband, no denying it.

White hot sparks.

But love? Michelle remembered the bond between her parents. Something so solid, so strong, so real, Michelle always felt that she could have held that bond in her hand, like a solid thing that connected them, that truly made the two become one. Love?

She thought of how smart she always claimed to be, but she just couldn't figure this one out.

"Zane," Josh asked, "how are we going to handle selling it?"

Zane opened his mouth, but there was a hard rap on the back door that drew him to his feet. When it was Shad, he normally knocked and came on in. The door remained closed.

Zane went to it, and a tall man in a black suit wearing a

lawman's badge stood at the door. "I'm US Marshal Trey Irving. Are you Zane Hart, owner of this ranch?"

"I am." Zane stepped aside and gestured for Irving to come in.

The marshal looked around the room until his eyes landed on Michelle and Jilly. "I talked with Margaret Stiles Beaumont and her daughter a week ago. I've been working on this case at the direction of Governor Booth."

"You work for Uncle Newt?" Michelle asked.

Trey shook his head a little too hard as if hearing the governor called Uncle Newt wasn't quite settling in his brain right. Michelle knew she needed to call him Governor Booth. She just kept forgetting.

Even Jilly forgot, and Jilly never forgot anything.

"I fired the judge who let Jarvis go, then I locked him up and had him transported to Sacramento to stand trial. I've been investigating him since I talked to . . . she must be your ma, she looks just like you, miss."

"I'm Michelle Stiles Hart, and this is my sister Jillian Stiles."

The marshal removed his hat and tipped his head. "I found plenty of reasons to arrest him. And I got a confession that implicates Horace and Jarvis Benteen. I've got warrants to arrest them both, but Jarvis hasn't been seen in the area, and Horace has a lot of tough cowhands at his ranch, including some known gunmen. I can't ride in there alone. And the governor has already appointed a man to fill the judge's office here. A man we can trust to be beyond the influence of Horace Benteen. The sheriff seemed downright gleeful about locking up the judge."

Michelle was finding herself downright fond of Marshal

Irving. She listened to him with growing hope. He was a tough man, very confident.

Annie warned him about how dangerous Benteen was, and they all sat through a thorough questioning that distracted them from gold hunting.

"YOU OWN THIS HOUSE, TOO?" Caleb looked in wonder at the mansion in a whole neighborhood of mansions.

He stared at Laura. "Just how much do you charge for those trees you cut down?"

Laura smiled and patted him on the arm as they stood on the porch of their San Francisco house. "This is California Hill, but it's gained the nickname of Nob Hill. Some say it's because nabobs live here."

"What's a nabob?" Nick muttered.

"Someone rich or powerful."

"Or both," Mama Stiles added.

"The name Nob Hill has caught on so well, I expect them to change the name officially one of these days," Laura went on. "Papa and Mama didn't build this house. They bought it when some railroad or other went bankrupt. It's beautiful, but you have to admit it's a rather boring rectangular thing. And half the size of most of the other mansions up here. It's not blessed with all the flourishes and turrets and porches most of the other houses have."

"I grew up in a three-room cabin." Nick looked around the street of lavish homes. "It seems real fancy to me."

"All this lovely architecture on our neighbors' homes here was an inspiration for our house on the mountain.

But ours out there is a fraction of the size of some of these." Margaret pointed to one down the street from hers. "I've heard that house has twenty-five bedrooms." Then Margaret smiled at Caleb. "And I can promise you my husband charged every penny the market would bear for his lumber."

Caleb was amazed at how much she looked like Laura when she smiled, even with her dark hair. Margaret bore a much stronger resemblance to Michelle, but that smile she shared with all her daughters.

A locksmith followed them into the house, intent on changing the locks. Margaret had already been to her bank and closed all her accounts, then reopened them in such a way only Laura could withdraw money.

Caleb had listened to her lament how low the accounts had gotten, but he'd heard the numbers. Mama Stiles still seemed plenty rich to him. He thought of those folks he'd ministered to in Purgatory. No food in their homes. Children around their knees.

He controlled his expression, but he felt sure he needed to discuss laying up treasures in heaven with the Stiles family. And do it soon.

Margaret strode into the house. Edgar stepped into the foyer to meet her.

His voice cold, Edgar said, "What are you doing in San Francisco, Margaret? I told you to stay on the mountain."

Caleb felt a chill at the tone. He didn't want to jump to any conclusions, but he suspected Edgar hadn't spent much time contemplating his soul.

The entrance hall was huge. So big that Edgar's voice echoed. The hall was two very tall stories high. Rooms opened to the left and right, and hallways led to the back of the house on either side of an imposing central staircase.

Caleb slipped his arm around Laura, and the two of them came up beside Margaret on her right. Nick stepped to her left side. Edgar's eyes narrowed.

Margaret said to the locksmith, "Can you please wait for us in that parlor to the right, sir? We'll be in to discuss what's to be done about changing every lock in this house."

The locksmith seemed nervous, and he was all too glad to leave the tension-filled room.

"My girls have married, Edgar."

Caleb noticed she didn't lie, but she didn't mention Jilly still remained single.

"The man you sent to harm them failed, and we've spoken to a US Marshal, the governor, and a lawyer the governor recommended to me. On his recommendation, we've stopped in at the bank that holds our company's funds. The girls have taken possession of the company, and the bank has seen the legal documents and understands they now have controlling interest. That includes Stiles Lumber and also the various companies my husband owned shares in. I no longer have any say in the company, and for certain, you don't."

Laura stepped closer to her ma. "This house and the one on the mountaintop are part of that company, and speaking on behalf of my sisters and myself, you are no longer welcome in either place. You'll find the company bank accounts all closed. The new ones we opened are expressly set up to block any attempt on your part to withdraw funds."

Stiles Lumber was a collection of many businesses. Caleb had watched Margaret change it all over. Each business had its own accounts, and its own tidy set of books. He'd also watched Laura very carefully conceal her dread at being in charge of the whole company. She still hadn't told her mother she didn't want to be an industrialist.

But with Jilly still in hiding and Michelle stuck on a ranch, it looked like Laura was it.

*Stuck* wasn't really accurate for Michelle. Being stuck on a prosperous ranch with a gold mine, well, *stuck* wasn't a fair word.

Anyway, Laura didn't want the job. Something she'd told no one but Caleb. Caleb should probably offer to take over, but he didn't want the job, either. He was a preacher. Called by God. One of these days, and it'd better be soon, Laura was going to have to be honest about what she wanted.

"I want you to leave now, Edgar." Margaret, as warm and kind as any woman Caleb had ever met, sounded cold and harsh. "As the owners, Laura and her sisters are changing the locks on the doors here and doing the same at the mountain house."

Laura took up her being-in-charge stance again. "I've sent word that your henchmen there are to be fired. I left a man I know I can trust in charge to carry out those orders."

Margaret said, "Send a messenger when you get settled, and I'll have your clothing packed and sent to wherever you're staying. I will add, I've filed for divorce. I'll forward those papers to you, also."

Edgar's eyes flashed with fury. He looked at Nick, who stood with his hand resting on his six-gun. Then he slid his eyes to Caleb. Two burly men stepped out of whatever room Edgar had been in. Caleb saw they had guns under their coats. Caleb didn't carry a gun. Maybe that was a mistake, and heaven knew he'd used one back east, though he wasn't a gunman. He'd used a gun to feed his ma until she died. After that, he'd fallen into a life of crime—but there was no shooting involved in his crimes.

But he was a good shot, and he knew it.

He braced himself to dive in front of Laura, leaving Nick to protect them all, and prayed it wouldn't come to shooting trouble.

That's when Old Tom and Carl came inside. They were still standing guard over the Stiles women. Both heavily armed. Glancing back at them, Caleb didn't see many qualms in Old Tom's eyes about buying into a gunfight. He looked eager for some retribution against Edgar.

Edgar saw he was outgunned, and with a sniff, he said, "We're leaving. But this isn't over, Margaret."

Caleb guided Laura and Margaret away from the door. Nick, Old Tom, and Carl stood in front of the women. Caleb tried to think of what God would have him say, and all he could think of was the futility. He prayed as the men went past, out the door, and down the front steps.

"I'm sorely afraid he's right about this not being over," Margaret said after Edgar and his men were gone.

Carl closed the door with solid finality.

"What now, Mama?" Laura leaned her head on her mother's shoulder, sounding exhausted.

"I need to personally visit and talk with every business enterprise we are involved with. That will be at least a dozen stops. Five . . . no, six of them here in San Francisco. We need to go out to the sawmill, especially, and make sure Edgar doesn't meddle there. I need to make sure my voting rights on all the company boards your father served on, or had part ownership of, are converted to you, Laura. Each of those many companies needs to be aware of the change of status. That may take days. Then we need to get home to the mountain. Or no, maybe we should go to see Michelle and Jilly instead. Old Tom and Carl could head back to the mountain and take charge there."

Margaret seemed frozen with indecision and had a look of exhaustion to match Laura's that dragged down the corners of her mouth.

Caleb didn't give anyone a chance to voice further opinions. "For now, we rest. It's been a long stretch of days. Tomorrow we'll plan for what's next."

Margaret nodded, then headed for the stairs. "I'll show you men where you can sleep."

"I'm sleeping across the front of your door, ma'am," Nick said.

"We'll watch the locksmith and make sure he does his job well, hands over every copy of the keys, and is on his way," Old Tom said.

From the startled look on Margaret's face, Caleb was sure she'd forgotten all about the locksmith.

"Thank you, Tom, Carl," Margaret said. "I'd be lost without all the help you've given me. Nick too." She smiled at Caleb and slid her arms around Laura's waist in a gentle hug. "Everyone. You've kept me going."

The men looked bashful and dragged off their hats.

"We'll decide what's next when we aren't nearly out on our feet," Margaret said. "Come on then, Laura, Caleb, Nick. We'll try and get some sleep."

She led the way up a sweeping staircase that rose before them with great majesty. When it reached the wall, the stairs divided to the left and right and went on to the second floor.

Margaret led the way to the right. By the time they reached the top, Caleb had one arm around Margaret and the other around Laura, practically carrying them upstairs.

Nick followed close and would have helped if the stairs had been just a bit wider.

CHAPTER

# EIGHTEEN

"A TRACTION ENGINE?" Zane tilted his head. He thought his mind might be addled, and viewing the world from a slightly different angle might clear things up.

"They're so useful. And we make them at California Iron-works," Michelle said.

"We?"

"Yes, my father was part owner, and . . . well, now my sisters and I are, and we sit on the board of California Iron-works in San Francisco. Laura is probably talking to them right now with Mama. I am sure I can get it for cost."

"Before we spend any more money, I need to tell you, Josh came in after the noon meal. He wants us to ride out with him and decide if he's found all the . . . *gold*." He whispered that single word. "He thinks he's reached the end of the vein, but he wants someone else checking, seeing if there are any other veins to be found and then . . ." Zane glanced all around to make sure no one was coming over to talk to them.

Michelle and Zane stood in the ranch yard, careful to be a good distance from any building where someone might accidentally overhear them. He hadn't brought her out here because of her wildly inventive ideas about his ranch. He'd brought her out to talk about gold.

"I've given it a lot of thought," he said. "We've tried to decide what to do about that . . . um . . . *ore*. So we don't start some kind of . . . stampede onto our ranch."

"And have you decided?"

"I want to go a good distance away from home, change it all to cash, and put it in a bank. I want a large enough bank in a big enough town that they don't have much trouble with bank robberies. In a city the size of, say, Denver, they'd have all of that, and no one would know me there."

"You'd have to identify yourself at the bank in order to write bank drafts."

"That's what I realized, so going that far serves little purpose. I'd prefer it if we could go a good distance, but we can't really hide who we are. Add to that, there are still train robbers around. We put days and days of travel on a train, and our chances for trouble go way up." Zane ran his hands deep into his hair and knocked his Stetson off his head.

Michelle caught it, smoothed his hair, and replaced the hat. "You've made a decision, then. Good. I knew you would. Necessity is the mother of invention."

"What?" Zane really couldn't keep up with his wife. "What are you inventing now and whose mother?"

"Sorry, sorry. Ignore that. Plato applies, but he's a distraction at this point."

Zane could agree with that.

"What have you decided?" She gave him an encouraging pat on the shoulder to get him to go on.

"We're going to San Francisco. All of us. My brother and sisters, you and Jilly. We've worried about an obviously heavy load. And we have probably two hundred and fifty pounds of"—he barely moved his lips—"gold." He was going to be glad to get this gold out of the house just so he could stop talking like a half-wit.

"I think if we split it up," he continued, "and pack five trunks and each carry a satchel, then no one trunk or satchel will be noticeably heavy. Especially if we take nothing else. I'll pull the wagon up to the door. Josh and I can haul the trunks out and load them. I won't ask the hands to help so maybe they won't notice how heavy they are. We'll go to Lodi and ride the train, just to make the trip as fast as possible. Then make our sale, and bank the money."

"And buy a traction engine?" Michelle asked hopefully.

"Can we talk about that later?"

Her eyes sparked. She quit asking, but he had no hope she'd given up.

"I SEE NO MORE SIGNS OF GOLD." Jilly had studied the rugged area to the north of the gold strike, which was very steep.

Michelle had gone west. No one went south. That led to the clearing where the Purgatory settlement had stood. East was fairly cleared because of the logs they'd cut down for the church, and they'd been over it for days before they found the quartz outcropping.

So north or west.

"I didn't see anything, either." Michelle and Jilly looked at each other, both analyzing all they knew about gold and the area and altitude.

"So that's it?" Josh hadn't learned to step back and let the Stiles sisters think. Michelle noticed that Zane and his sisters had gotten used to the long silences.

Josh just had no patience, or maybe he just couldn't shut up.

Jilly's eyes fell closed.

Michelle held up a staying hand. "Just give us a few more minutes." She asked for minutes, but she prayed for seconds at least.

"Why do you—"

Zane caught Josh under the arm and dragged him toward the short stone wall, where Jilly had started building another church after the first one had been burned down. She'd gotten it about three feet high before their mission group abandoned the settlement.

Michelle had all the time she needed. Beth Ellen and Annie sat on boulders while Caroline hunted up rocks to build with. Michelle noticed and wondered if the little girl would like to go to engineering school to develop her construction skills.

"No sign of gold. No more quartz. No soil or rock that looks like it might yield up gold should we go to digging." Jilly crossed her arms and waited for Michelle to respond to that.

"If we cast stones about here and there, fill in holes, generally cover the digging, I don't think anyone would come up here and recognize this as a mine."

Jilly nodded in silence, then turned to study the ground. "It's so rugged and broken up here, it only looks different because we know what it looked like before. Some of the rock looks freshly axed, but we can hide most of that with dirt. If we have just a bit of time, a month maybe, the grass will cover what we've excavated. The edges of the rocks will weather. Should we wait that long before we take the gold to town?"

"The risks of waiting are as big as the risks of acting now, I'd say. One of us will let it slip." Michelle's eyes went to where Josh and Zane talked. Well, Josh talked. Zane not so much. "Then the danger will come right to the ranch house."

With a near violent shake of her head, Jilly said, "There's never been a good solution to this. No sense driving ourselves batty trying to come up with one. Let's get that gold out of here."

Michelle turned to Beth Ellen. "Which bank is that cheating, lying fiancé of yours connected with?"

Beth Ellen's eyes glinted with temper as she named a large one.

"We'll pass over that one, then. Let's use Wells Fargo."

Jilly looked at the ground again as if she could see the trouble coming. Then she picked up a shovel and began scooping rubble into the hole. She'd been at it about twenty seconds when Zane and Josh came and took over.

With a smirk, Jilly handed Josh the shovel while Zane grabbed a second one.

Michelle knew Jilly enjoyed hard work. But she wasn't opposed to letting someone else do the heavy lifting if they were available.

She and Michelle concentrated on rubbing dirt by hand over exposed rock that was obviously recently broken off by a pickax.

Annie and Beth Ellen picked up every tool and did their best to cover tracks and any other evidence that they'd spent time up here.

They headed out in the middle of the afternoon and were home in plenty of time to make supper. Michelle even helped a little.

"You know, baking is a bit like chemistry." Jilly stirred a batter that would be a cake before long.

"It is not." Michelle was peeling potatoes and felt no scientific wonder at the task.

"Sure it is. Adding carefully measured ingredients, flour to thicken, yeast or eggs or soda for leavening, sugar or other flavorings to turn boring flour and milk into something delicious."

"Keep talking." Michelle tried not to sound glum. "I'm sure this will spark my creative energy in a few seconds if you tell me about it just right."

Jilly chuckled and continued to talk science. Michelle was left remarkably unsparked.

THEY LEFT FOR SAN FRANCISCO the next morning before first light.

When they reached Lodi, Josh and Zane did a good job of refusing help as they loaded the overweight trunks in a baggage car, tucked well back against the wall with other trunks and crates in front of them all.

As they headed for the closest passenger car, a man shouted, "Beth Ellen!"

The whole group turned to see a man carrying a satchel rush toward them.

Beth Ellen jerked as if she'd been stabbed by a tack.

Michelle watched an incredibly handsome man, dressed in the finest clothing, a dark suit with silk-lined lapels. A vest with a row of brass buttons. A white shirt with a dark bowtie and a top hat. He wore boots that shined until they gleamed. Michelle knew a wealthy, well-dressed man when she saw one.

The man had slightly overlong dark hair and brown eyes. A nose and cheekbones that looked like they'd been carved by an Italian master artist. He swept off his top hat and clutched it to his chest. His expression was one of joy, and yet Michelle didn't like something in his eyes.

Beth Ellen stiffened until Michelle wondered if her spine would crack.

"Beth Ellen, I was just getting off the train." He reached for her, and she stepped back until she pressed against Josh, who was just behind her.

"I'm heading for San Francisco, and I have no wish to talk to you, Loyal."

Jilly leaned forward and whispered into Michelle's ear, "Loyal Kelton, former fiancé."

Michelle had heard the name exactly once. Through Beth Ellen's sobs the night she'd returned to the ranch. She'd've needed a bit to dig it out. But not Jilly.

"I'll be right back." The man rushed up to the conductor, standing at the front of the train car.

Michelle saw him pull money from the satchel he carried

and hand it to the conductor, who nodded and hurried toward the baggage car.

Loyal came back to Beth Ellen. "Please, I need to talk to you. Please give me a chance to apologize. I've changed. I love you and—" Loyal looked at Josh with a faint blush on his cheeks, then his eyes slid to Zane.

With a formal bow of his head, Loyal said, "Zane. It's been a long time since we've spoken."

"My sister told me why she broke things off. How you intended to keep a mistress and a wife at the same time. She has no wish to speak to you."

Loyal swallowed hard as he studied Zane, then he looked back at Beth Ellen. His expression practically shouted regret and loneliness. A broken heart walking around wearing a top hat.

"Beth Ellen, you were right about me. Right about everything. Please, if you won't consider giving me another chance, at least allow me to make a true and thorough apology. Your brother and . . ." He looked at Josh, then back at Beth Ellen and arched a brow.

"This is another brother, Mr. Kelton."

Seeming to relax now that he'd eliminated a suitor for Beth Ellen's hand, Loyal said very quietly, very sincerely, "Please, can I ride with you? I'm returning to San Francisco. My only reason to come out here was to talk with you. Please say you'll at least listen to my apology."

Michelle would have pitched him off the station platform, but then, no one ever accused her of being overly nice.

"We can talk for a time, Mr. Kelton. I might even accept your apology. But I can promise you it won't change the status of our former relationship."

Nodding, Kelton followed Beth Ellen onto the train.

The rest of their group boarded the train, each with a heavy satchel. Michelle did her best not to look like what she carried was overweight as she led the way down the aisle, with Jilly next, and Annie right behind her.

"I wish she'd have just kicked his backside," Annie whispered.

They were the first to board, and no one seemed to pay particular attention to them, either with the trunks or the satchels. But Michelle kept her eyes open, and she knew Zane and Josh were both on edge, watching everyone who came near them.

They all found seats. Annie with Caroline in the very back. Jilly beside her. Michelle and Zane in the next seat. Beth Ellen and Kelton ahead of them, and Josh alone ahead of Beth Ellen.

Michelle watched Beth Ellen closely and hoped she wasn't being charmed into forgiving this cheating scoundrel.

So far, Beth Ellen seemed to want to sit next to her former fiancé in order to scowl at him. Which, despite his fast, sweet talk—Michelle eavesdropped on every word—never convinced her to stop frowning.

"Our talk is over, Mr. Kelton. I'd like to sit with my brother for the rest of the ride."

"But, Beth Ellen, darling—"

"You're to call me Miss Hart from now on. Your use of my first name is too familiar, and I don't like it." Beth Ellen stared at Kelton until he finally gave her a solemn nod and stepped out of the seat he was in. He walked forward a few paces and sat down in another vacant seat, but turned to watch Beth Ellen with the eyes of a puppy who'd just been kicked.

Josh rose from his seat to take the place next to Beth Ellen. Michelle saw Beth Ellen's eyes glisten with tears. They all settled in for a long, quiet ride.

---

The train finally pulled into the San Francisco station, and Kelton watched and waited until Josh rose and stepped into the aisle. He then came to face Beth Ellen. "I left my valise behind," he said as an excuse. "Beth Ellen, consider what I've said, please. I swear I'd be faithful to you if you gave me another chance. You know where to reach me." He bent to reach under the seat, grabbed his satchel, and strode straight out the door as the train pulled to a stop.

Jilly leapt to her feet before the door slammed shut. "He picked up your satchel, Josh, not his. He stole it."

Zane charged after him. "Josh, stay with the women—and the bags."

Michelle wasn't going to sit here while Zane took on that thief alone. "Watch my bag, too." She ran after Zane and reached the station platform just as Zane dove at Kelton and tackled him. The two of them were too close to the platform edge and went tumbling to the ground below.

Michelle dashed down the steps as Loyal staggered to his feet and aimed one of his fancy boots at Zane's head. She screamed.

The noise distracted him for a split second.

Michelle screamed again, "Stop! Thief!"

Zane rolled sideways as Kelton's boot swung at him and grazed his shoulder instead of landing square on his head.

Michelle, wishing she had a trusty volume of Tolstoy, slammed into Kelton with her shoulder. The man was solid. He barely staggered back a pace.

Then a conductor responded to her screaming. Zane was on his feet and slammed a hard fist into Kelton's face. Michelle thought he was swinging with the desire to avenge his sister as well as to get his gold back.

A second punch knocked Kelton back so hard his feet flew out in front of him, and he landed hard on his back. His head hit the wooden sidewalk with a sickening thud. He didn't move again.

Zane's lip was bleeding, and he clutched at his shoulder. Under his breath, he said to Michelle, "I think we need to move fast more than we need to get the law involved with this."

She heard the question in his statement. "It doesn't sit right, but we do need to move fast."

She turned to the conductor. "He stole my brother-in-law's satchel. It was very deliberate, not a mistake. He took it and ran. Since we got it back, this can end here if it's all right with you. Do you want us to call the law?"

"We'd prefer to have no trouble with this," the conductor said.

A crowd had begun to gather, including their own group, with Josh and Jilly each carrying two satchels. Michelle had to wonder when Kelton had noticed the overly heavy bags. Had he really come to Lodi on his way to Beth Ellen? Or had he seen her, recognized the bags as weighty enough to be suspicious, and faked his apology to get close to the satchel?

Michelle suspected Kelton would pretend it was all an innocent mistake. He'd picked up the wrong bit of baggage. She doubted they'd even be able to have him arrested if they'd had the time.

"I'll hire a wagon." Josh left quickly, carrying Zane's and

Annie's satchels. Michelle took hers from Jilly, and Zane took the one Kelton had dropped.

"We'll meet Josh at the baggage car. Let's move." Zane led the way.

"His father should be arrested for naming his son so poorly," Beth Ellen muttered.

"Why would the son of a wealthy banker steal from us?" Zane reached the car that held their trunks of gold and stood at the door.

Michelle watched Josh come toward them leading a wooden wagon pulled by two tired-looking Percherons.

"I asked the driver to let me handle the reins. I paid him well to pick up his horses at the Wells Fargo bank. He'll follow along. We need to get out of here before we draw any more attention, or Kelton wakes up and decides to try again."

## CHAPTER NINETEEN

LAURA ARRIVED AT CALIFORNIA IRONWORKS to find she was early for a board meeting. She had no idea they met today and had come to talk with Eric Barritt, the company president, about the new power structure of Stiles Lumber.

She, Caleb, and Mama were ushered into Mr. Barritt's office. He listened to Laura explain about taking control of all aspects of Stiles Lumber. About Edgar's no longer having any say in any company business, including no longer having a seat on the board here.

He asked a lot of questions, and Laura did most of the talking. She didn't know Mr. Barritt well, but she knew Papa and Mama considered him an honest man who led a dependable company. When they were done, it was time for the board meeting, so he led the way to the boardroom.

Laura walked beside Mama. Caleb was just a pace behind with his hand resting firmly on her back.

He could probably feel Laura shaking, but she hoped everyone else was fooled. She was afraid she'd gotten so good at pretending she wanted to be in charge of an industry that everyone believed her completely.

Only Caleb knew how much she dreaded it. Had always dreaded it. And how right it felt to serve God at Caleb's side.

She searched the room, relieved to notice that Edgar wasn't there. Had he not come, knowing he might face humiliation? Or had he tried to get in and been stopped? Laura hadn't seen Mr. Barritt give such an order, but the man was nothing if not subtle and completely in charge.

Laura heard a quiet grunt of disdain from Mama. Laura quickly scanned the table. Horace Benteen sat straight across from where Laura had entered. She'd only seen him a few times. Then her eyes went to two other men among the dozen or so there. Royce Carlisle sat on Benteen's right. Small and bald with wet-looking blue eyes, he was known to own one of the largest banks in California. He'd been chosen to marry Jilly. And Myron Gibbons to Benteen's left—the man Edgar chose for Laura. A fat man, tall with beefy hands and thick, slack lips. He wore gold wire-rimmed glasses, but they didn't disguise the blaze of hunger in them when they locked on Laura.

"My daughters have married." Mama spoke softly, but there was steel in her well-modulated tone, and no one in the room could fail to hear it. "As married women, according to my husband Liam Stiles's will, they are now owners of Stiles Lumber and all the investments contained under that company's banner. That includes a seat on the board of California Ironworks."

Mama, with every man in the room listening to her every word, gestured softly toward Laura. "My daughter Laura is here to sit in the board meeting with proxy voting authority.

I accompanied her. As you know, I used to sit on this board before Edgar stepped in. Now Laura has that honor. Her husband, Parson Caleb Tillman, and I are here merely to listen. Please proceed with the meeting."

The last she said to Mr. Barritt.

Laura wondered if Mama and Caleb would be kicked out. But Mr. Barritt had an amused gleam in his eye and didn't demand they leave.

He gave a formal little welcome speech to Laura, then they got on with the business. Business Laura knew nothing about and had no interest in learning.

Until she knew better, she'd follow Mr. Barritt, and if there was a vote, she'd wait until he indicated how he'd vote, then she'd join with him.

If that was wrong, Mama had better intervene firmly.

MICHELLE WAS SHAKEN by Kelton's attempted theft. They piled in the wagon Josh had rented and set out for the Wells Fargo bank. It had a supposedly uncrackable vault. They bragged about it, lured in customers with it. Michelle certainly hoped it was true.

"What do you think made Loyal Kelton steal from us?" Beth Ellen had a cold look in her eyes. Michelle was sorry life had taught her to be this chilly.

Shaking his head, Zane said, "I can't imagine. That satchel wouldn't touch the wealth he already has."

"He must have seen us when we approached the train," Beth Ellen said. "He must have known the bags were too heavy."

Zane looked around them. In the bustle of the city, there seemed to be a threat everywhere. "I suppose a banker would have experience with such things as that."

"I'm going to ask Mr. Tevis about it at the Wells Fargo bank." Michelle never let her eyes rest on one spot. She scanned the crowd constantly for trouble. "I'll ask if he's heard of any rumors about the Keltons."

Their gold, once converted to bills and deposited, would be safe. Then Michelle was determined not to lay it up on earth. She was going to use the money to make life better for her husband, his men, and, if her inventions proved out, the whole world.

She prayed to keep her heart in the right place. She didn't covet this money. And she knew she'd lived a life of comfort few people did. Until Edgar of course.

And that was the biggest reminder of all.

Money had failed them. No amount of it had protected them from being unwise.

As they rode along, eyes wide open for another attempted theft, Michelle whispered to Zane, "'How much better is it to get wisdom than gold, and to get understanding to be chosen rather than silver!'"

"Proverbs." Zane looked sideways at her from where he sat in the back of the wagon with her.

Michelle leaned against him. "God always says what most needs saying before we even think to need it."

"Well, seeing as how you're so smart, I reckon you can count yourself as wise."

Shaking her head, Michelle said, "Smart isn't the same as wise. I think of Edgar and the way he tricked us all. I don't think I have any great claim to wisdom."

THE MEETING WENT WELL. Laura listened very carefully and never suggested a thing. Though she had to admit there was a point or two she might have spoken about, but she hesitated because she knew she didn't have a full understanding of California Ironworks. Still, she did know quite a bit about machinery, and she thought there were areas the ironworks could be innovated a bit.

She'd think these ideas over and maybe talk them through with Mama before she got further involved.

And maybe by then the sister with the greatest understanding of machines, Michelle, could take over at least this one small part of the family industry.

Laura intended to slip out of this yoke and leave everything to Michelle and Jilly. But she had to pick her moment.

They reached the door to the street in the echoing entrance to the magnificent office building, and Caleb caught her arm. "Let me go out first, Mama Stiles."

Mama, a pace ahead of them, turned and smiled at Caleb.

"Let me make sure no one's waiting out there to cause trouble." Caleb sounded worried and more than a little dangerous. His grim expression wiped the smile off Mama's face, Laura's too.

Caleb reached for the heavy door. It opened to a small entryway with a second door to the street. Caleb went to the second door, opened it, and stepped out. Laura let Mama go ahead of her.

As Mama stepped into the entrance, a vise closed over Laura's upper arm and a hard hand came around from behind to cover her mouth. In a dizzying whirl, she was dragged sideways and inside an office. It all happened so quickly, Laura could barely register that she'd been grabbed. She heard a key turn in the lock. Then she was pushed back against the door they'd just come through with that hand still solid on her mouth. She looked straight into Edgar's cruel eyes.

He spoke with utter determination. "One noise from you, and I'm going to kill your precious mama."

The vicious promise in his voice told her this was a threat that he was willing to carry out. More than that, he *wanted* to. He was looking for an excuse. Her mouth still covered, she watched those cold eyes.

"I've got her." Edgar spoke loudly.

A second door in the office opened, and three men emerged.

Horace Benteen, Myron Gibbons, and Royce Carlisle.

The four men arrayed before her struck her with terror so deep it was like a fist gripped her heart and froze her mind. All she knew was fear.

Though different in build, the dreadful men were exactly alike in how they reacted to having her in their power. Their polished clothing was like putting a gilt finish on filth. All four of them looked at her with hungry rage.

"We've already paid the bride price," Carlisle said to Edgar in a voice that dripped with contempt.

Laura fought hard to find her usually sensible brain, but nothing was there for her to say. She knew any words would be useless. All she could do was trust that Caleb was already searching.

She prayed for him to find this room. But the front hall was lined with office doors. Even she wasn't sure which one she'd been dragged into.

Edgar eased his hold on her mouth as if expecting an answer.

Her throat bone-dry, she swallowed hard. "Wh-whatever you paid is between you and Edgar."

Her air ran out as the three studied her wolfishly. Like they refused to be denied one of the Stiles sisters now that they had their hands on her.

"We'll see about that," Carlisle said. "I consider this a breach of contract, and the three of us may well see you in court. We'll settle this somehow."

Caleb shouted her name in the hallway.

Edgar's hand tightened once again on her mouth.

Carlisle's tone made an icy chill run up Laura's back.

"That is your husband seeking you." Carlisle, the smallest and weakest looking, was doing all the talking for the group, and they seemed to accept that. "Not all men live long, healthy lives."

Laura felt another chill, colder, more terrifying.

Laura made the loudest noise she could with her mouth covered. She doubted it was enough. And the thought of what might happen to Caleb when he found them terrified her.

"I told you your mama would die if you made any noise." Edgar looked ready to kill whoever came through that door.

Footsteps pounded toward the office they were in. They must have heard her.

Edgar gave her a cruel smile. "That worked so well to shut Jilly up. Be careful then, Miss Laura. You're going to need to be."

Benteen opened the second door. Edgar released her, and all four men filed out. The door closed and locked as Laura sagged against the first door, then her knees gave out, and she sank to the floor. The doorknob over her head turned but didn't open.

She remembered Edgar locked it.

Caleb slammed a fist against the door.

Only knowing Caleb was right there gave her the strength to get to her knees and twist the key in the door to unlock it. Caleb nearly plowed over her.

He saw her still on her knees and bent to lift her up high in his arms. "What happened? Laura? Are you hurt?"

Laura, her head leaning against Caleb's strong shoulder, managed, "I-I'm not hurt."

She had to tell them, but the terror nearly strangled her.

She heard again Edgar's ugly words spoken nearly with humor. "*That worked so well to shut Jilly up.*"

What had he done to her?

Movement behind Caleb finally put strength in her neck. She worried Edgar might be coming to stab him in the back. She saw Nick was a pace behind Caleb with his gun drawn. Across the vast entry hall, Mama had a security officer by the arm and was dragging him over. Old Tom was with Mama. Carl was coming hard after Nick.

"What happened?" Caleb looked past her, studying the room.

Her heart quaked when she watched Mama, watched Caleb.

She looked right at Nick and spoke low enough those men couldn't hear her even if they had their ears pressed to the door. "We've got to get to Jilly. You've got to marry her without delay."

Nick was holstering his gun, and he dropped it the last few inches as he tripped over his feet and slammed into the doorframe.

"What?"

"Shh!" She pressed her fingertips to Nick's mouth.

From behind her hand, Nick's eyes flashed with fire. Quietly, he said, "I thought you Stiles women were supposed to be smart."

Caleb pulled her tightly against him. "I want to hear every word they said."

"Get me out of here. It was Edgar. I'll t-tell you everything."

"*One noise from you, and I'm going to kill your precious mama.*"

She couldn't tell.

But she had to tell.

The agony of indecision nearly ripped her in half.

Keeping silent was foolish, though. They were all in danger no matter whether she told or not, but somehow those words were powerful, and to tell what happened risked everything she most loved. She'd have to face that risk and overcome it.

Laura couldn't stand the thought of decent, honest Parson Caleb Tillman facing such vile men. She'd seen Caleb fight and knew he was tough. But he might be too fair, too honorable. And these were the type of men to come as back-shooting cowards, who hired evil done.

Laura wanted to grab Caleb and Mama and run as far and fast as the train would carry them. "N-not here."

Nick moved past her. "Where's Edgar?"

"Th-they went through that door. I heard it lock."

"They?" Caleb said much louder than Nick had talked. "Who was in here?"

Nick ducked past her and went to the door, tried it, then kicked it hard.

Mama reached them with the security guard. "Tell us what happened, Laura."

From the terror on Mama's face, Laura knew she'd feared Laura might disappear. Vanish never to be seen again. Even with strong men at hand.

"*One noise from you, and I'm going to kill your precious mama.*"

For the first time ever, or at least more profoundly than ever, she understood Mama's fears, Jilly's fears, because now they were her fears.

Whether she faced them and spoke of them or not, they were all in deadly danger.

## CHAPTER
# TWENTY

DRIVING A WAGON DOWN San Francisco's busy streets was always slow going.

Michelle was jumpy, expecting armed gunmen to erupt from the alleys or open fire from the second-floor balconies nearly every building featured. Or Kelton to come at them again.

No gunmen, no attacks. They reached the bank and rounded the corner, then pulled into an alley behind the bank.

"Michelle, you and Jilly hurry in and get permission for us to carry the luggage into the nearest secure room."

Since Michelle had mentioned knowing the bank president, Lloyd Tevis, she and Jilly were the most likely ones to get quick cooperation, and Josh, Zane, and their sisters could stay with the wagon, guns close to hand.

Michelle went in the back door. She wasn't familiar with the bank, because they'd met Mr. Tevis and his wife and their four children when they'd come visiting in the Stiles home, or when the Stiles family had gone to their home.

Michelle and Jilly were quickly directed to the president's office. His secretary tried to stop them, but he had a large window in his door, and she saw he was alone. Hurrying through the door, she said, "Mr. Tevis, I need your help and quickly."

"Michelle, Jilly, what's the matter?"

Michelle rushed to his side to whisper, "We've got gold in a wagon outside your back door. I'm married, and my husband made a gold strike. A nice little vein that we completely dug out." Michelle was eager to get that bit of information out. Mr. Tevis probably wouldn't talk about this, but when it came to gold, word spread. She certainly hoped the fact there was no more spread right along with talk of the discovery.

"We want to get it in here, get it exchanged for cash, deposit the cash in your bank, and walk out of here with hopes we won't be robbed. There's already been one attempt by Loyal Kelton, the son of your competitor."

Every word she spoke seemed to send Mr. Tevis staggering a bit. But he was a fast-thinking man. Papa had admired his mind.

"I've heard Kelton senior cut his son off. He was furious the boy wasn't more discreet with his mistress until after he got his fiancée to the altar."

"So he saw no chance with Beth Ellen," Michelle said, "but somehow realized what we were carrying, and he acted."

Tevis nodded, then said, "Let's go." When they left the office, they were met by two security guards, no doubt alerted by his secretary, a young man who also stood ready to save his boss. Except since it was two young women charging the man, they probably hesitated to stage a rescue.

"All of you, come with us." Mr. Tevis led the way at a near

trot to the back door of the bank. Michelle and Jilly on his heels. The three men following close.

He opened it to see Zane and Josh standing in the wagon, alert but with no one robbing them. No guns drawn.

"Tell these men what to carry." Mr. Tevis took charge.

Soon they were all locked in a back room with a harried-looking man weighing gold on a scale made just for that purpose. Mr. Tevis's secretary offered them refreshments, but Michelle glanced around and then declined for all of them. "We'll be meeting Mama for a meal soon. I think we're all too anxious to eat a thing."

Annie and Beth Ellen diverted Caroline's curious exploration of the small and overly crowded room.

Jilly, Zane, and Josh watched the weighing like a hawk. Jilly had already estimated to within ten dollars how much their gold should be worth, and she seemed suspicious of the man working over it, which seemed to make him nervous.

Michelle listened to Mr. Tevis talk about the uproar around San Francisco that came with Laura's taking over all the holdings of Stiles Lumber, waving around the proxy that gave her power and voting rights for the company and the various boards Papa had sat on.

"I should have been here to help her. But I'm planning to live on Zane's ranch, so Laura said she'd handle things in Sacramento and here. And besides, there's been trouble all around us, some of it concerning Horace Benteen and his son, Jarvis. It was safer for me to stay on Zane's ranch."

Mr. Tevis furrowed his brows. "I know Horace well. He's a sharp one."

Mr. Tevis was sharp, too, so it wasn't exactly an insult. But the way Lloyd said it wasn't a compliment.

They talked while his man weighed and counted. Finally the gold was handed over to the Wells Fargo bank, and four accounts were opened. One for each of the four brothers and sisters. Zane felt Jilly should have a share of the gold, but she adamantly refused. "That's Hart gold, and you've been feeding, sheltering, and protecting me for a good length of time now. That's all the payment I'm willing to accept."

Then Jilly got a calculating look in her eyes. "Although you really could use a bridge over the river in your southernmost pasture. That river gets too fast moving for the safety of your cattle." She gave Zane a smile so sunny it looked completely phony. "You could let me build a bridge across it."

Zane rolled his eyes. "Let's go see your family."

They shook hands with Mr. Tevis and left.

MICHELLE LEAPT DOWN from the back of the wagon, Jilly just a step behind her. They ran up the steps to their home. Mama stood at the door, waving at them. She called over her shoulder, and Laura, Caleb, and Nick came out.

Michelle wanted to weep. She wasn't a crier in the normal run of things, but it was more than seeing her mother and sister, it was being home. Just as that mountain mansion was home, so this was home. This lovely house on Nob Hill that they'd lived in since shortly after Papa had sent for Mama and the three girls, still very young. He hadn't lived in a place this nice at first. But his lumber business was booming, and soon they'd moved here. Only when the girls had gotten older and Papa's business had expanded to a dynasty had they built the house out in the mountains.

Michelle threw herself into Mama's arms. Jilly hugged Laura.

Michelle stepped away from Mama to give Jilly a turn at hugging her. Zane shook hands firmly with Caleb, then the men started talking as they moved inside.

When everyone was caught up on the news, Caleb said, "Laura, you haven't told us yet what Edgar said to scare you half to death."

Michelle wheeled around to face Laura. "You saw Edgar?"

"Can we have tea, maybe? Mama, can we figure out a meal? I haven't eaten all day. I'd like us to settle down before I start—"

"No." Caleb cut her off. "We agreed to get you away from those men. Then we agreed to wait until we got home. Then before we could more than get inside, here came your sisters and Zane's family. We've waited long enough."

He slid an arm across her back and hugged her. "Please tell us what happened. You were trembling and white as a ghost when we got to you. No matter what threats he made, this isn't something you can keep to yourself for our safety."

"Let's go into the sitting room." Laura leaned against him. "His main threat was to Mama. Talking about it is terrifying."

Mama came and caught Laura's hand. "Edgar is a threat to me, to you girls, to your husbands, no matter what you say or don't say. Come, let's sit down, and you'll tell us. I'm glad we're together so we can make plans, arrange for guards, whatever we need to do to make you feel safe, Laura. To make us all feel safe."

ZANE LOOKED AROUND THE ROOM. Except for Nick, this was his whole family. His sisters and brother. Michelle's family. It was an impressive group for a man who had been living alone for years, with the occasional brief visit from Annie and Beth Ellen and even less occasional drop-ins by Josh.

Nick had tried to leave with Old Tom, but Laura had interrupted his exit with a question, and he'd been drawn into the group with an oddly wary look in his eyes.

Nick handled most things with a steady hand, so what was he worried about? Probably about someone trying to kill Mrs. Stiles and maybe the rest of the family. It was a heavy load that Nick seemed to have willingly taken onto his own shoulders.

"How do you hire a bodyguard in a city this size?" Zane drank deep on his coffee. It was good, but he preferred to drink coffee from a tin cup, boiling hot from the stove. Now he held a porcelain teacup. "How do you know who is trustworthy?"

"We could ask Uncle Newt to recommend someone," Michelle suggested.

Zane had to stop himself from slapping his face. Uncle Newt. The governor. And the head of the Wells Fargo bank treated them like they were his children. He'd heard how the head of California Ironworks had welcomed Laura, Caleb, and Mrs. Stiles into the board meeting. No, he had no idea just how rich his wife was. But he'd opened a bank account today that made him mighty rich, too. And he probably had snagged a wife who knew just how he should spend his money. Lucky him.

"Why don't you do that. Talk to Uncle Newt. Maybe talk to Marshal Irving." Zane went back to his fussy coffee cup.

Caleb took a lemon tart off the tray of pastries included in their afternoon meeting, looking thoughtful. "Marshal Irving struck me as a fine man and a good judge of character."

"What we need," Laura said, "is to get Jilly married and do it fast."

Jilly, sitting in a chair near the unlit fireplace, choked and spit coffee on Laura, and some might've hit Michelle, who sat next to Laura on the sofa. Fortunately, the coffeepot and pastries were out of range.

Laura swept her hand across the fine mist of coffee on her dress. Michelle rolled her eyes.

"We own controlling interest in the company." Jilly dabbed at her lips as if she hadn't sprayed her sisters. In fact, it was possible to describe her expression as quietly satisfied. "You both seem to have married fine men, and I'm glad of that. But there is no need for me to marry. When and if I do that, it will be a thoughtful decision, not because I'm afraid or feeling coerced."

Mama Stiles spoke up. "I think that's wise, Jilly. You girls had to escape from Edgar. There was no other choice. When we decided you needed to marry quickly, I felt as if it were a life-and-death situation. But once you were away and, I had to believe, safe I wished I had only urged you to run. I regretted pressuring you to marry quickly. I am living proof that a poor marriage can be ruinous, dangerous, even deadly. We're blessed to add Caleb and Zane to our number. But no, Jilly, you will not be expected to marry quickly. You can marry to suit yourself and take all the time about it you wish."

Jilly eased back in the overstuffed chair. The wingback seemed to cradle her. A smug smile settled on her face.

"Now, we've had our reunion, but we've got three more

stops to make this afternoon," Mrs. Stiles said. "Beyond that, I'm sure word has spread about Edgar being blocked from Stiles Lumber. Eric Barritt assured me he'd help get the word out." She rose from her chair.

Afraid she would leave without them, Zane hurried to gulp down the last swallow of his coffee and grabbed a scone. A very determined woman, Margaret Stiles Beaumont.

They were on the street again, and this time they walked down Nob Hill and caught a horse-drawn streetcar for their afternoon of waging war against Edgar.

Margaret said she refused to ride one of the streetcars up any of the steep hills in San Francisco because it was so brutally hard on the horses. A smaller horse-drawn cab with a less unwieldy carriage behind it made the trip up all right, but the heavy streetcars were terrible. There was talk of running a cable of some sort that could draw the streetcars up and down the hills, but so far it was only talk.

Zane couldn't imagine such a thing working. He wondered if Michelle had a notion to try to invent that.

While they traveled, Zane found himself on edge in the bustling city.

After the way Edgar had snatched Laura almost from under Caleb's nose, he didn't put anything past that vermin and his friends.

He didn't mention it in the group, but tonight he was going to tell Michelle he had to go home, and she was coming with him.

# CHAPTER TWENTY-ONE

BUT WHAT ABOUT OUR TRACTION ENGINE?" Michelle shook Zane's shoulder.

She knew Zane had gotten very quiet this afternoon. He was very alert for trouble, as they all were. But in the city, well, it was almost impossible to notice everyone. And as a man who'd rarely left his ranch, trying to notice everyone in a madhouse like San Francisco had to be nearly overwhelming. Still, she'd thought he intended to stay awhile. He'd definitely mentioned shopping.

"Do we have to decide this now?" Zane sounded more than half-asleep.

She'd noticed he tended to fall asleep quickly after they'd spent some time doing married things in the night. She did too.

But go home tomorrow? Tomorrow? "The last time I saw Mama and Laura we barely had a day with them. I thought maybe we'd have a bit longer."

A rustling stirred the bed and suddenly the lantern on the bedside table, which was kept turned down through the night, went brighter as Zane turned it up. He rolled onto his side to face her.

"Michelle, I thought you knew when you married me, we'd be living at the ranch."

She swallowed. She had known that. Yes, he'd agreed to lengthy visits during the slower seasons on the ranch. She didn't think summer was one of those, as Zane and his men were out working from dawn to dusk every day, doing . . . she wasn't sure what.

The silence stretched, but she wasn't upset with him. She was upset with herself.

"I did know that. You're right. We've been away long enough. The train makes the trip to Lodi daily. We'll head home tomorrow. It would be best especially to get Jilly out of here since she's still vulnerable. Though I do feel as if I'm leaving Mama and Laura in danger, too."

"They should probably get back to the mountain as soon as they possibly can. They're not safe here. There is no way to know who might be on the payroll of one of those men you talked about." Zane yawned. "It also occurred to me, you're familiar enough with ironworks and waterwheels and other such things that you can place your orders with a letter. We don't have to go to the businesses to buy them. You could even write the letter before we leave tomorrow so they'd receive it right away and could make arrangements to ship things. I really like the idea of a waterwheel. Do you think we need to hire skilled men to put it in or can you and Jilly do it? With my men's help, of course."

That coaxed a smile out of her. "Thank you for trusting me with such a big project. I've looked at the waterways on your property, and Jilly has done a thorough inspection of your pastures. Small waterwheels will do the trick, so we're not talking about massive projects with terribly heavy rock work, although the streams will have to be temporarily rerouted, and that's always a big job. Yes, the orders can be done with letters more quickly than if I went to the businesses individually. The traction engine can come later. As a matter of fact, I heard of a new development in the engines that makes them even more useful. I can give them a few months to work on it and get the most up-to-date device. We can head back. There's work to do at the ranch, and the drought is stretching on. We need that irrigation."

"Thank you, Michelle." Suddenly, a very warm and friendly Zane was kissing her. She had pleased him. It surprised her how much she enjoyed doing that. She wrapped her arms around his neck and held on tight to the man she was choosing over her childhood home, her mother, her dreams of how she'd live her life.

That was all as God commanded, and it pleased her that God's way suited her.

THE WHOLE FAMILY LEFT TOWN the next day. Once Zane spoke of his concerns, it spread like wildfire.

Yes, they needed to get to a safer place. Yes, trouble could follow them. Jarvis's breaking into Zane's house proved that. Much had been done to make them safe, but risks still remained.

Mama Stiles, Laura, Caleb, Nick, and those with them would stop at a few more businesses, then head for the mountains. Michelle wrote her orders and sent the letters, and then she, Jilly, and the whole Hart family went to the ranch.

Rather than whine about missing her mama, Michelle

had acted like getting to see her family was a treat that she appreciated and would get to enjoy again. Zane's heart was warmed by hearing Michelle speak of the ranch as home.

Jilly agreed easily to leave the dangers of San Francisco. But for her it was more. Zane saw the spark in her eyes when Michelle talked with her about waterwheels, windmills, copper boilers for hot water, and lots of pipes. There were plans already being discussed to erect a special building for Michelle's experiments.

A woman who got this excited about boilers and pipes might have some trouble finding a husband. Especially a woman as hostile to the idea of marriage as Jilly. Zane had hoped she might turn her eyes toward Josh, but the two seemed to have no interest in each other. Jilly was prone to rolling her eyes when Josh got started about his travels. And Zane had to admit his brother could get very long-winded. Oh, all right, he was boring.

Mama planned to head for home through Sacramento for an additional meeting with Governor Booth. Zane absolutely refused to think of him as Uncle Newt. While in the state capitol, they were going to talk to the US Marshals about additional guards, hoping the marshals could be trusted.

Before the sun was straight overhead in the sky, Zane and his family were on a train headed for Lodi.

The ordered items would be a while shipping to Lodi, and Zane planned to arrange for them to be hauled by wagon at least to Dorada Rio, while some of the larger pieces that needed specially built heavy wagons and mule teams would be hauled all the way home. No reason he had to ride all over creation tracking them down. The orders were to be shipped as they were ready, so Michelle and Jilly could get to work on whatever arrived first. Not all of the overwhelming order would come at once, thank heavens.

The trip home took them until nearly sunset. Only an almost desperate need to get Michelle to safety pushed Zane on. He considered the Two Harts safe, even knowing it had been attacked before.

It might have been wiser to stay overnight in Dorada Rio rather than risk riding in the waning light when they had men after them with reputations as sneaks and back-shooters. But tiring as the train ride was, he'd done little but sit all day. He was full of restless energy.

Michelle was riding side-by-side with him, everyone else strung out behind on horseback, when the Two Harts came into sight.

"It's nice to be home." Michelle sounded genuinely relieved to be here.

Zane turned and smiled at her.

"What?" She sounded confused, and she didn't like being confused. Michelle liked to know everything.

"You called this home again. It makes me happy to hear it."

Michelle smiled. She reached across the space between their horses. He took her hand. He'd never held hands while riding before. He found it suited him.

Men came out of the bunkhouse at the sound of approaching hooves.

Zane led his parade of family toward the barn, but Shad rushed up and grabbed the reins. "Let us take over, Boss."

"I see to my own horse."

Shad waved him off. "Get inside. You look like you've been rode hard and put up wet."

Michelle laughed out loud. Jilly giggled. She was riding just behind Annie, who had Caroline asleep on her lap. Josh and Beth Ellen brought up the rear.

Zane felt tension unwind inside him that he hadn't realized was there.

MICHELLE BUZZED WITH EXCITEMENT. She might have actually heard a buzzing sound in her ear.

She and Jilly found a large map of Two Harts Ranch and sketched out smaller maps focused on the areas where they wanted to put the waterwheels.

"We don't have to finish this tonight, do we, Michelle?" Zane asked.

Michelle had to force her eyes away from the map of Zane's largest pasture. They'd ordered small waterwheels. They didn't need to run a huge saw or a gristmill, after all. They just needed to pump a steady supply of water from the available waterways to each of Zane's pastures. The largest pasture had a curve in its stream and that was where they'd—

"Michelle, it's late." Zane drew her away from the map. "Gretel has a meal on, God bless her. Let's eat and get some sleep. I've got a big day tomorrow. We're going to start cutting the herd, getting the cattle separated so we can drive the older steers to market. We need to sleep now and get a jump on the day tomorrow."

Michelle looked with longing at the maps. Then it occurred to her the buzzing might not be excitement. It might be exhaustion.

She set everything aside. Jilly laid down her pen more reluctantly than Michelle.

"I am hungry. I should have helped get the meal. I'm sorry." She'd come inside and headed straight for Zane's office. And she'd expected somehow a meal would be placed in front of her. That wasn't right. It was selfish, and she prayed for God to direct her in more thoughtful ways.

She had big plans, and there was a lot of work to do. But the family had to eat. Beth Ellen had traveled today just as far as Michelle. Annie had done it while wrangling a young child. Gretel, though she was a paid employee, had left her own home and family to come and help cook a late meal.

And Michelle had walked away without offering to help.

Almost worse, Gretel, Beth Ellen, and Annie had expected her to. They'd accepted they couldn't depend on her and Jilly for any of the normal tasks involved in running a house. And Michelle had to change that.

She followed Zane out of the room. He let her go past him through the door, then slid his arm around her waist. "I'm excited about your plans, too, Michelle. All of us are. That grass staying green is going to make all our lives better. The cows will thrive on it, which is a kindness to them."

"Don't talk too much about being kind to the cows you're planning to eat. It doesn't exactly ring true."

Zane laughed as he and Michelle led Jilly into the kitchen to sit at the table there. Gretel had returned to her own home. Caroline had been fed and put to sleep already. So Annie had to do that as well as help make the meal.

There was a simple stew made with beef jerky, so no need to cook it for a long time. Michelle knew that stew was often left to simmer for hours to make the beef tender.

Instead, this meal was done as fast as the potatoes, onions, and carrots in the stew were cooked through. Almost as fast as biscuits could bake.

Grateful to the soles of her feet, Michelle sank down in the chair to Zane's right. He was at the head of the table. The house had a nice dining room with a big, dark wood table, but they'd never yet used it.

The prayer was spoken and the stew and biscuits passed. Once they were eating, Josh, at the foot of the table, asked, "Do you think word will get out about our gold? Do you think there'll be trouble because of it?"

Without answering, Zane asked, "Do you think I should give each of my cowhands a big bonus? They've been doing extra work so we could dig."

"You were only over there a couple of times, Zane." Annie buttered her biscuit. "You've kept up with the ranch."

"Which means you *don't* think I need to give them a bonus?"

Annie smiled. "I was just trying to make you feel better about being gone. Yes, I think you should give them a bonus."

"Maybe you could give them a raise instead of a bonus." Jilly scooped stew onto her plate. "Is the going wage thirty a month, plus the bunkhouse and meals?"

"That's what we pay," Zane said.

"Well, raise it. Make it thirty-five a month. That would be a nice steady reward."

Jilly set to eating as if the matter was settled.

Judging by Zane's smile, Michelle thought it well might be.

"And then"—Annie picked up the idea and expanded it—"give them a bonus, say, for Christmas. Maybe hire a few more men, too, instead of working with a skeleton crew through the winter like Pa always did."

"I don't fire them in the winter, a few just always wander off, and that leads to a shorthanded crew, which is fine because there aren't so many chores."

"A few more might stay if you're paying the best wages around." Josh was cleaning his plate like a man glad to be back at home.

"Which would ease the load for the other hands and us. If you give them a bonus of . . ." Josh shrugged. "A couple of hundred dollars, well, it'll be the most money they've ever had at one time in their lives. They might run off just because they have it to spend. Good reason not to give it to them now. It's a busy time of year."

"We need to separate the cattle out for the drive. Then drive the cattle to Sacramento. Which isn't too long of a trip. Maybe I'll give them a raise tomorrow, then tell them they're getting a bonus at the end of the drive."

"Maybe you could do two bonuses." Jilly chewed thoughtfully. "Give them vacation time during the slower seasons. They could get away, do their wandering, knowing they'd be welcomed back."

No one quite agreed on how to do it, but they agreed it needed to be done.

The meal was finished, and as they began to gather plates, Michelle jumped in, working as fast as any of them.

As they cleaned, Michelle asked, "What do you think that Bible verse about money being the root of all evil means? Do you think it somehow applies to us?"

"The verse," Annie said, "is 'for the love of money is the root of all evil: which while some coveted after, they have erred from the faith, and pierced themselves through with many sorrows.'" She vigorously scrubbed the empty stew pot. "So the *love* of money, and coveting after money to the point you turn aside from your faith, *that's* what the verse warns against. It's not strictly money that is the root of all evil."

Michelle nodded, relieved to hear that because she had money, but she didn't believe she coveted it, nor had it turned her away from God.

"What about the one about laying up treasures in heaven?" Jilly stacked dried plates in a cupboard.

"Nope," Annie said, sounding sure, "you've got that one wrong, too, or incomplete. What it really says is to lay up treasures in heaven where moth and rust cannot corrupt. If you fail that, whatever you did, or laid up here, it's all useless because heaven is our goal, our only true wealth."

She quoted, "'Lay not up for yourselves treasures upon earth, where moth and rust doth corrupt, and where thieves break through and steal: But lay up for yourselves treasures in heaven, where neither moth nor rust doth corrupt, and where thieves do not break through nor steal: For where your treasure is, there will your heart be also.'"

"I find myself a little embarrassed that Jilly and I have misquoted the Bible twice in a few minutes," Michelle said.

Annie set the clean pot aside and turned to give Michelle a hug. "I'm glad you're in our family. Thanks for marrying my half-wit brother."

"Hey." Zane snorted, but he was fighting a grin.

Michelle went to him and slid an arm around his waist. "So we need to make where our heart is the most important thing, and it needs to be with God."

"Um, we should probably tithe from the money we got from the gold." Zane looked from his two sisters to his brother, then down at Michelle.

She had a fourth of this newfound wealth through marriage to Zane, just as he shared in all she owned. She liked that Zane included her in the family's decisions.

They all nodded. Annie said, "We rarely get into town for services, but that little church could use some money."

"I wondered about Caleb," Jilly said. "I think he still sees a mission field in his future. We could ask him about his plans, and once he's made them, we could help finance that. And help him be generous with the people he ministers to."

Michelle remembered talking with her youngest sister. "They've only been home a short time, but Laura said he speaks on Sunday mornings to the lumberjacks. He uses a sawed-off tree stump as a pulpit." Michelle grinned at Jilly. "Remember how he wanted to do that when we came to the Purgatory settlement, but you started right in building him a church?"

"It was fun."

"Laura said quite a few have come to his services, and in true Caleb fashion, he's reaching out to them beyond just Sunday mornings. He's trying to meet their needs. Trying to show love. None of that sounds like it's costing him much."

Jilly's eyes lit up, and she stood straighter. "I wonder if they need a church built out there?"

"We'll find a way to make the money support God's work." Zane nodded, looking determined. Right in that moment, Michelle felt like she fell deeper in love than she'd known a woman could fall.

He was a good man, and he was hers. To show him, she'd

work at his side, build her irrigation system, get hot and cold water flowing in his cabins, and use this gold to support the ranch and beyond.

Then the kitchen was in order, and they all headed to bed, and Michelle thought of another way to show him she loved him. Smiling, she led the way to their bedroom.

CHAPTER

# TWENTY-TWO

"THIS LITTLE BEND IN THE CREEK IS PERFECT." Michelle had decided the stream in the largest pasture needed to be prepared for a waterwheel first.

Zane wasn't sure why she thought that, and he couldn't think of any questions that didn't just slow everyone down, so he assigned five men to Michelle and Jilly, including Josh, and went to help the other cowhands start separating the herd.

Three men had also ridden in who used to work for Annie. Zane hired them on the spot.

Before he assigned the day's jobs, he mentioned how much the irrigation was going to add to the workload and raised every man's salary to thirty-five dollars a month.

He had a happy crowd with him for the day.

Shad was riding beside him to the first pasture.

"I want to push ahead with the cattle drive this year, Shad. I know we usually wait and get more weight on the cattle before we thin the herd."

"You're worryin' about the drought, aren't you, Boss?"

"Yep."

"We got that fence up you wanted in the small pasture."

"We can start separating there. Drive out the cows and this year's calves into the next pasture south. Keep the steers in there and drive in more."

"We got the cattle moved off that south pasture, so the grass is in fair shape, dry but not eaten down."

"Thanks, Shad. You're getting a raise, too, you know."

As Zane's foreman and a hand who'd been here through most of Zane's growing-up years, Shad already made real decent money, and he was a man with simple needs. But if the money was going to be spread around, Shad would get a share.

"Thanks, Boss."

"We can spend the next couple of weeks pushing the older steers into that little pasture, and I might cut a little deeper than usual."

"Mrs. Hart is gonna get you some water flowing. You'll be fine."

Zane thought he probably was going to be more than fine. Between his thinning the herd, Michelle and Jilly irrigating his pastures, and finding a gold mine, he was going to be great.

"She's gonna reroute the stream?" Shad glanced behind him as if he might be able to see through the miles to where Michelle had headed to work.

"That's what she says. And dig some shallow canals for the water to spread out over the field, then put in a waterwheel so the water comes out of the stream and flows into those canals. There might be pipes involved, too. I lost track. For today, I think the plan is to pick a site, then start hauling rocks in to reroute the stream. It's why she picked that stream to start on. It's got the easiest bend and a good supply of rocks nearby. She and her sister spent an hour mulling over maps this morning before they came out."

"She's a wonder. Mrs. Hart and her sister."

"I am fortunate in my wife." Zane's heart seemed overly warm as he thought how she came into his arms at night. How she listened when he talked. How she'd called the Two Harts home. It all suited him right down to the ground.

"I'd've liked to watch," Zane said. "Try and see how those two are going to manage irrigating my pasture."

"Go on back. We can handle the herding."

"Nope, she'll do what she's good at, and I'll run my ranch. It's an arrangement that suits us both."

"I've had a talk with the men, so they'll keep their eyes open for trouble. We let Jarvis Benteen get into your house, and that should've never happened."

Then they reached the small pasture and were too busy to talk further. All Zane thought of was no, that should've never happened. He worked hard. And while he worked, he prayed hard that they could keep it from happening again.

Because there was no doubt in his mind that the Benteens hadn't accepted defeat.

MICHELLE AND HER CREW spent a whole morning digging. They needed to reroute the stream and had to dig a temporary waterway for it to follow.

Next, they'd fill a wagon with rocks, haul them to the stream, and drop them just so to block the waterway and reroute the stream into the new path. Then they would set up the waterwheel and turn the water back to its original course. The wheel would pump water out, and it would flow into a series of trenches they still needed to dig to carry the water to the grass. It wasn't complicated, just a whole lot of hard work.

Michelle expected it to take at least a week for this pasture, and Zane had nine of them. The waterwheels weren't here yet. Michelle hoped when they got here, she would have everything ready for installation, and they could start watering a few pastures.

Rocks to haul, ditches to dig. Honestly, Michelle was finding it all a trial. She'd much rather concentrate on the train car braking system she'd already patented. She had a dozen ideas for improvement and more ideas for passenger cars to make the undercarriage system absorb bumps and rattles and make them more comfortable for passengers.

And if she could just figure out that four-stroke cycle engine, she'd be rich. Which she already was, but money wasn't her motivation. Achievement was. Maybe a twinge of power. She hoped that didn't count as laying up treasures here on earth. Could power be a treasure? She thought of Benteen and suspected it could.

Jilly seemed to love the ditch digging and rock hauling far more than Michelle, so at least her sister was happy.

"Let's stop digging for a while and eat the noon meal," Michelle announced.

The men straightened from their shovels with a sigh of relief. They were cowboys, not ditch diggers, but they'd been given a big raise and were in high spirits.

Michelle sat down with a plate of beef, beans, and biscuits

the cowhand cook had brought out. It was a relief to rest her back while Josh built a fire and the men made coffee. Michelle felt like she was a true rancher. Maybe she ought to learn to rope.

"Do any of you know men who are looking for a job? Men willing to do hard work for top wages?"

One nodded. "And with men getting married and such, there's room in the bunkhouse."

Another said, "I can think of a few."

"Benteen has a lot of men on his payroll. Be careful who you talk to, but if you bring in more men, we'll hire them. Otherwise, we'll be spending the rest of the summer on this."

The men had been involved in holding Benteen, and some had ridden as guards to town with him. They all knew he'd been let go. Zane trusted them and considered his men loyal. Michelle would trust them, too.

Smiling as Josh started one of his overly detailed stories, she let her mind wander to the details of the irrigation she planned. And to the gold they now had in the bank. And the work Zane was doing.

She thought of how nice it'd been to see Mama and Laura.

She'd already seen them twice since the wedding. Josh handed her a cup of coffee. She took it and thought of how happy Jilly was to be working at this hard labor.

Was she, though? Was Jilly happy?

Michelle caught her sister's eye and tilted her head, then moved away from the men until they were well out of earshot.

When they came upon a couple of thigh-high boulders beside the stream, Michelle headed for one and sat.

Jilly stayed standing. "My back feels better if I'm on my feet." Then she drank deeply from the tin coffee cup.

Her vividly red hair was in a tight braid, twisted into a bun at the base of her skull, but it had unruly curls and plenty of them escaped and hung in wispy ringlets around her face and down the back of her neck. Her green eyes caught the color of the grassy meadow and the backdrop of the leaves on the trees climbing the mountain nearby.

Michelle watched those eyes and considered and discarded several of the questions she wanted to ask.

"Jilly, what are you going to do?"

Jilly didn't answer. Instead, she concentrated on drinking, but Michelle saw the wheels turning in Jilly's head. She understood the question. She just needed to organize her thoughts.

"Did you see how exhausted Laura looked after that meeting at the ironworks?"

Michelle didn't accuse her of avoiding the question. She guessed the answer was going to be a long one. And a serious one. "She's not suited to it."

"You are."

Michelle knew that to be the truth. "You could manage a seat on the board, too."

"I could manage it. But you're the one who understands what California Ironworks is creating. You're the one who could push them. It's an excellent company, but you'd guide them in the way of raising the quality of their products. You could make it the finest ironworks in the state, maybe in the country."

"But it's not our main purpose." Michelle would love to get involved in the board meetings of the ironworks. "Stiles Lumber is our main purpose. Yes, I could do a lot with that foundry, but now that we've taken control of the lumber company, we need to find out what damage Edgar has done and go to work fixing it. And you can do that just as well as I can."

"You were always raised to take over. I was supposed to be the builder. You were supposed to make sure I had all the iron and lumber I needed to build my bridges and trestles. And invent new and better machines to make our trains run. Hauling logs down steep mountainsides is serious business."

"Now that we've talked about our history and parents' plans for us—things we both already know—I'd like to find out what you're planning."

Jilly looked away from Michelle, toward the mountains and trees. As a woman might look for an escape route.

"You're welcome to stay here, but it's no longer a hiding place. You can go home to Mama if you wish. They're as capable of protecting you there as I am here. Maybe more capable because of how remote the mansion is. You could get married."

Jilly's eyes snapped back to Michelle's with a fire in that green that looked ready to burn. "I'm not planning to marry."

"You're not safe unless you do."

"I'm not safe if I do."

"I'm safe. Laura is. She can't be forced to marry someone."

"You both got very lucky, and I think you know it."

"I do. Though I knew what kind of man Zane was when I married him. What's more, even though Laura married so precipitously, she knew Caleb was a good man. She didn't know how strong he was. How capable of protecting her he was. And she didn't know some of the secrets of his past. But she knew he was a good man."

"We *knew* Edgar was a good man, didn't we?"

"Looking back, though, I can see that we were in a position to be plucked like geese for Edgar. Caleb didn't come around the rich Stiles sisters and act sweet and charming like Edgar did. We descended on him. And poor Zane got both of us and our whole mission group landed on his head. He didn't come slithering up to us wearing a fancy suit in San Francisco."

"Neither of you knew anything. And what's more, you still don't know what unkindness your husbands are capable of. It's early days. We all still liked Edgar a month after the wedding."

Michelle bristled to hear a single word against Zane, but she controlled herself. Mainly because she still wanted an answer to her first question. She'd been patient, but Jilly was dodging. Michelle had seen her dodge this before, but now things were serious.

"You'll never be safe, not as long as you're unmarried. Even if you stay unmarried until you inherit the company at twenty-five, as long as Edgar is in our lives and has his plans, you're in danger. You need to pick a husband and do it quickly. So what are your plans, Jilly? Don't tell me you don't know, because thinking ahead is as natural to you as breathing."

Jilly's green eyes dropped to the ground. Dodging the question again? Or too upset to look her in the eye with the truth, whatever that was? Michelle wasn't sure.

"I've thought about it long and hard. I . . . well . . . I understand the dangers of remaining single." Then Jilly looked up, determination in her eyes. "I'm going to face those dangers. Because no. I will not marry. Ever."

"Why? Did Edgar do or say something to you?"

Another extended silence before Jilly said, "He just opened my eyes."

She turned and walked away. Michelle knew it was a waste of time to chase her down and try to shake the truth out of her. It looked like Jilly didn't believe she was safe. Not yet.

# CHAPTER TWENTY-THREE

JUST AS THEY WERE FINISHING the noon meal, a big wagon drawn by six mules pulled into Zane's yard, hauling the first waterwheel. The factory had enough orders they were running double shifts to make the wheels, and this first one showed up almost before Michelle expected it. They'd finished rerouting the stream and digging out the trenches only the night before.

"I told the men we will all go out and work on the wheel. Everyone is eager to see how it's going to work." Zane smiled. "Including me."

The women and children even came. It was almost a party. Michelle had the mule skinner take the wagon straight out to the stream. She was glad they could have the skilled driver maneuver the huge wagon as close as possible. They had a tree trunk of the proper width ready to thread through the center hole of the waterwheel. It was hard work to line everything up just right and get the wheel in the trench Jilly had directed the men to dig.

By the time they had the wheel off the wagon, Zane had

stripped to the waist, and was sweating along with his men as they heaved the wheel—one of the smaller ones the ironworks made but still a heavy machine—into the hole prepared for it. Then they threaded the log and seated it deep into the bank of the river. The log stretched the width of the river and was anchored on both sides.

When Jilly was satisfied that the wheel would turn rather than be swept downstream, she said, "Let's open up that waterway."

The men had to wade into the stream and heave out rocks. The cool water was better under the burning summer sun than working on the banks had been.

They didn't have to move all the rocks before a trickle of water surged back into its natural course. As the rocks were thrown aside, the trickle grew faster. Finally, when the waterwheel was hit with a strong enough current, it slowly began to turn. It worked a pump that sent water gushing out onto the ground. The first of the water seemed to soak into the thirsty ground, but soon the shallow trenches they'd built filled with water and flowed out through the pasture.

Zane dipped his hands into the water as it flowed through the chinks in their manmade dam. The water flowed around his waist as he turned to watch the cascade pour out of the wheel onto his dry land. He stopped moving the rocks and cupped his hands into the water and drank deeply. Then he laughed, and the men, still getting soaked along with him, joined in. Zane waded out of the water and went straight to Michelle.

"You did it." He dragged her into his arms, soaking her dress.

"You're all wet!" She squealed and slapped at him, but there was laughter in her voice.

"Stop playing and get to work," Jilly said. "We need to move rocks until we drop below that trench we dug, so all the water will flow into its natural banks and turn the wheel at full speed."

Jilly, still working, still building. But she smiled at the flowing water.

The other women watched the water with wondering eyes. The few children toddled for the shallow trenches filling with water, and their mothers let them splash.

The men smiled as they went back to work with renewed energy.

Everyone's spirits were sky-high.

THE REST OF THE WATERWHEELS were hauled straight to the ranch, but the boilers were smaller and delivered to the general store in town.

Zane was in a good mood from watching the grass turn green in three pastures now as August crept along. He had several to go, but it was enough to get them through the summer. And by next summer, they'd have every pasture irrigated.

A few times a day, Zane caught himself thinking about how much he loved the supply of hot water that flowed right into a tub. All Michelle's ideas so far were great ones. Now she was talking about something called a shower bath. Hot water pouring down on your head instead of pooled in a tub. That really would be a wonder.

When he got word that his boilers had come in, he and Michelle decided to ride to town with Shad coming along behind in the wagon.

As they rode, they passed grazing land that was pure brown, the grass crisp.

"No stream in this one." Zane swept his arm out to include the whole meadow. "This one and a couple of others have springs in them that give the cattle enough water to survive, except in a drought year like this. This year the springs have gone dry."

"That's what the windmills are for. We can water the cattle with tanks or build a pond, and we could irrigate using the water the windmill will pump out."

"I'm going to have to cull my herd even more because of the drought."

"How long does it take for the herd to grow back when they're culled deep?"

Zane tilted his head a bit. "We'd be set back some. I'd probably just not have many cattle to sell next year. So a year with very limited income. But this year's income will be high."

He smiled at Michelle. "And your irrigation is already helping. Before you did that, I was going to have to sell a lot more cattle. Thank you. And a windmill could get up and working fast. We've always had decent rains here, and I've gotten by in other dry years without putting one up."

They continued on their way, and Zane mentioned finding water using a water witch, a forked branch of wood that dipped toward the ground when it passed over water. That was the usual way to decide where to dig a well.

Michelle launched into a talk about geological surveys,

water levels, aquifers, and the capillary rise of groundwater. His head started to spin from her complicated explanations.

And now she wanted a traction engine that drove itself around on wheels so they could use it here and there. No such thing existed to his knowledge, which he admitted to himself might be limited. She talked about a threshing machine and a baling machine—and how a traction engine could run them. Threshing made no sense because he didn't grow wheat or oats. He just cut down prairie grass that grew wild, stacked it, and forked it up in case the forage got short in the winter. But Michelle was excited about how much better oats and wheat would be for his cows, which were gaining weight just fine as they were. And she wanted to turn his big haystacks into dozens . . . no, hundreds of small hay bales. Why would he do that?

Labor saving, she had said. Machines that took over a lot of the backbreaking work. But baling was work he didn't even do, so how could doing it save any work?

He wouldn't have to have so many hired men. And he knew they often quit with little notice, leaving him shorthanded. Cowboys were a bunch of wanderers, for a fact. But new ones always came in, and he liked having men around. They needed jobs, and he liked their company.

Zane knew Michelle was really smart, but even so, he decided to use small words. "I run a ranch. I have helped with this ranch since I was knee-high to my pa. I have no idea why you think I need a traction engine."

"We have one in each of our sawmills. And there's one in the lumberyard in San Francisco that runs a saw strictly for doing finer work." Her eyes practically glowed with excitement. "Once we're done with the waterwheels and windmills setup and the threshers and balers running, I want to work on my four-stroke cycle engine. I've told you about Rochas's theory on how his engine would work. But no one has ever figured out how to truly create it. If I could invent it and apply that engine to Lenoir's internal combustion engine, I could—"

If he heard the name Alphonse Beau de Rochas or Etienne Lenoir one more time he might . . . he might . . . good grief, it was too late. He already remembered them.

Twenty minutes later, Michelle was talking about the shed she wanted for inventing. She called it a laboratory, but it sounded like a big shed to him.

Jilly was excited to have something new to build. With all the trees she was cutting down, he probably oughta invest in one of those two-man crosscut saws. Michelle said that's what they used in their lumber business. Maybe he needed a sawmill. He sure enough wasn't going to suggest that, or he'd find himself with a mill so fast his head would spin quicker than a paddle wheel.

He respected Michelle's excitement about machines, but Zane was a little hurt by her urge to improve and organize a ranch that was already one of the best in northern California. Not that he'd visited others to compare. But he knew it.

Instead, she was determined to invent things the world had been getting along without since God created the heavens and the earth.

They finally reached Dorada Rio, well ahead of Shad. The wagon was a slow-moving thing, and Michelle had errands she wanted to run and letters she wanted to mail with more orders before they loaded the boilers.

"That's Marshal Irving." Zane pointed to the man riding into Dorada Rio from the other side of town.

"He looks tired." Michelle frowned as they closed the distance between them.

Marshal Irving, wearing brown broadcloth pants and a dusty blue shirt, instead of his usual black suit, caught sight of them and straightened in his saddle. He picked up his pace and rode up to Zane and Michelle, his eyes sparking with urgency. "Follow me over to that hitching post."

He guided his horse to the front of the general store, the nearest place to tie up. He dismounted and was around his horse before Zane's feet hit the ground.

"Glad to see you," Irving said. "I've got a lot to tell you, but it has to wait. For now, I could use someone to guard my flank."

"What's going on?" Zane asked.

Michelle came around her horse and was clearly listening in that sharp way she had. She didn't miss a thing. She had a memory for names and details, and she always had an opinion.

"I've been keeping watch over Horace Benteen's ranch. There's a good spot for a lookout. I can lay on my belly up on a hilltop with my spyglass and see what's happening there."

That explained the dust, and it probably explained the two tied-down guns. A man expecting trouble.

"Horace rode out yesterday with about six riders. Then last night, I saw Jarvis ride in."

"He's out at his pa's ranch right now?" Zane hadn't seen or heard a whisper about the man since that crooked judge had let him out of jail.

"Yes, and his pa didn't take all his hands with him."

"You want me to go along with you out there and help you round 'em up?" Zane wondered where he could put Michelle while he took a long ride out of town. The Benteen ranch was as far from town to the south as Zane's was to the east.

"Nope, I followed Jarvis here. He and two men from his ranch just rode into town as bold as you please."

"He must think he's untouchable," Michelle said, crossing her arms tightly. "And after he broke into my bedroom and tackled me to the floor. That can't be allowed to stand."

"He thinks it, ma'am, but he's wrong. I have some marshals riding in. I've warrants to arrest Jarvis and Horace over the theft of Mrs. Lane's land. I contacted the marshals a few days ago, figuring I needed more men if I had to take Horace at the ranch. Now I've got Jarvis here in town with only two men to back him."

"Where are the other marshals?" Zane glanced around the town, wondering where they were waiting.

"They're not here yet. That's why I was keeping watch over the Benteen ranch, studying the situation while I waited for help. I figured we'd arrest Horace, then comb the hills for Jarvis. But he came right into the place, probably because he knew his pa was gone.

"Now that he's here in town, I'm going to grab him. It'll be a sight easier here than when he's at home. I'd prefer having my men with me, but I can't wait. He might head home at any time." Irving looked down the street in the direction Zane and Michelle had come. "He's in the Red Boot Saloon. No idea what else he's come to town for. I was riding to the sheriff's office. I'll get Sheriff Stockwood and his deputy, but another man would help things go smoother, Zane."

"Glad to help, Marshal. My foreman, Shad, is trailing

along behind us, driving a wagon. Do you want to wait for him?"

"I'd as soon not wait a minute longer than we need to."

With a firm nod, Zane said, "Let's do it fast. A man drinking in the saloon before midday might not stay long."

With a one-shouldered shrug, Irving said, "And he might settle in for hours. In which case, he'd be easier to arrest later. But I don't want to chance it. Let's get Stockwood."

"Michelle, do you want to wait in the sheriff's office?" Zane hesitated to call it the jail for some reason. Probably because he could so easily picture himself swinging the iron door shut on her to keep her away from the danger.

"I'll walk along to see the sheriff. While you're arresting Jarvis, I'll go to the general store and discuss a few orders I want to place."

Zane shuddered to find out what he was going to own next. In fairness, he had to admit most everything Michelle ordered, she paid for herself. Still, her money was his, wasn't it? So he oughta have some say in how it was spent.

For now, if ordering something kept her away from armed men, he'd encourage it.

## CHAPTER
# TWENTY-FOUR

IT DIDN'T TAKE LONG TO GET THE SHERIFF—his deputy was out of town. The three men walked down the long boardwalk, their spurs clanking. Zane glanced behind to see Michelle standing out front of the general store, her arms crossed, her expression grim.

She was supposed to be inside ordering mysterious things that Zane didn't even know existed. But Zane didn't have time to go back and scold her. And scolding didn't work worth a hoot anyway.

The saloon was at the north end of two blocks' worth of stores, and the general store was on the south end, so she was probably out of range if any gunfight cropped up.

Irving was trying to explain what was going on to the sheriff.

"I figured you'd have to drag him out of some hidey-hole up in the mountains." Sheriff Stockwood walked closest to the storefronts, while Zane walked closest to the street.

"The fool rode into town and went into the Red Boot." Irving pointed to three horses—two brown, one black—tied up in front of the saloon. "I'm sure he's in there having a drink. He has a couple of the hands from Horace's ranch with him. I've been spying on the place, every man out there wears two guns. I'm glad to have some help, it oughta keep things from turning into a turkey shoot."

The marshal, one pace ahead, pushed open the batwing doors to the Red Boot Saloon.

Three men leaned against the bar, Jarvis in the middle of the row. Red, the bartender, stood back, leaning against a counter lined with whiskey bottles and little else.

Zane knew Red just a little and saw the man's eyes go to the sheriff. He sidled down the bar a few paces. He knew trouble when he saw it.

"Jarvis Benteen, you're under arrest." The marshal's voice boomed like thunder. A man prepared for trouble—he came in with both guns already drawn. He strode into the room straight for where Jarvis and the two others shared a bottle of whiskey.

Both of the men with Jarvis must've figured themselves to be salty, because even with aimed guns coming at them, they slapped leather.

Red dropped to the floor.

Jarvis knocked the whiskey bottle aside as he vaulted over the bar and threw himself flat so he was out of sight, leaving his men to fight while he hid.

Irving's gun was blasting. The sheriff a second behind him. The two men with Jarvis sent bullets tearing across the saloon.

Zane was a man cool under pressure. He had a fast draw but not lightning quick. He'd fired his gun plenty of times but never at a man. Now the world seemed to slow down.

He heard each separate shot from the blasting of the lawmen's guns. He saw the two men with Jarvis flailing and crying out with pain under the impact of bullets as they fired wild. The sulfuric smell of gunpowder burned Zane's nose.

Zane was on Irving's left. He couldn't go after Jarvis without running straight into the gunfire, so he backed up and came around behind Irving and Stockwood.

Bullets whizzed toward him, but they all went high or low or wide.

In all the mayhem, Zane's only thought was for the man who'd put his hands on Michelle.

The other two men collapsed in a blaze of blue gun smoke.

Irving rushed toward them. Zane rushed for where Jarvis hid. The bar was an *L* shape with the short side blocking Zane's path.

Just as Zane went to vault it, Jarvis lunged to his feet with his arm around Red's neck.

"Back up, or I swear I'll kill him." Jarvis's roar was laced with panic. His gun trembled as he shoved it against Red's temple.

"I'll shoot him dead, then use him to block your shots while I kill every one of you." Jarvis sounded vicious and desperate enough to do just what he said. He backed to the swinging door at the end of the bar and dragged Red through it.

"Stay back." Jarvis's voice sounded near hysteria. Zane knew a cornered man, especially one as afraid as Jarvis, could do most anything.

"I'll kill him." His voice echoed from behind the door. "I'm warning you."

Zane was quiet about it, but he slid over the bar and approached the still-swinging door.

The sheriff and Marshal Irving came right behind him. Zane heard something, soft so he wasn't sure. It wasn't a gunshot at least. Slowly, staying to the side of the door, he reached out and pushed it, expecting to hear gunfire. When none came, he peeked around the edge of the door to see Red unconscious on the floor and the back door wide open.

Zane rushed past Red, hoping he was just down from a blow of some kind. He looked out into the alley that ran along behind the row of storefronts. He saw nothing. Jarvis had vanished.

Zane turned back. "See that he doesn't get his horse."

Stockwood pivoted and raced for the hitching post out front of the saloon.

"I'm leading this search." Irving pushed past Zane and strode farther into the alley. He looked left and right, then said, "We have to split up. If he's rounding the building to get his horse, Stockwood will get him. I'll head for the livery stable. That's his most likely choice." Irving pointed with his gun to the left. "You make sure he hasn't ducked into one of those businesses, but those are just more places to get cornered."

Zane took off in the direction he'd been sent. He looked in the back rooms of three stores before he remembered Michelle.

And remembered Jarvis was panicked. He'd be thinking to get a horse and ride for home. There were few horses on the quiet main street, but Zane's was tied up in front of the general store, along with Irving's and Michelle's. And if Jarvis was thinking, he knew that if he didn't go to the livery stable, his best chance of finding a horse was in front of that general store. Zane stopped searching and ran.

MICHELLE HEARD THE GUNFIRE. She froze, her arms crossed so tightly they were a clamp. Everything in her cried out that she run for Zane, protect him, fight for him, fight *with* him.

Instead, she stayed. He'd told her to and for good reason. This was a hard business confronting and arresting an armed man. It was no place for an unarmed woman. She'd just be someone else to protect.

The shooting stopped.

No one came out. Fury overcame fear. She'd buy a gun and bullets and go save her husband.

Behind her, a scream ripped through the store. Something crashed and shattered. She whirled.

"You're paying for that damage, Benteen." The general store clerk rushed to block Jarvis.

Michelle's blood ran cold. If Jarvis was loose, that meant he'd bested the sheriff, the marshal, and Zane.

Michelle rushed for the front wall of the building. With no time to hide, she hoped he'd run right past her. Steal a horse maybe. Then she'd get a gun and—

"Stop where you are." The clerk was probably the owner. No mere clerk would stand his ground against Jarvis.

Peeking around the window, she saw Jarvis slam into the clerk, who didn't budge. He was a big, brawny man who wanted his money. Jarvis staggered back, then turned and hurled himself at the store window.

"No! You're paying for that, too!"

Glass crashed around Jarvis. Shards rained down on his head, slitting his clothes, hands, and face. Bleeding, he landed on his side, then fought his way to his feet, and his gaze landed on Michelle. Cruel satisfaction blazed in his eyes as if he'd been coming for her all along. The ugly scar on his face now ran with blood. His golden tooth gleamed like a weapon. His gun came up. He aimed at the clerk who'd come barreling out. The brawny man froze when he faced the gun.

"Get back, or you'll die."

The clerk hadn't seen Michelle, so she didn't consider it running rather than staying and defending a woman.

Jarvis rushed at her, grabbed her by the arm, and said, "My pa's been wanting to get his hands on you. Let's go."

He tore the reins loose from the hitching post and threw her up on the buckskin stallion Zane rode. A big horse strong enough to carry two. Probably why Jarvis had picked it. He swung up behind her just as she dove for the ground. Jarvis's big hand caught the back of her dress and held her in front of him, straddling the saddle, as he wheeled the horse and kicked it viciously. The horse took off, galloping with the first leap.

"Jarvis!" The roar from behind her was Zane.

Michelle's heart lifted to hear her husband sounding furious, frantic but alive.

She struggled to escape a choking grip. She nearly got both feet on one side of the galloping horse. Better to fall from the tall horse at a full gallop than go wherever Jarvis intended.

He shouted ugly threats over the raging sound of the horse's hooves as he dragged her back, then draped her across his lap, the saddle horn gouging her belly. The buckskin's muscled front legs moved under her face as she hung down with Jarvis's hard grip on the back of her dress.

Knowing not to escape was to face something terrible, she went mad fighting and clawing. Her fists punched up and back. Her legs kicked as she screamed and wrenched against his hold.

Jarvis clung to her. "Stop fighting me. I'll carry you home unconscious, and my pa will thank me even if you're not in good shape." His rough laugh was laced with hysteria.

Michelle was barely capable of lifting her head a few inches, but she was able to see past Jarvis's leg.

Zane. Riding hard, bent low over the saddle on her horse.

Behind him, she saw Marshal Irving and Sheriff Stockwood. All coming to save her.

How far was it to Benteen's ranch? The horse was breathing heavily, carrying a double load and being driven hard.

Benteen growled and cursed as he kicked the poor horse mercilessly. If he got her to his home, he'd have . . . what had the sheriff said? Michelle, who rarely forgot anything, couldn't remember. But Irving hadn't wanted to go out there alone. Men, Jarvis would have a crowd of men to fight for him.

The saddle horn gouged her with particular sharpness, and she twisted to escape Jarvis's grip.

Wanting to stop this however she could, she thought of the knife she kept in her boot. No way to reach it. She could only think of one weapon. She turned so she was facing his leg and saw his pants had been ripped from knee to ankle by the glass. His bare leg was right there. She sank her teeth in hard right below his knee.

He roared and jerked, but she hung on as if her life depended on it. It very possibly did.

He slammed a fist into her face. She refused to let go, just dug her teeth in deeper, wanting to tear him apart.

Another blow knocked her hard enough that her grip was torn loose.

Dazed, dizzy, in agony from Jarvis's battering fists. The thundering hooves, the dust, the smell of a terrified, furious, brutal man, the pain from his blows to her head. The gouging of her stomach. It all overwhelmed her, and she felt every muscle go limp and saw the world go black.

ZANE URGED EVERY OUNCE OF SPEED out of Michelle's little bay mare. The mare was no match for Zane's stallion. His teeth gritted with rage as he saw Michelle fighting, hitting at Jarvis, kicking, trying to break his hold.

Then he saw Jarvis draw back to strike Michelle with his fist.

Michelle, Zane's wife. Zane's to protect.

Yes, the buckskin was a bigger, faster horse, but Jarvis had his hands full subduing Michelle and wasn't getting top speed out of Zane's stallion.

Zane closed the distance, but it was taking too long. He didn't dare draw a gun. He couldn't risk hitting Michelle. On a galloping horse his bullet could go anywhere, including into Michelle. Her brilliance, her beauty, her flood of ideas, silenced forever.

It was an unthinkable risk.

He bent lower over the mare's neck. Pressed her with his thighs. They inched closer, closer. Benteen's ranch was a long way off, but Zane knew the stallion's endurance, and he knew this little mare's. This chase couldn't go on much longer without Zane falling hopelessly behind.

Then it came to Zane: the one thing a cowboy could do to get into a fight when he couldn't risk a deadly weapon. He reached back and, with a lifetime of experience, untied the leather thongs that held a lariat on the back of the saddle.

He had it in his hands as he closed the distance. He widened the loop, and knowing his own horse, he blew a shrill whistle and yelled, "Whoa, Buck!"

The buckskin, in full gallop, skidded, nearly sitting down. Jarvis twisted in the saddle just as Zane dropped a loop over his shoulders and yanked it tight. Buck reared up as Jarvis fought the rope and tried to get to his gun. All the jostling shook Michelle free of the hold Jarvis had on her, and she fell headfirst to the ground.

With a shout of fear, Zane tore Jarvis free of the saddle on the side away from Michelle. Zane saw the fall carry her, rolling away from the hooves of the prancing buckskin. Then the trembling stallion turned and came to Zane.

Zane leapt to the ground, leaving his nerve-rattled horses as he dashed to Jarvis's side and hog-tied him like a spring calf. Only with Jarvis, Zane wasn't nearly as gentle.

Jarvis roared and struggled.

Zane had no time for him and didn't like the noise. He dragged Jarvis's neckerchief up and used it to gag him, then Zane rushed to Michelle's side just as Irving and Stockwood caught up to them.

Dropping to his knees, Zane rolled Michelle to her back. Her face was bleeding. Her lip split.

Her head lolled to the side as he lifted her into his arms.

She needed his attention, or he'd have fallen on Jarvis and torn him to shreds with his bare hands.

He quickly pressed a hand to her chest and felt her heartbeat. Felt her chest rise and fall. But she was out cold. Her face an ashen white under the ugly swelling bruise left by Jarvis's fist.

Irving was there, kneeling across from Zane.

At a glance, Zane saw the sheriff replacing the rope Zane had tied with shackles on Jarvis's arms and legs.

Trusting Stockwood to handle Jarvis, Zane went back to tending Michelle. Irving jumped up and was back in seconds with a canteen. He dampened his own kerchief and pressed the cool cloth to Michelle's battered face.

Zane ran his hands over her, carefully checking for broken bones. Her feet flexed as he felt her ankles above her half boots. It gave him hope that her back and neck weren't broken.

"I think she's just knocked cold." Irving had a look in his eyes, like a man with experience in this kind of thing. It helped Zane steady himself. He'd been praying like a devout monk the whole ride out here. Now he started again. Asking for God's care, God's healing hand.

"Can we move her? Or should we let her come around out here?"

"Carry her back to town," Irving said. "The doc can have a look at her. I reckon she just needs time."

Zane looked around again to see the sheriff had rounded up the horses and thrown Jarvis over the saddle of Michelle's mare. Zane lifted Michelle with utmost care, then carried her to Buck, who stood on trembling legs, sides heaving. Irving held the reins.

Zane stroked the stallion's neck, gave the critter a little time to calm. When the horse had its nerves under control, Zane went to the saddle.

Stockwood came up and said, "Let me hold her while you mount up."

Because it would jostle her around less, Zane let go of her. It took every ounce of willpower to do it.

He swung up, then Stockwood handed Michelle over, and Zane began a slow, even ride to town. It was the longest ride of his life.

CHAPTER

# TWENTY-FIVE

MICHELLE'S EYES FLUTTERED OPEN as she felt the world tilt around. She looked up to see she was being held in the arms of Marshal Irving.

"Howdy, ma'am," Irving said. "You're back with us, I see."

Zane was there, taking her into his own arms. She saw his horse behind him, and the town around them. Back in Dorada Rio. Right now, she didn't like this town very much.

"You're awake!" Zane kissed her so gently she feared for how badly she was hurt. "I'm taking you in to the doctor."

Michelle didn't like being afraid, so she launched herself at Zane. Wrapped her arms around his neck and clung to him. Everything hurt, but her arms worked.

"Michelle, you're going to be all right." Zane staggered under the assault, tightened his grip on her, kissed her neck, then kept walking.

Irving opened the door. A bell tinkled overhead.

Zane swept inside. "I need a doctor! Now!"

Honestly, all the urgency seemed dire. "Am I badly hurt? Do I have broken bones and a cracked skull?"

She hurt in every muscle and joint. Head to toe. Head especially.

Then someone else was there. A man she'd never seen before wearing a black vest and a white shirt. Gold wire-rimmed glasses framed kind brown eyes. Well, Zane had hollered for a doctor. She made an assumption.

"What's happened here?" the doctor asked.

Zane explained, and it all made more sense. She didn't remember falling off the horse. Probably landed headfirst. "That vicious scoundrel Jarvis Benteen punched me."

It gave her some faint satisfaction to know she'd bit him hard enough to make him holler. "Doctor, can you let me leave for just a while so I can punch Jarvis in the face?"

"Maybe in a little while."

She turned to Zane. "Can you please hold Jarvis while I pay him back for this pain?"

"I might make you stand in line." Zane's concern felt like soothing balm to her wounded pride. Her wounded body, unfortunately, kept hurting. "But you can definitely have a turn, and it would be my pleasure to hold him down while you stomp him good."

She reached to touch her face and felt a swollen cheek, a fat lip.

For a second, Michelle furrowed her brow, which, to her surprise, hurt terribly. She relaxed her brow just to make the pain stop.

She squeezed Zane's hand. "You got to me in time."

The sheriff came in. "I have Jarvis locked up. How are you, Mrs. Hart? I'm sorry that low-down coward got to you."

She turned to Zane. “I stayed at the general store just like you asked.”

“You did.” He took her left hand with his right. “Like the worst kind of yellow-bellied villain, he ran while his two men shot it out with us. I don’t think he was coming for you. He knew there’d be horses outside the general store. When he saw you, he—he—” Zane shook his head, his jaw so tight words seemed to be beyond him.

“He said he was taking me for his father.”

Zane kissed her cheek, as gentle as a warm summer rain.

“Let me see to her now, Zane. Ease back a bit.” The doctor worked over her awhile.

It all hurt.

“Am I going to have a black eye?”

“You’ll still be the most beautiful woman I’ve ever seen.” Zane never let go of her hand.

Which Michelle took to mean yes.

“There are no broken bones,” the doctor said.

“He draped me over his saddle. The saddle horn gouged me.”

He’d inspected her belly by unbuttoning the fewest possible buttons on her shirtwaist. “Nothing seems to be injured internally, though your stomach is bruised.”

Michelle didn’t like that idea much, but she was vain enough that the black eye bothered her more.

“With a fall like that, added to the blow to your face, you probably have a concussion.”

“I’m not seeing double. Except for the fall, my memory of what happened is solid. No nausea. It’s hard to judge dizziness when I’m flat on my back, but my thoughts are clear. If it’s a concussion, it’s a mild one.”

The doctor looked startled. "Are you a doctor, Mrs. Hart?"

"Michelle performed surgery to remove two bullets from my brother-in-law." Zane kept holding her hand, kept watching every flicker of her eyes, every movement of her mouth. "And one bullet from my sister."

"Oh, well, my goodness, you *are* a doctor then?"

"No, though I have studied anatomy, and I once watched and briefly assisted Professor Othniel Marsh assemble a pterosaur skeleton."

"What?" It was Zane's turn to look surprised.

"Papa liked to bring in tutors," Michelle said. "I've had a few other classes that helped."

"And how did it go? How is your brother-in-law?"

"He's dead," Zane said it absently. Maybe he didn't quite know that he wasn't complimenting her skills.

The doctor's brows rose behind his wire-rimmed glasses.

"It wasn't my fault." Michelle would have glared at Zane, but she supposed that would hurt, too. "The man's situation was very serious. I wasn't able to save him from two abdominal bullet wounds. No one could have."

"You're exactly right." The doctor patted her on the hand. "Stay calm. I've got a cool cloth I want to rest over the right side of your face. The bleeding has stopped, but you're going to be very bruised."

Black eye. She knew it. And no, no, she *wasn't* a vain woman. Heaven knew she dressed for comfort, and her main interest in her hair was keeping it out of her experiments. But surely this was a level of ugly over which no woman would be other than dismayed.

Jarvis deserved at least one good punch. She had a lot of aches and pains, but her fists were feeling just fine.

"If it helps, Mrs. Hart," the sheriff said, "there's a bite on Jarvis's leg that would need medical attention if I didn't plan to hang him before he could heal up."

"It does help a little."

The sheriff stood at the foot of her bed, his hat in his hands. "You can't kidnap and batter a woman in California and expect to get away with it."

Michelle didn't bother to mention Jarvis had done so before, just recently.

"And you sure as certain can't steal a horse." The sheriff sounded more upset over the horse thieving than her getting kidnapped and punched.

"Does that hanging rule count if you get the horse back right away?" Michelle had studied the law, but mainly as it pertained to business. And anyway, her thinking was a little muddled. Maybe she *did* have a concussion.

"If they don't hang him, they'll send him straight to San Quentin. His pa isn't going to be able to clean it up. Not this time."

She relaxed, and let the cool cloth ease a bit of her pain while the doctor brewed her some concoction and served it to her as a tea.

When she felt able, she sat up and said, "Let's go see Jarvis."

## CHAPTER
# TWENTY-SIX

LEANING HARD ON HIS ARM, Michelle let Zane support her as they followed the sheriff to the jail.

Marshal Irving stepped out as they reached the boardwalk in front of it.

The marshal studied Michelle's face, his expression grim. Zane suspected it matched his own.

"When they get here, my men are going to transport Jarvis to Sacramento. He'll be tried and convicted before his pa comes in with another crooked judge to get him set free. And he wouldn't dare try that right under the governor's nose anyway. Horace and Governor Booth are mortal enemies."

"He and Uncle Newt don't get along?"

Sheriff Stockwood said, "Uncle Newt?"

"Yes, Newton Booth, the governor, is a personal friend of my family," Michelle said. "I should probably ride along to Sacramento. Uncle Newt won't like seeing what Jarvis did to me."

Zane tightened his grip on her to keep her from hopping on a horse and riding off.

"I'll make sure and describe your injuries very well, Mrs. Hart. I witnessed him hit you. It was a cold-blooded, terrible thing to watch."

When Zane pictured it, which he seemed to be doing every minute, it made him killing mad. He couldn't believe she was on her feet, alive and going to heal. His whole life hadn't been as long as that single horse ride chasing after Jarvis.

"We can hold him, try him, and jail him without your testimony, Mrs. Hart. He'll end up in San Quentin, probably before the end of the week."

The name of the notorious California prison sent a shudder up Zane's spine. It'd been built about twenty years ago in response to the violence that came along with the gold rush. He'd heard tell it was a harsh, crowded place. It was supposed to be an improvement over the prison ships that used to anchor off the coast of San Francisco. But harsh and brutal or not, bad men had to be held somewhere. Zane thought it was a stern warning to stay on the right side of the law. Jarvis, with his arrogance and being accustomed to wealth and comfort, wouldn't do well in that prison.

"Don't forget he stole a horse," the sheriff said.

Irving cracked a mean sort of smile. "I won't. And I'll make sure he doesn't forget, either."

"Trey, I'm letting Mrs. Hart come in and see Jarvis while I ask him some questions. I'm hoping the sight of what he did to her, and what we're going to do to him because of it, will get a few answers out of him. I'd sure like to hear him say a few words about attacking Zane's sister's ranch and shooting Todd Lane. That's an ugly business, and Horace Benteen's land grab can't be allowed to stand, but a land grab isn't ordering murder. I'd like Jarvis to slip up and mention that."

Then Sheriff Stockwood turned to Michelle. "I'll apologize here and now for any foul language you might hear. You might prefer to not be exposed to that."

"I'll come." Michelle squared her shoulders and reached for the doorknob.

Zane regretted what she might hear but didn't bother to try to stop her.

"Then come right along, Mrs. Hart," Irving said. "Glad to goad Jarvis any way we can think of." He took over opening the door and gestured for her to enter.

"Let me go first, ma'am." Stockwood went inside.

Michelle went in ahead of Zane, but he was glad Stockwood was already in there.

"The last time I was in this jail, I'd brought Jarvis in for breaking into my house and assaulting my wife and her sister. Too bad you didn't hang on to him when you had him."

Stockwood looked back at Zane, scowling. "Too bad for a fact. I had to open fire on two men today because of Jarvis and his pa. I lay a good bit of that at the feet of the judge who forced me to let him go."

The door clicked firmly shut behind Zane.

"He's not getting out this time. I guarantee it." Irving came up beside Zane, then passed on ahead to follow the sheriff through the door to the room where the cells were.

Michelle gasped quietly. Zane suspected he was the only one who'd heard it. Then he saw Jarvis and understood why. The man had apparently fallen really hard off his horse. Hard enough to blacken both eyes and break his nose. There was a rough bandage around his leg just below his knee. It looked like Jarvis had tied it on himself. And he had a few stubbornly bleeding cuts from that window he'd crashed through.

He was flat on his back on the cot inside one of two cells. The other cell was past Jarvis. Its door stood open.

Only one prisoner today.

"We've got someone here to see you, Benteen." The sheriff rattled the bars.

Jarvis turned to look, and his eyes went straight for Michelle. For the first time Zane wondered how he got that ugly scar on his face. Beyond that scar he was a decent enough looking man, dressed in fine clothes, though western clothes, not city suits.

Right now, he looked terrible. His clothes ripped to bloody rags. Zane could see the gold tooth was missing. The scar was the least of his problems.

Swinging his legs off the cot, he sat up, still staring. Zane suspected the man had regrets. Not that he'd kidnapped a woman. Not that he'd punched her. But he sure as certain regretted getting caught. And here stood proof of his guilt.

Jarvis gave the sheriff an arrogant smirk as he rose to his feet. "I won't spend a single night in jail. I've got friends."

The exact words he'd said last time. Last time he'd been right.

Michelle crossed her arms. "You can't blame him for believing that, Sheriff."

"He's not getting out, ma'am." Sheriff Stockwood didn't show an ounce of worry over Jarvis's confidence.

"You're sure you'll be able to hold on to him this time?" Michelle sounded stern and skeptical.

Jarvis's getting out before wasn't Hugo's fault, but Zane

decided he liked Michelle scolding someone besides him. And besides, he wondered the same thing.

Zane knew Horace owned a vast tract of land right next to Annie's ranch. When the man wanted to expand, there was one prime piece of pastureland nearby, and he coveted it. He also owned a house in San Francisco and who could say where else. But that was Horace. A separate problem. Jarvis they had a firm grip on this time.

"I'm expecting my men in town anytime," Marshal Irving said. "Now all they need to do is keep you under guard on the long ride to Sacramento." Irving went up to the bars. "You're guilty of kidnapping and assault. You did it right in front of witnesses, including me and the sheriff. And I fired the judge who let you go last time. Matter of fact, I fired him, then arrested him. He's in Sacramento right now awaiting trial. And the governor appointed a new judge. The new judge is a personal friend of Governor Booth. He won't be siding with your pa. Maybe you can share a cell with the old judge in San Quentin."

Jarvis's arrogant smirk slipped. His eyes again went to Michelle. "You can't blame me for running scared from the Red Boot when you two opened fire on me and my men."

"You bet we can." Stockwood leaned against the wall straight across from the locked cell door, his thumbs hooked into his belt. "Running when a lawman tells you he's got a warrant for your arrest is a crime. The least of yours."

"And yep, I grabbed ahold of her, but here she stands. It ain't kidnapping if you get her back this fast."

Stockwood and Irving both turned to look at the swelling on Michelle's face.

"For a fact, it *is* kidnapping." Irving leaned right on the bars of the jail, his left hand raised to hold a bar as casual as if he were standing in someone's kitchen chatting.

"And she fell off the horse. That's not assault."

"I know the law, and if she gets kidnapped and gets hurt in the course of that, it's assault, but I saw you punch her. I saw it, the sheriff saw it, her husband saw it, and she was right there and lived to tell us all about it. You knocked Red cold, too. That's another assault."

"Stole a horse, too." Stockwood shook his head. "You've had a bad day, Jarvis. You may not make it to San Quentin. They may decide to hang you instead."

"Hang?" Jarvis lunged for the bars and clung to them. "No!"

"I'd say the *best* you can hope for is spending the rest of your life in San Quentin, though I think the judge you're going before in Sacramento may decide hanging is a better punishment to fit all these crimes." Irving laughed, and it was the coldest thing Zane had ever heard.

"You're listening now, aren't you, Jarvis? Yep, hanging. And if kidnapping and stealing a horse isn't enough, they'll hang you for attacking Todd and Annie Lane's ranch. Especially because Todd Lane is dead. That's what Zane brought you in here for to begin with, figuring you'd broken into his house to finish the job of killing the Lane family. Those charges are going to hold."

"I didn't kill Todd Lane."

"There's some that say you did. Those men who had the guts to stand and fight at the Red Boot tell a different story."

Since Zane knew they were dead as fence posts, he realized Irving was trying to get a confession out of Jarvis.

"I didn't kill anyone! Those men are lying to shift blame for a murder onto me. Pa sent two of his men on ahead.

Two-Toes was one of them. Pa and I stayed back at the ranch."

And that was it. Zane relaxed just a bit, though all he had to do was look at Michelle to get upset again. But Jarvis had just told them that his pa had ordered murder, and in the eyes of the law, that was the same as committing the murder yourself. That was enough to arrest Horace Benteen, already a wanted man, but now he'd be wanted for murder.

"Two-Toes? You said a couple of men. Who else, Jarvis?" Stockwood's face didn't show a flicker of the satisfaction this confession must give him. "You'd better get your side of the story in before those two are done with the doctor."

"Pa's got gunmen hired. Len Beedle and Two-Toes Parker. It's them that were sent ahead. Beedle's out at the ranch. Two-Toes and Nevada Miller were with me in town."

"Len Beedle is out at your ranch right now?" Irving looked like a hungry wolf. "We've got wanted posters for him. He's a known killer. A couple for Parker, too. Who else is out there riding the hoot owl trail?"

Jarvis's eyes narrowed with calculation. "I'll tell you names, but I want your word there'll be no hanging. And no kidnapping and horse thieving charges, either."

"Maybe, if you write it all down and sign it, you can avoid the murder charge. But no judge is going to let you all the way off of kidnapping and horse thieving. But they might not give you a life sentence if you write out your confession fast, before your two saddle partners get their version of the story down."

"Sure, I'll write it." He looked past Michelle, worried as a man could be. "I'm sorry you're hurt, ma'am."

Jarvis was a while writing his story, and everyone stayed and watched him.

Michelle sniffed, her arms crossed. Her eye mostly swollen shut. "You're sure you're not going to let him confess and apologize so sweetly that you swing open the jail doors and set him free, right, Sheriff?"

"That's right, ma'am."

The two lawmen stood together reading the confession, slightly turned away from Jarvis and not paying attention. Zane eased around them on one side and Michelle on the other. Zane's hand snaked through the bars, grabbed Jarvis by the front of his shirt, and yanked him hard. His head struck the bars with a dull thud.

Zane said with quiet menace, "You'd better hope they lock you up tight. If I ever see you again, I'll kill you on sight."

With no real plans to kill anyone, Zane took some pleasure in watching the color drain out of Jarvis's battered face.

Michelle took the opportunity of his being so close to punch him in the eye.

Jarvis started to howl.

Zane and Michelle stepped back.

The lawmen looked up at the noise, then went back to reading.

Zane wasn't one bit convinced that these two savvy men hadn't noticed the little exchange between the Hart family and Jarvis Benteen.

Satisfied with the confession, the four of them went into the front office just as the front door swung open and six US Marshals came in.

Jarvis was on the road to Sacramento long before he figured out his two saddle partners weren't going to be coming in to tell tales against him.

All six marshals, seven counting Irving, said they'd be back as fast as they could ride, with a few more marshals, to clean up the varmints at Horace Benteen's ranch. In Jarvis's confession, a few more notorious men were identified.

Horace Benteen himself had to be arrested, too, and for that, they had to find him.

It was all settled, and Michelle still had time to contact the California Ironworks and order a traction engine.

At this rate, all that gold wasn't even going to make him rich, unless you counted being loaded down with machines as wealthy. Frankly, Zane didn't count it.

# CHAPTER TWENTY-SEVEN

"LOOK AT THAT WATER FLOW." Michelle felt a pleasant chill, even in the California heat of August, watching the cool water pour out of the waterwheel onto the ground.

Everyone had come out to see the water start pouring onto the land from the newest waterwheel. But work waited for them all. Michelle had seen some wobble in the wheel, and she and Jilly had stayed to tighten a few bolts while everyone else headed back. It was touching really, the way Zane trusted her with these things.

"We did it." Jilly slung an arm around Michelle's neck. "Now a few windmills and we can turn our attention to hooking up the hot water boilers to all Zane's cabins."

There was already one in the house and one in the bunkhouse, but there were five other cabins that needed running water. They all now had to go to the bunkhouse, the ranch house, or the spring that flowed cold out of a rocky stretch near the ranch yard. That's where the ranch house water was piped from, but a windmill would be much more efficient.

"Jarvis is really headed for San Quentin." Michelle watched the water but thought of the letter they'd gotten just today from Marshal Irving.

"I can't believe his father didn't find a way to get him out of it." Jilly let go of Michelle to run her hands up and down her arms as if she had goosebumps. "Ten years. That's brutal for a man as used to comfort and wealth as Jarvis."

Standing silently side by side, each with her own thoughts, they watched the wheel turn and the water pump.

With a firm shake of her head, Michelle said, "He brought it on himself. He was so arrogant, he thought he could assault a woman, break into a man's house, even kidnap me, and steal a horse and walk away from it."

"His father did him no favors raising him in such arrogance. It sounds like Horace shares the same attitude. To think you might have ended up married to him."

"Laura described Carlisle. You had a lucky escape from him, too." Michelle didn't mention that Jilly hadn't fully escaped. And wouldn't until she was married.

Michelle hugged Jilly tightly, then stepped away. "I want you to build my workshop before you start with the boilers."

"Have you gotten Zane to stop calling it an invention shed yet?"

"No." But talk of Zane put a smile on her face. "He wasn't even listening when I said laboratory, but I'm hoping *workshop* will stick in his mind."

"I'd rather build the workshop anyway." Jilly jerked her head at the waterwheel. "Watching that water flow is really satisfying, though."

Michelle rested her eyes on that beautiful cool flow. "I can feel the grass taking a big drink and imagine the cattle drinking deeply. It is satisfying."

"This workshop is going to be pretty complex. I mean, sure, the building itself will go up fast, but you're going to need things like a forge and a supply of steel, things like that."

"I used to go down to the ironworks and use their equipment. It's going to be much harder to set it all up here."

"Is it worth it?" Jilly studied the water.

Michelle considered the question. She really did want to create a four-stroke cycle engine. Then she wanted to hook that engine to everything that moved. Maybe even a sewing machine.

"Should we put it off? Or should I focus on inventing something else? I have some ideas for springs under the carriages of train cars that will make the ride smoother. They already have them, but I can make them better. I think."

"And brakes. You've got the patent on that. You could do a lot more work there."

"When the traction engine comes, I can use that engine to modify machines to work with it, but it's still too large. The key to true progress is making the engine smaller."

"I'll get started on the invention shed tomorrow." Jilly grinned, and the two of them headed for the horses tied nearby.

"SO YOU DON'T THINK IT'S SELFISH to want my workshop built before we put running water into the cabins?" Michelle was peeling potatoes for dinner and talking to her two sisters-in-law. She was getting better at it, peeling potatoes, that is. She'd always been good at talking.

It was simple enough, making the potato and its peel part company, but not very interesting. And she did have a tendency to nick her finger a bit too often. Annie and Beth Ellen never did. She was forced to admit that, boring or not, there was skill to this job. And since everyone had to eat, there was importance to it. Add in that Annie and Beth Ellen would almost certainly someday marry and leave Michelle to run the house. Beth Ellen was rather testy on the subject of marriage right now, and Annie mourned her husband. Still, chances were good they'd each eventually find a man and move into their own homes, so she'd better learn.

"What you're doing sounds so interesting." Annie filled a pot with hot water with a look of delight on her face. "I know you have big ideas, about trains and tunnels and powerful machines that have not yet been invented, but there is so much you could do in little ways. Things to make running a home easier. I'm not sure what, but having the water run into the house, already hot, well, it's just a wonder. Washing clothes is backbreaking work. Maybe you could find a way to hook an engine to a . . . a . . ." Annie stopped and turned with a smile and pink cheeks. "I can't even quite imagine hooking an engine to laundry. Foolish idea." She turned back to her pot and hefted it to the stove.

"No, don't be embarrassed. All inventions start with an idea. I've thought about washing clothes somehow using a waterwheel. A smaller one, powered by the force of the water that flows in hot through our pipes. If we had a little tub with the wheel in it, threw the clothes in that tub, then let water flow in and turn the wheel . . ." Michelle shook her head. "I'm stumped, but it's a good idea. Waterpower, steam power, these are the underlying forces that drive most engines. I've ordered the parts for a shower bath. You're going to love that."

But her mind was caught. Michelle thought everything small needed that small of an engine. And she believed the four-stroke cycle was the foundation of that. But was that wrong? Even the smaller waterwheels they'd used to pump water in the pastures were huge, and of course, the company she ordered them from made them. But what if—

Michelle set her potato and paring knife down and darted out of the room, frantic to get her ideas down on paper before they slid away.

Yes, all inventions started with an idea. Maybe she didn't need a four-stroke cycle engine to change the world. Maybe she needed a really small waterwheel.

A knock at the door drew her out of her frantic note-taking and sketching. She lifted her head to see Zane.

"What time is it?" The office where she worked had north-facing windows, and she could see by the slant of the sunlight that time had passed. She looked down to see pages and pages of writing.

"Annie sent me to call you to dinner. Can you get away from your work?"

Work.

Peeling potatoes.

Learning the skills a woman needed to run a ranch house.

She'd failed again. Sheepishly, she rose from the desk. Zane's desk. She'd taken it over. She followed him to the kitchen to be waited on by two women who were bright enough, but Michelle realized she harbored inside her the firm notion that she was much smarter. But all the smart in the world wouldn't feed this family. And these two seemed to have more common sense than she did.

MICHELLE, THRILLED TO BE WORKING in her new laboratory that Jilly had built, finished the small waterwheel and faced the moment of truth.

She had a long morning ahead of her to get the water flowing, make sure it hit the paddles just right, had enough force to turn the axle at a high enough speed to give the waterwheel power. She'd studied Archimedes. She knew about the physics and mechanics of torque and how it brought force to rotation. She needed force, torque, linear momentum, and angular momentum. By adjusting all those factors, she could get a stronger force or a milder one as needed.

It worked with large waterwheels. Of course it would work with a smaller one.

About ten jobs in all, and everything had to be done and work just right. She was so excited she was giddy. Surely someone else was using the power of water for little jobs, but she'd never heard of it, and if she was copying other work, she didn't know it. This was all her own.

She looked forward to a long quiet morning that might lead her exactly where she wanted to be.

Then Zane stopped in to see if she wanted to get out of the shed and ride out to check the cattle with him.

After she politely but firmly said no, Rick came to see if she needed help. Michelle thanked him and sent him away.

Beth Ellen came to see if she wanted to come in to coffee and cake.

Knowing she should be learning how to *make* coffee and cake, Michelle urged the sweet young woman along.

She was almost afraid to try to focus on her work. It was as if she were *inviting* interruptions.

Finally, silence reigned.

Silence. Blessed silence.

ZANE KNEW HE'D LEFT PLENTY of people around the place. He and his men mostly rode out every day. But Neb, the cowhand cook, was in the bunkhouse, and Rick was around. Besides all the women. And anyway, no one would bother them in the middle of the day.

And Zane hoped there was no one left to bother them.

Jarvis would spend years in prison. Marshal Irving had written them that there was an intensive search for Horace Benteen, now officially wanted for murder. The man hadn't been seen by anyone in the places he regularly frequented.

Irving wanted him but admitted in the letter that it was possible the man had left the state.

The marshal's office had made up wanted posters and offered a reward. Either they'd catch him, or he'd be on the run. Either way, he should be out of the area, and it was safe for Annie to go home.

Which Annie seemed to have no interest in doing.

"Something's moving up there, Zane." Shad pointed to a rugged stretch that the cows usually avoided.

Zane studied the rough, steep stretch. It wasn't bad to get

in there from the north, but the cattle were to the south. He could see a patch of fur and some motion through the heavily forested hillside. "We get calves up there once in a while."

"They might've gotten to running or been spooked by a wolf."

Zane couldn't see enough to be sure. The coat wasn't quite red enough for his Herefords, but the trees cast shadows that could make it look darker.

"We'll need to take him out to the north," Shad said. "It'll be hours bringing a calf around the hills. But it's gotta be done. I doubt it'll make it on its own."

"I'll hike in there. I don't want a horse breaking a leg on those boulders." Zane reined his horse toward the spot Shad pointed to.

Cattle rarely went into that tight stretch of steep woods, but a calf or two made its way in once or twice a year. Zane considered that it might be worth the work to put up a fence so it wouldn't happen again.

He hitched his horse low so it could graze, then climbed over boulders, around massive tree trunks and downed logs, and pushed through bramble that he'd've never tackled if he didn't have a calf to save.

He broke through the heavy woods only to see a horse tied up, tucked back here where no saddled and bridled horse should ever be.

And he saw the brand on its flank. Horace Benteen's brand. A man with no good intentions toward Zane's wife and maybe downright evil intentions toward his sister.

A man who was missing. A man who'd left the area . . . or gone into hiding.

And here was Benteen's horse hidden on Two Harts property.

Zane forgot caution. He turned and ran.

IT WAS STIFLINGLY HOT IN THE WORKSHOP.

Michelle unbuttoned the top button of her shirtwaist, rolled up her sleeves, and, beyond that, accepted the heat as part of summer life in California.

Instead of fretting about what she couldn't change, she tightened the water pipe and turned a valve. Water gushed in with great force, and the wheel spun.

A smile bloomed on her face. She dipped her hands in the cool water, splashed her face, and enjoyed the dribble of water that went down her neck. The dampness turned cool as the fast-spinning wheel created a bit of a breeze.

Could she make a fan of some kind? To cool a house down?

What else?

This water had a lot of force. The wind was pumping the windmill fast, and that wouldn't always be true. The windmill was also slightly higher than the workshop, so that increased the water pressure. Maybe she could build a water tank and set it even higher. They had water towers in some cities. Then her modest little waterwheel would have even more power. She could find a way to use the waterwheel to pump the water back to the tank and circulate it over and over through the machine it was running.

What else could she hook up? What could she run?

What things could she invent that had never been invented

before? Her only limits came from a limited imagination. And her imagination was excellent.

It would take time, but she had an endless supply of that. Nothing would stop her.

Her spirits soared.

ZANE'S TERROR SOARED.

He fought his way out of the steep, nearly impenetrable woods.

Shad had gone on ahead. He was within earshot but only just.

"That's a horse from the Benteen ranch!" Without wasting another breath, Zane charged for his buckskin, tore the reins loose from the low bush, and vaulted into his saddle.

He galloped toward home, squeezing every drop of speed he could out of his stallion, and the buckskin was a game critter. He heard shouting behind him and hoofbeats coming.

Michelle wasn't alone. Annie wasn't alone.

Zane knew it. But Horace Benteen was a crafty man and a cruel one. Who might he kill to get what he wanted? He'd had Todd killed. Why couldn't he slip up behind Rick and knife him in the back? Same with Neb.

Same with Michelle and Annie, any of them. All of them.

Zane had been so confident just moments ago.

All his confidence had turned to ash.

He leaned low on his horse's neck and urged Buck on.

THE DOOR BEHIND MICHELLE clicked open and closed.

Though annoyed at the interruption, she thought whoever it was tried to be quiet. Gave them credit for that.

She continued working, focusing completely on the small waterwheel she'd built and the piped water forcing the wheel to turn. It had surprising power. She was suddenly glad to have someone to share this with.

"This is going to work. This is going to—"

A hard hand landed on her shoulder and spun her around.

Face-to-face with Horace Benteen.

JILLY HEARD A SOFT MOAN from behind the ramrod's house. She intended to put a boiler on it today and add pipes that would carry hot water from the boiler to the house.

Wondering what she was hearing, Jilly slowed down. She'd learned caution under the cruel hands of Edgar Beaumont.

The evil men who'd paid handsomely for the right to marry the Stiles sisters were still out there. Edgar was still running around loose.

Her sisters had married and were safe.

But Jilly wasn't. She needed to marry, but the idea of it set off a deep, shuddering dread she couldn't control.

The day might come when she had no choice but to marry. She'd put that day off for as long as she could.

Approaching the ramrod's house as quietly as she could manage, she peeked around the corner and saw Rick face down on the ground, stirring, moaning, as if he was just now regaining consciousness.

His head was bleeding.

Jilly rushed to his side. "Rick, are you all right?"

She helped him roll onto his back.

His eyes fluttered open. With slurred speech he asked, "Wha happ'n'd?"

She leaned over him until his dazed eyes locked onto hers.

He was asking the same questions she was. "What happened, Rick?"

"D-don't know. I-I heard something back here. A-a noise. I came around the back to see what it was and . . ." Rick fell silent, as if speaking caused him pain.

"Someone must have hit you. To have the back of your head bleeding when you fell forward, that's not where you'd be hurt if you tripped over something."

"Didn't see anyone."

"Let me get you up." Jilly couldn't leave him lying here. But the last time they'd had an intruder—and she could only believe they had one now—the man had assaulted Michelle.

She got Rick to his feet as an almost frantic need to see Michelle beat against her chest like the wings of a trapped bird. *Hurry, hurry, hurry.*

She got him moving, got him around the corner of the house, then left him leaning against the house but on his feet. "I've got to go. Tell Gretel you need medical care."

"No," Rick said. "I'll come with you."

He straightened, then staggered until he fell against the building. That was the only thing holding him up.

*Hurry, hurry, hurry.*

Defeated, he said, "Go to the bunkhouse and get Neb. You need someone searching with you."

"You go on in. I'll get Neb."

*Hurry, hurry, hurry.*

Rick staggered toward the door, dazed enough to accept that she would do as he asked.

After one terrified moment when all she could think of was to get to Michelle, Jilly forced common sense to rule. She spun toward the bunkhouse.

MICHELLE CRIED OUT, and Horace slapped a hand over her mouth and cut off the sound. He'd moved too quickly. She hadn't made enough noise.

As she twisted against the strong grip, he shoved her against the table, where she'd been working. The edge of the table cut into her back. The noise of the spinning waterwheel sounded behind her. The pressure of his hand bent her backward until she could feel the breeze created by the waterwheel.

And that's when she smelled him.

Benteen, a wealthy, influential man. When she'd seen him in society in San Francisco, he'd always been exquisitely dressed, clean-shaven. His hair neatly trimmed.

Now he was filthy. His eyes bloodshot. Hair greasy and overlong. His face thick with gray bristles. The collar of his white silk shirt was brown with grit and sweat. His coat was worn and tattered. He must've been wearing it day and night for weeks.

Striking out, she clawed at the hand over her mouth.

The coat tore at the shoulder as she gripped it, until the sleeve dangled around his wrist.

This wasn't the kind of filth that came from falling in mud or working with animals. It was built-up, ground-in filth that only came with time and neglect. And his sweat wasn't the clean, healthy smell of a hardworking man, it was the sweat of fear, anger, and desperation.

She could picture this well-dressed man stepping out of some board meeting and realizing he had to run.

She knew without his saying a word that he was ruined. The US Marshals were after him, and he couldn't go where he usually went. The fine restaurants. The elite clubs. His high-priced tailor.

He couldn't even go home to his ranch.

Benteen shook her hard, like a wolf shakes a rat to kill it. His grip hadn't loosened one whit on her shoulder or her mouth.

She wouldn't win like this. The fight went out of her. Or at least the fight of her hands. She still had her mind.

Benteen leaned close enough that his nose almost touched hers over his smothering hand. She smelled his foul breath. But under all of the filth and stench, she saw fury.

"Are you going to be quiet?" His voice was little more than a growl. He had her head pushed back until her neck was bowed and her spine twisted.

She nodded to the extent his painfully tight grip on her mouth would allow.

She didn't mean it. She'd scream her head off given a chance, but the man seemed to think she'd keep her word, even while he was attacking her. Or maybe he just thought he had her in his power and could keep her quiet even with this small amount of freedom.

Maybe he was right.

He slowly lessened the pressure on her mouth. She remained silent. He watched too closely. She'd get one chance to scream, maybe a chance to fight or run. She had to pick the right moment and make it count.

Her voice broke in her bone-dry throat, and her words were little more than a whisper. "What are you doing here?"

"You're mine." His voice was little more than a growl. He seemed more animal than man. "I paid good money for you."

She swallowed to wet her throat, then said, "Whatever deal you made with Edgar has nothing to do with me."

"Oh, that's where you're wrong. It has everything to do with you. You're coming with me."

The very thought wrenched her stomach until she feared she'd lose the food in her belly. "I'm a married woman. Taking me gains you nothing."

He grabbed the front of her dark blue shirtwaist and dragged her onto her toes. He was a big man, tall and good-looking when hate wasn't warping him from the soul out. He tightened his fist on her dress until she could hardly breathe. It silenced her as effectively as his hand over her mouth.

She looked into those crazed eyes. This was a man who used to have everything. All she could see was want. Hunger. He never stopped wanting more. And suddenly she knew what the Bible meant when it said the love of money was the root of all evil. Because this man loved money above God. He loved power above God. He loved his hate above God.

Loving hate. Strange thought, but with Horace, the truth of it struck hard.

Loving anything above God was the root of evil. And Benteen had made a religion of his desire for more.

Michelle prayed as the thoughts flooded through her. She turned to God and knew that if she died today, she'd be with her heavenly Father. And if Benteen died, he'd be separated from God for all eternity.

Quietly, barely able to whisper, she said, "Horace, what has happened to you? You've always been a hard man, but have you so completely lost your grasp on reality that you think you can grab an innocent woman, threaten me, and take me away from my husband? Do you think the law will step aside while you do such a thing? Your son is already locked up for that. Your power and money couldn't stop it. If you harm me or take me, no amount of money or power will protect you."

She reached up and rested her left hand on his right where it choked her.

"You had everything." His grip wavered as she touched his hand, and she drew in a deep breath. "And you've squandered all you had over some sick desire for a woman you don't love, don't even care about. A woman who is very much in love with her husband. You need to face the ugliness inside you and recognize the sin. You need forgiveness and repentance. You need to accept God and turn from this horrid path."

Red veins arched in jagged lines across the whites of his eyes. His fist tightened. Michelle had to fight for every breath.

As she prayed, she accepted that this very day she might stand at the feet of her Savior. As she began to feel lightheaded from lack of air, she became aware of the running water behind her. The spinning waterwheel.

A noise that had gone on steadily this whole time. But suddenly the noise breached her fear. She looked at her hand, resting on his wrist, and saw the dangling sleeve. With a sudden shift of her grip, she grabbed the torn fabric, tugged it behind her, and let the waterwheel catch it. The cloth wound around the center axle of the waterwheel and jerked Benteen's hand straight into the paddles, then wrenched it tight.

Benteen screamed. The wheel stopped.

He let her go and grabbed for his wrist just as the door behind him banged open.

Zane was shouting before he got inside. "Michelle! We found a horse with Benteen's brand—"

Michelle jumped away from Benteen and charged for Zane.

Zane had his gun drawn but quickly holstered it and pulled her into his arms.

Benteen's screams were so loud he might not have heard Zane shouting his warning.

Shad, just a pace behind him, stopped, then strolled over to Benteen and studied the man, who was screaming terrible, ugly words, his hand held tightly in the waterwheel.

Jilly came up fast with Neb armed and ready just behind her. Neb was white haired and stocky but as tough as any Western man.

"So, no hurry, but maybe we should turn this thing off?" Shad turned from Benteen and arched his brows at Michelle. Still shaking, she studied the situation and thought Shad was probably right.

With one last hug for Zane, she headed for the valve she'd opened to let the water flow. With a quick adjustment, the water shut off. Shad tugged on Benteen, which made him scream louder. He was well and truly stuck.

Zane had a firm grip on Benteen's free arm, but the man wasn't doing any damage, except to himself.

Michelle had to do some work to get the waterwheel to ease its pressure. Benteen's arm was bent at a dreadful angle, though the skin wasn't broken.

Thinking of the surgery she'd performed on Annie's husband, Michelle decided her career as a doctor was done.

Benteen could just ride to town like that.

Shad dragged Benteen, still mewling with pain and spewing profanity, out of the workshop.

Michelle threw herself back into her husband's arms.

"Michelle, did he harm you? Are you all right?"

Neb followed Shad, his gun still drawn.

Hugging Zane, loving him for the concern in his voice, listening to Benteen's fading filthy language, Michelle said, "I'm fine. He didn't hurt me. But he threatened to take me away from here."

She looked up at Zane. "Away from you."

Zane leaned down and kissed her. "So you fed his arm into that waterwheel?"

Jilly rolled her eyes at the kiss and Zane's question. "I'm going to go tell Annie and Beth Ellen what happened. To the extent I know."

Jilly wandered off to leave Michelle alone with Zane.

Michelle shrugged. "I tried to reason with him first. I was preaching to him. Telling him he needed to admit he was a terrible sinner and repent."

"Have any luck?" Zane asked as Benteen's vile language continued even from a distance.

"What I had was inspiration. God made me hear a sound that had been going on all along. Suddenly, that waterwheel, turning behind me, was loud. Benteen's sleeve was torn and dangling. I grabbed the fabric and shoved it into the waterwheel, and it sucked him right in. I believe it was a heavenly message."

Zane wrapped both arms around her, lowered his head, and kissed her again. Longer this time. Deeper.

When the kiss ended, Michelle said, "When I was talking to Benteen, one of the things I said to him was that I had a husband, and I was in love with him."

Their eyes met. Silence stretched between them.

"And did you mean it?"

"I meant every word."

And this kiss lasted until Shad came and pounded on the workshop door to tell them he had their horses saddled.

"I DON'T KNOW WHY YOU WON'T MARRY JILLY." Laura jammed her fists on her waist and glared at Nick. They were back in the mountain mansion. The worst of Edgar's henchmen were fired, including that dreadful cook.

They'd hired more men, including a few to guard the house.

The logging business was running well.

But their troubles wouldn't be over until Jilly was safely married.

Nick, who still spent most of his time around the house, not satisfied that anyone could guard Mama as well as he could, blinked those odd eyes at her. The three of them sat at the breakfast table. Mama had gone to the office to work on the account books.

"Uh, because, uh, well . . ." His face had a helpless look on it as he searched for words. "I don't know her. Don't love her. And . . . uh, don't want to."

Laura didn't think those were good enough reasons. "Caleb barely knew me, hadn't begun to love me."

Caleb said quietly, "I'd begun to love you."

"And honestly probably didn't want to."

"I wanted to marry you something fierce. Having known you for less than a month, I had my doubts that it was what *God* wanted. But, oh yes, I wanted to marry you."

Laura's eyes narrowed as she considered what they said. She knew her thinking went on for an uncomfortably long time, but the men remained quiet, giving her time. They'd gotten used to this. They'd gotten to know her.

"She needs a husband, and you might not know her, but you know Mama. Wouldn't you like to have her for your own mama?"

Nick studied Laura. She realized this tough man, devoted to protecting Mama above all else, was smart. Not as educated as she was but plenty smart. Now he looked at her with kindness, maybe even pity.

"We'll make sure everyone is safe," Nick said. "Your mama, Jilly, you, everyone. Don't carry around this fear, Laura. Do your best to hand it over to God." He took a drink of his coffee, then wiped his mouth on a snow white napkin that lay beside his plate.

He looked at Caleb and solemnly said, "You need to pray with her more. Help her to ease this burden of fear she bears."

Caleb took Laura's hand and tugged until she looked at him.

He smiled.

She couldn't help smiling back. "You wanted to something fierce, huh?"

"I absolutely did."

"Do you think we should bring Jilly back here? Is she safer here than at the ranch, now that everyone knows she's hiding there?"

Caleb lifted one shoulder. "I know Jilly well enough to be sure no one's going to *bring* her anywhere."

"I have to give you that."

"And," Nick said, "no one's going to marry her without her full permission and cooperation."

Laura studied him again. "You could try to convince her."

Nick politely stood from the table. "I'm going to go try to convince Old Tom to teach me about running a logging camp."

Old Tom already taught Nick all day, every day. When he could get Nick away from guarding Mama.

Laura sniffed. Caleb laughed. Nick left.

"OUR TROUBLES AREN'T OVER until Jilly gets married and Mama makes sure Edgar isn't able to harm her," Michelle said. "But we've come a long way."

Nodding, Zane said, "Do you think we can get Josh to marry Jilly?"

They were riding to town with their moaning, wounded prisoner in tow.

Michelle and Zane in front. Shad and Neb behind with Horace between them. Someone had put his arm in a sling, but it sure hadn't been Michelle.

Michelle had preferred to get back to work, but Zane convinced her the sheriff would want her to stand as witness to all Horace had said and done.

It probably wasn't true. Horace was a wanted man, after all. But Zane couldn't stand to be separated from her right now. When he thought of her being in Benteen's clutches, alone, helpless, he nearly started to howl with anger.

Well, not quite helpless as it turned out.

"No," Michelle said.

"Why not? He's right here handy."

Michelle gave him a strange look that told him her thoughts toward his brother might be ones he didn't want to hear. Unfortunately, they probably followed along with his own thoughts.

His brother did tend to bore everyone senseless.

Jilly, bright and energetic and fascinated by most everything, tended to wander off when Josh started in on his stories.

And since his stories were of exotic places and far distant lands, wicked weather at sea and dastardly pirates . . . it wasn't that easy to bore everyone into going to bed just to escape him.

Josh could manage it with no trouble at all.

Zane rode up close to her as they walked their horses toward Dorada Rio. He reached across the space separating them. She took his hand, and they rode along in harmony.

"When you told me you loved me, I didn't say it back."

Michelle turned to him, her hand tightening on his. "Can you say it now?"

That got a smile out of him when he was feeling mighty solemn.

"When I saw a Benteen brand on that horse, well, it could have been someone he sent, but I knew it was him. I was in a flat-out terror racing to you. All I could think was that if

I lost you, that would mean I'd lost the love of my life. The fear told me more than anything that I loved you. I reckon I have almost from the start. I feel blessed by a loving God to have ended up married to a precious, brilliant, strong woman. You saved yourself, and knowing you can do that gives me peace. Yes, Michelle. I love you."

And they rode along to town to put one of their biggest troubles behind them, knowing that whatever came, they'd face it together.

# ABOUT *the* AUTHOR

Mary Connealy writes romantic comedies about cowboys. She's the author of the BROTHERS IN ARMS, BRIDES OF HOPE MOUNTAIN, HIGH SIERRA SWEETHEARTS, KINCAID BRIDES, TROUBLE IN TEXAS, WILD AT HEART, and CIMARRON LEGACY series, as well as several other acclaimed series. Mary has been nominated for a Christy Award, was a finalist for a RITA Award, and is a two-time winner of the Carol Award. She lives on a ranch in eastern Nebraska with her very own romantic cowboy hero. They have four grown daughters—Joslyn, married to Matt; Wendy; Shelly, married to Aaron; and Katy, married to Max—and six precious grandchildren. Learn more about Mary and her books at

*maryconnealy.com*
*facebook.com/maryconnealy*
*seekerville.blogspot.com*
*petticoatsandpistols.com*

# Sign Up for Mary's Newsletter

Keep up to date with Mary's latest news on book releases and events by signing up for her email list at maryconnealy.com.

# More from Mary Connealy

After learning their stepfather plans to marry them off, Laura Stiles and her sisters escape to find better matches and claim their father's lumber dynasty. Laura sees potential in the local minister of the poor town they settle in, but when secrets buried in his past and the land surface, it will take all they have to keep trouble at bay.

*The Element of Love* • The Lumber Baron's Daughters #1

# You May Also Like . . .

Assigned by the Pinkertons to spy on a suspicious ranch owner, Molly Garner hires on as his housekeeper, closely followed by Wyatt Hunt, who refuses to let her risk it alone. But when danger arises, Wyatt must band together with his problematic brothers to face all the troubles of life and love that suddenly surround them.

*Love on the Range* by Mary Connealy
BROTHERS IN ARMS #3
maryconnealy.com

Falcon Hunt awakens without a past—or at least he doesn't recall one. When he makes a new start by claiming an inheritance, it cuts out frontierswoman Cheyenne from her ranch. Soon it's clear someone is gunning for him and his brothers, and as his affection for Cheyenne grows, he must piece together his past if they're to have any chance at a future.

*A Man with a Past* by Mary Connealy
BROTHERS IN ARMS #2
maryconnealy.com

British spy Levi Masters is captured while investigating a discovery that could give America an upper hand in future conflicts. Village healer Audrey Moreau is drawn to the captive's commitment to honesty and is compelled to help him escape. But when he faces a severe injury, they are forced to decide how far they'll go to ensure the other's safety.

*A Healer's Promise* by Misty M. Beller
BRIDES OF LAURENT #2
mistymbeller.com

# More from Bethany House

While Brody McQuaid's body survived the war, his soul did not. He finds his purpose saving wild horses from ranchers intent on killing them. Veterinarian Savannah Marshall joins Brody in an attempt to save the wild creatures, but when her family and the ranchers catch up with them, they will have to tame their fears if they've any hope to let love run free.

*To Tame a Cowboy* by Jody Hedlund
Colorado Cowboys #3
jodyhedlund.com

When her brother dies suddenly, Damaris Baxter moves to Texas to take custody of her nephew. Luke Davenport winds up gravely injured when he rescues Damaris's nephew from a group of rustlers. As suspicions grow regarding the death of her brother, more danger appears, threatening the family Luke may be unable to live without.

*In Honor's Defense* by Karen Witemeyer
Hanger's Horsemen #3
karenwitemeyer.com

Del Nielsen's teaching job in town offers hope, not only to support her three sisters but also to better her students' lives. When their brother visits with his war-wounded friend RJ, Del finds RJ barely polite and wants nothing to do with him. But despite the sisters' best-laid plans, the future—and RJ—might surprise them all.

*A Time to Bloom* by Lauraine Snelling
Leah's Garden #2
laurainesnelling.com

BETHANYHOUSE